PARADISE
PARK

PARADISE PARK

A WILLIAM MULDOON NOVEL

L. MAD HILDEBRANDT

RoseQuill Press

Copyright © 2017 L. Mad Hildebrandt

Cover Design: Gabrielle Felts
Cover Illustration: from the New York Public Library Digital Collections, image 430676

ISBN: 978-1976057410

RoseQuill Press
PO Box 1784
Socorro, NM 87801

www.rosequill.com

Acknowledgements

This book is dedicated to the two wrestlers in my life: my son Dominic and my grandfather Edwin. In various ways, they influenced the development of William Muldoon's character. For that, I am grateful.

I also thank my husband Richard for his unwavering belief I could complete this project, and my daughter Gabrielle for all the hard work she's put into editing and formatting—she's a computer genius. I want to thank Bonnie Hearn Hill who taught the first Writer's Digest class I ever took, so giving amazing advice for this novel.

And, last but not least, Lori Wilde, who makes me remember to always believe in myself.

Pronunciation Guide

The following Irish words appear in this book.

Leanbh (child)—LANN ov
Shillelagh (paddling stick)—shi LAY lee

PARADISE
PARK

PART ONE

"When you march up to attack a city, make its people an offer of peace. If they accept and open their gates, all the people in it shall be subject to forced labor and shall work for you. If they refuse to make peace and they engage you in battle, then lay siege to that city. When the Lord your God delivers it into your hand, put to the sword all the men in it. As for the women, the children, the livestock and everything else in the city, you may take these as plunder for yourselves."

—Deuteronomy 20:10-13

CHAPTER 1

New York City, April 16, 1867

LIGHTNING split the darkness, temporarily illuminating the corpse. The dead man was nude, arms and legs spraddled as if he was a child's rag doll, dropped to the ground and forgotten. He had been shaved smooth, from head to toe, and bruises of various shades, ranging from faded yellow to the most recent—livid purple—marked his pale flesh, pummeled into the man's chest in a vague five-pointed star pattern. William Muldoon squatted beside the dead man. Kelly. The name entered his mind unbidden, and he shook his head. He raised his hand to shut the corpse's bulging eyes, closing his own eyes for a moment.

A movement across the body drew his attention, and Muldoon glanced up at Sergeant O'Malley as he stepped close. "There's only one kinda man who could kill a guy like Schneider," said the Sergeant. "That's another wrestler . . . maybe a boxer. But I don't think so. I've never seen a boxer take down a wrestler like this." He stared intensely at the star-shaped bruise, superstition clouding his expression. He crossed himself quickly, whispering, "Father, Son, n' Holy Ghost."

"Mmm," agreed Muldoon, pulling a sheet across the dead man. But, silently, he disagreed with O'Malley. He'd seen man's savage side during the war. What lay before him was man's handiwork . . . not the devil's. "It would take another wrestler, and a strong one at that. Maybe a couple of men." Kelly flashed into his mind again. No, he shook away the damning thought.

"Did you know him well?"

"Just a bit. He was pretty good on the mat." He rose to his feet, darkness shrouding the body in its drab gray cover. Muldoon glanced about, surveying the scene. The night was dark, spring clouds blotting the moon and stars. He could see little in the inky blackness. A lone gas lamp at the end of the block shed weak, yellow light, barely breaking the dark. A shadowy figure stood below the lamp, young Davey Flynn, O'Malley's partner.

He glanced again at the sheet-covered body. It took a strong man to steal life from the big German. He knew several in the Points large enough, but he wasn't sure of their skill. Karl Schneider was a good fighter. Few men could take him down, but if he'd been attacked from behind . . . well, perhaps. Kelly might have been angry enough . . . He pushed away the thought.

Taking the lantern from O'Malley, he searched the ground nearby. Circling out farther and farther, he looked for clues, but didn't see any. The loose dirt was pockmarked from thousands of passing feet. Muldoon couldn't see any particular sign of scuffling, at least not recent. The Points was a constant battleground, home to gangs like the Dead Rabbits and the Plug Uglies. They fought one another on their own turf, and then turned to the B'hoys or other gangs from Mulberry Bend, the Docks, or the Bowery.

O'Malley shrugged beside him. "There's nothing," he said. "Leastways nothing we'll ever see in the dark."

Muldoon agreed. And with morning's light, the whole area would come alive again with urchins and beggars, street vendors and ruffians. If any clues were left, they would be gone before the police could take note.

"All right if I take him?" called a voice somewhere in the darkness behind them.

Muldoon spun about. A second lantern lit a small circle, a short, round man lifting it high.

"Mmm . . . yes," Muldoon said. "I'm done with him here. I'll come round in the morning to take a closer look at the body."

Whatever secrets it held, he knew they'd tell best in the light. He yawned, handing the lantern back to the sergeant. "I'm going home for a little shuteye. The morgue can wait. I've still got a couple of hours before I'm on duty."

"Sure you have, now," O'Malley said with a rueful grin. "But the Captain's got me working a double shift. I'll be seeing you when you get in."

"All right," Muldoon said. They parted company, O'Malley and Flynn back toward Paradise Park. Pulling his coat tight against the chill night air, he headed toward the Points district border. The morgue van clattered past, and he wished he'd asked for a lift. It wasn't safe, even for a cop, to walk alone here at night.

As the wagon passed the far corner, a shadow separated from the darkness behind it. Muldoon slid deeper into the shadows and watched as the figure followed the cart several steps, then turned toward him. Weak light filtered from the lamp, barely illuminating the man . . . but his eyes. Crimson orbs, like those of a night beast, flashed angrily where his eyes should be hidden in the dark. His gaze seemed to burn into Muldoon. Then the man donned a top hat, and with a flip of his cape, he disappeared into the night.

CHAPTER 2

WIND rushed up the steps, pushing against Muldoon as if to keep him from leaving the boarding house porch. Stepping into the street, he pulled his hat tight and turned toward police headquarters at 300 Mulberry. He shoved his way through the crowd. Ladies in bright dresses fought the breeze, and men wearing top hats and boots chased wayward hats and parasols. The poorer folk mimicked the wealthy with gaudier, brighter fabrics and mixed patterns. Here and there, a street vendor cried out, "Apples, apples, buy me apples."

Across the street, a soldier passed through the crowd. Muldoon glanced toward him, then quickly away again. At the corner, he paused momentarily while a wagon passed, a huge bay draft horse straining in its harness, each heavy hoof plodding forward. Behind it, a young woman darted into the street, sweeping away the mess the horse had dropped. She nodded with a smile as Muldoon pressed a penny into her hand. He crossed the street quickly, before a fast-moving carriage could draw near. The street sweeper darted into traffic again, clearing the way for pedestrians. A few blocks on, in the poorer district, there would be no sweepers.

An imposing structure loomed ahead. It stood five stories high, a sturdy cube, undecorated aside from two Greek columns on each side of the door and a cornice jutting out like a shelf along the top front. A wrought iron fence and broad sidewalk separated it from the street, the fence lining the steps as they rose to the front entrance. The gas lamp was unlit this time of day, standing like a solitary sentry before the halls of blue.

Muldoon climbed the steps and entered the front foyer just as the first drops of rain hit the ground. A sergeant at the high desk tipped his head up then back—a small sharp movement—acknowledging the newcomer.

"The Captain's looking for you, Muldoon," he called, his Irish brogue thick.

"Great," Muldoon said with a grimace. He took the steps two at a time, not so much because he was in a hurry, but because it was his custom.

He strode down the hall, paused at the Captain's office door, and lifted his hand to knock. It was slightly ajar, muffled voices inside just audible.

"So, that's that," said Captain Hayle beyond the door. "Take McAllister into custody."

Muldoon thrust the door open, abandoning the knock. "Are you talking about Kelly McAllister?" he demanded, his tone fueled by his own guilt. Kelly had been his first thought, too.

"Muldoon!" Hayle roared, half rising from his desk. He paused for just an instant at the sight of the angry sergeant. Quickly he regained his composure, sat down again and leaned back in his chair. He ran a hand through his graying hair. "Sergeant Muldoon," he began, particularly stressing that first word "sergeant," reminding the younger man of his position. "Detective Graham here has determined that Kelly McAllister killed Karl Schneider. His motive? Why, of course, that humiliating defeat a couple of days ago."

Muldoon turned to Graham, who sat in the sole chair this side of the big desk. The room was pristine, not a file, not a paper to be seen, aside from the one clutched tightly in the detective's fist. Even the heavy shelves, lined with books, were neatly arranged, as though they never moved from their designated positions except when dusted.

"It had to be McAllister." The detective leaned back and placed one foot over the other knee. He looked down his long nose as best he could, tipping his head sharply back and just to the side to glare up at Muldoon. Heavy lids dropped low, his pale blue eyes were barely visible. "He lost his match and was quite mad about it. He spouted off in the bars last night. I went to several, and each time it was the same. He threatened to get even . . . and he did."

He said it so matter-of-factly. Muldoon raged inside, but he knew his place. They were English, he was Irish. In order to do any good for his people, he had to work within the confines of the job. And if that meant keeping his tongue, so be it. But he wasn't about to let Kelly McAllister, a man he thought of as a brother, take the fall. The boy hadn't killed Schneider, Muldoon was sure of it. But niggling doubt whispered that he could have.

"It couldn't have been McAllister," he said, and turned toward the Captain, appealing for help. "Of course he wanted to get even. On the mat! But he was too beat up to kill Schneider. If you'd seen him after the match . . . "

"Well, I didn't see him, Muldoon," grated Hayle. "I wouldn't go anywhere near that kind of entertainment. Of course, you frequent the low taverns quite often, I hear. Even wrestling yourself! It's not a bad thing . . . keeping in condition . . . but to wrestle down in the Points? You can wrestle against the other policemen, if you want."

"I've beat every man on the force," Muldoon said. "None of them'll fight me anymore."

"I don't want you, or any of my men, taking part in the matches down there. And yes, I know you were at the Schneider—McAllister bout. You should have been with the men who came to break up the scene . . . instead of sneaking off with your boy."

Muldoon controlled himself with an effort, his face growing warm. He spoke through gritted teeth. "Sir, McAllister was beaten down by Schneider. He was badly bruised. I had to help him home."

"All the more reason to kill Schneider later," said Graham from the shadows.

"He didn't kill Schneider!" Muldoon spun about and pinned the detective with his glare. "I can promise you that!"

"How?" asked Hayle. "Were you with him all night?"

"No," Muldoon admitted. "I left him in his bed. But he wasn't going anywhere."

"There." Graham leaned forward, planting both feet on the ground, a wicked gleam in his eye. "That proves it. McAllister was alone . . . unless you're going to say it was the devil that killed Schneider . . . like some are saying out on the streets."

The Captain nodded. "Sorry, Muldoon." He pursed his mouth tightly, pushing out his bottom lip. "There's enough evidence. Graham has witnesses who'll testify to McAllister's statements. We'll be picking him up today . . . if he can be found." He turned quickly to the detective. "And I'll have no more of that 'devil' talk, Graham! Leave the super- stition to the Irish!"

" . . . And Muldoon," Hayle continued as the sergeant turned to leave. "It'll go easier on McAllister if he comes in himself. I don't ex- pect . . . ah . . . 'anyone' will talk to him . . . encouraging him to run, per- haps. We'll find him, no matter where he hides in this city."

Muldoon nodded. He knew this advice was for him. But he was too good a cop to encourage anyone, even his young protégé, to flee. If he could find a way, justice would be served, and it didn't include the hanging of Kelly McAllister.

He hurried through the building and paused at the front desk to tell the sergeant he was going out to join Detective Benson on a case. He knew Benson would cover for him. They'd worked together often during the past couple of years, and Benson had come to rely on the younger officer. Muldoon knew where he'd find the detective, anyway. He'd be sitting in Harry Hill's, clutching a drink, drowning the tragedy of his life. Muldoon could use a stiff drink himself . . . but that was somewhere he couldn't go. He shoved through the door, letting it slam behind him. The morgue would have to wait. He had to find Kelly McAllister before it was too late.

CHAPTER 3

WILLIAM Muldoon strode toward the Points. With a quick glance over his shoulder, he noted the man trailing him. He wore street clothes, one of Graham's henchmen, or maybe an off-duty cop. Muldoon didn't recognize him, but that didn't mean anything. Just that he wasn't from the district. He sped up, and took another look back. The man kept pace. Graham wanted this collar any way he could get it, but he'd be damned if he'd lead the detective's man straight to Kelly McAllister.

He entered Mulberry Bend and took a sharp left into a filthy alley, the dirt road quickly becoming muck in the rain. He could see the plain clothes copper turn the corner behind him. He smiled wickedly. These were his streets. It would take a brave, or foolhardy, man to follow him. He hurried down the alley, past grimy, large-eyed children and a woman carrying a basket of limp vegetables. It was the best she could get, he knew. Down here, you bought what was available, even if it was half-rotten. A person had to eat.

Muldoon stepped into the shadow of a heavily leaning building. It tipped worse than most of the others, its unpainted boards warped and broken. The door hung crazily from its hinges, but held when he pushed it open. He glanced back, then slipped into the darkened hall and ran quickly through the building and out the other side, but not before rapping on the first door to the left. One, two, three . . . four knocks.

He knew it opened to a cramped apartment, just a room, really. It was barely large enough to hold one person, let alone the family of six he knew occupied it . . . the O'Shaunessy's . . . mother, father, and four nearly grown sons. They were tough scrappers, every one of them. Muldoon had got a job for Brian, the oldest boy, clearing tables at Harry Hill's. This time of day, the boys could be found at home, not emerging 'til later, along with the rats, roaches, and riffraff of the night.

He ran through the hall, and out the far door. "Ay!" cried a man, followed by a loud commotion as the young men responded to his coded knock, entered the hallway and filled the small passage with their big, sweaty bodies. A scuffle broke out as his pursuer tried to push past. The boys would be obstinate, playing dumb, as if trying to get out of the way. But as one stepped aside, another would block the man's progress. They'd keep it up until Muldoon was safely away. It was a trick he'd used more than once.

He strode off confidently, a wicked smirk on his lips. He'd easily lost his pursuer, and now he walked down Mott Street, heading toward Chatham. He needed to check at the McAllister home first, and then search around town if he had to. His gaze flicked from face to face as he moved through the crowd. Even in the rain, the streets were filled with people going places, heads tipped low, water dripping off hat brims, umbrellas, or newspapers clutched overhead. He imagined accidentally walking right past Kelly on his way across town. But, he knew he wouldn't. The war had taught him a vigilance he would never lose. As he passed a newsstand, he caught a glaring headline: MURDEROUS DEMON STALKS THE NIGHT.

THE McAllisters lived in a rundown building, not unlike the many ramshackle structures in this part of town. This one was brick instead of wood, its federal style a remnant of a much better past, when George Washington had visited these same streets. Muldoon entered the building and made his way up to the fourth floor. He passed a pile of garbage someone had dropped over the rail. It had fallen a distance and splattered where it hit, its unwholesome contents spread across the landing. He leapt over the refuse, disturbing a rat, but it only sat and stared at him, its whiskers flicking. It claimed the mess for its own, and not even a man Muldoon's size was going to scare it off without a little effort.

He gave a halfhearted wave toward the rat. It started to move, shifted its shoulders, and then touched the ground with one tiny hand-like paw. But it didn't run. It held its place defiantly. Muldoon needed the same kind of spirit if he was going to help Kelly McAllister.

He stopped in front of the apartment door and rapped lightly. If Kelly was lying sick in there he didn't want to disturb him yet. He hadn't seen him since the fight, but the kid had been hurt pretty badly.

The crooked door opened a crack, the bottom hinge hanging uselessly. He'd have to remember to get back here and fix that. With Kelly locked up, Meg McAllister would be alone. Her face appeared through the thin space between door and jamb.

"It's me, Ma," Muldoon said. She insisted he call her that. His parents were long since gone, and she'd become something of a replacement. For that matter, he regarded Kelly as a younger brother, one who needed his protection at the moment.

Meg's face lit up, but he could see the worry in her eyes. He pulled the door open to where it always got stuck, just wide enough so he could get in. "Is Kelly here?" He yanked the door shut, and turned to her.

"No." She wrung her hands. "I mean, he was . . . up until about an hour ago." Her despairing tone couldn't dampen the dancing lilt in her Irish born voice.

Muldoon sighed.

"Ah, William," she said. "He's not so good. Had his ribs cracked in that last fight, he did. And not a dollar to show for it! We can't afford a doctor. Lord knows, he needs one to tape up his ribs. And now he's gone to fight again."

Muldoon glanced across the tiny room. An empty peg told him what he needed to know. Kelly had taken his wrestling tights. A small portrait of Mrs. McAllister hung next to the peg. He'd seen it so many times before, but this time he looked back at her. Agitated, she stroked her gray hair, unconsciously pulling it loose from its bun. She seemed but a shadow of the girl in the portrait, before she'd left Ireland. She stood proudly in the picture, her face tilted at a jaunty angle, full, curly hair over an impish grin. Her gown was of the best fabric and cut, the daughter of a wealthy man. He gazed down at the wreck of her former self. Hard living and poverty had broken her.

He pulled a dollar out of his pocket and slipped it into her hand. "You don't have to worry, Ma. I'll find him, bring him to his senses."

"If you aren't too late," she said. "The tea leaves don't look good for him." She gazed down at the shining coin in her hand. "You know I can't take this." She lifted it between finger and thumb . . . raised it slowly . . . hesitantly, to return it to Muldoon.

He took her hand inside his big fist and folded her frail fingers over the coin. "You can, and you will," he said. "You'll be needing it for your rent. I'll bring you what I can tomorrow. And I'll come and fix that door."

"And I suppose you'll be getting the cash in the usual way?" she asked, a slight, reproachful tone in her voice.

"Of course," he said. "Wrestling . . . or fisticuffs."

Meg harrumphed, but slipped the coin into her apron pocket. She studied his face. "You're looking tired. You're not sleeping?"

"Enough."

"Your dreams again?"

He shrugged. She was the only one who knew about them. She knew because she'd taken him in after the war, when he was so ill he'd nearly died. And she'd helped him learn to ignore, or attempt to ignore, the soldiers who walked through the crowded streets. Soldiers invisible to everyone except him . . . faces of the men he'd fought beside in the war . . . or against. The men who hadn't made it.

She turned partially away. "There's a shadow over you, William."

"Did your tea tell you that?" He couldn't stop the skepticism that entered his voice.

"No. I can see it on you. Mind it, will you? Now, you'd best be getting along if you're going to stop Kelly before he gets into trouble."

Muldoon nodded. He couldn't bring himself to tell her Kelly's troubles were only just beginning. The door opened with a shudder as he scraped it against the floor. He pushed it to and passed quickly down the stairs. He knew where to find McAllister; he just hoped he'd get there before Graham or one of his boys.

CHAPTER 4

MULDOON went down the stairs into the basement of 153 Bleecker Street. A fat whore in a gaudy, floral-print pink dress met him at the door. Her alabaster cheeks were bright with rouge, lips painted a harsh shade of red, clashing violently with the florid dress. "Why, boys," she screamed with obvious delight. "It's the champ! He's honoring us with his presence this afternoon."

He hadn't eaten since early that morning, and suddenly Muldoon realized he was hungry. The Black and Tan wasn't his first choice in eating establishments, but he wasn't going to be choosy.

"Hello, Mable," he said, wrapping one arm about the woman's thick waist. "Got anything good to eat?"

"Sure," she said and steered him across the full room toward an empty table. Even at this early hour, the saloon was lively. Several more prostitutes entertained the men, and dancing girls paraded in their show dresses, slit high in front for the can-can, layers of lace peeking from underneath.

Men packed the room. Most were black. Freed from slavery, the city had become a magnet, and the African population had exploded. All eyes turned toward him, leery at first, taking in his police blues. As they realized who wore the uniform, they relaxed. Muldoon frequented the taverns and saloons of the Points. It was where he wrestled and earned the extra money that bought him the nice clothes a Bowery man yearned for, money he intended to hand over to Meg McAllister while Kelly was put away.

As he glanced over the faces, Muldoon's gaze paused at Frank Stephenson. The saloonkeeper leaned against the bar. A tall, thin man, he stood stiff and erect. Even after knowing him for years, Muldoon couldn't help but stare at the proprietor, looking for some sign of humanity. His pale face seemed drained of blood, corpselike. Strikingly dark hair leapt from his forehead, swept back. It seemed all color had been reserved for the man's hair and eyebrows. His dark eyes glowered as he kept watch over the room.

Muldoon sat quietly at a corner table and watched the scene at the bar while awaiting his meal. Kelly McAllister had arrived and stood at the bar speaking earnestly to Stephenson. Trying for a match, he thought. The boy was more beat up than he'd thought . . . it was obvious even from across the room. He wouldn't be fighting today. Muldoon ate slowly when his pork pasty came. It wasn't the best, but it wasn't bad, either. While he ate, he debated how he'd approach his friend. He didn't think Kelly would give in that easily. I wouldn't, he thought. Just thinking of the Tomb's cold prison interior sent a shiver along his spine . . . and he was a cop. He sent men there.

As he finished his meal, a commotion began across the room. Not much, at first, just a slight rise in voices. Anticipation moved across the saloon like a tidal wave.

"There's gonna be a match!" someone shouted over the racket.

Surprised, Muldoon glanced up at the figure of Frank Stephenson. The proprietor no longer stood at the bar, but had returned to his accustomed place, high on a tall chair at the center of the room. He surveyed the tavern like a king over his land. The piercing, soulless eyes turned toward him and caught him in their gaze. The corners of his frowning lips just barely lifted as he looked across at Muldoon. He nodded, almost imperceptibly, a silent challenge meant only for him.

Muldoon shifted his gaze toward McAllister. The younger man still stood by the bar, stripping off his shirt. He could see the soreness in the boy's movements. Quickly he lifted his bulk from the chair and strode across the room.

"What are you doing, Kelly?" he asked.

"I'm gonna fight." Kelly lay his shirt on the bar, and turned quickly to face Muldoon. He grimaced with pain. "Don't try and stop me." He continued stripping down to his tights.

Muldoon looked pointedly at the deep purple bruises visible on the young man's body. "I don't think you're in any condition for fighting."

"It's not up to you, William. I've got to earn some money for my Ma."

He wondered what Kelly had done with his share of the kitty from his last match. Gambling, no doubt.

"She doesn't need it," Muldoon said. "I gave her a dollar this morning."

"She does need it." Kelly scowled. "And it's my business, not yours. I have to take care of her. I provide for mine, and you provide for yours."

"You know I can't do that."

Red flared across Kelly's face. He knew Muldoon's family had been killed during the war. "I . . . I didn't mean that! You know I didn't."

"I know, Kelly. And you know I can't let you fight. Not in your condition."

"But I've got to! It's a matter of honor now. It's already been arranged."

Muldoon shook his head. "Sorry, Kelly, but you've got to come with me."

"I don't think so," a deep, gravelly voice interrupted them. It came from a large man behind the bar. "The crowd's expectin' a match."

His ebony skin glowed from the lantern that hung just to the right. He reached up, pulled a huge bludgeon down from its place on the wall, and tapped it suggestively against one hand. The bartender to his left stepped closer and drew a long knife from its sheath. At the far ends of the long bar, the final two bartenders stepped out, each held a club at the ready. Four against one . . . and an injured boy.

Muldoon raised an eyebrow. "Who's he supposed to wrestle?"

The first bartender motioned with his head. A giant African stepped from the back room, stripped to his undershirt and a pair of vivid red tights. Muldoon smirked as his gaze slid around to the tall chair at the center of the room. Stephenson had swiveled the seat around to give himself a clear view of the scene at the bar. One eyebrow twitched noticeably. He rarely made any response at all. Eyes locked with Stephenson's, Muldoon removed his policeman's hat, and placed it on the bar.

"No! This is my bout." Kelly grabbed Muldoon's arm hard.

Muldoon broke from Stephenson's heavy, challenging stare, and turned to his friend. "No, Kelly," he said. "This was never your fight."

"I'm gonna take this one, William," Kelly said. "You don't understand! I've got to make the rent." He wrenched Muldoon's arm, but with the sharp movement, the younger man bent nearly double and grasped his broken ribs.

Muldoon grabbed hold of Kelly. The boy's face had gone sheet-white, his skin cold and clammy. He held onto him, and kept him from sliding to the floor. "Sit down, Kelly," he said, hooked an empty stool with his right foot and pulled it toward him. He eased the young man down, turned toward the bar, and motioned the bartender close. "Make sure he doesn't go anywhere," he said. "Or this match will end a bit too quick . . . "

The man glanced warily toward Stephenson. "Mmhmm," he mumbled through clenched lips.

Muldoon smirked. He'd give the saloonkeeper his show. He set his short daystick on the bar next to his hat. The long nightstick followed, and then his handcuffs and his braided leather and wire come-along. He imagined wrapping that light strap around Kelly McAllister's wrists, leading him from the bar, and booking him for murder. He sighed, then laid his heavy belt on the growing pile. Slowly he unfastened his brass buttons; he began at the neck, revealing the curly red hairs of his chest. He shrugged the uniform from his shoulders, but left his undershirt in place. It stretched tight across his barrel chest, and his muscles bulged and flexed as he moved.

"Sorry," he said loudly. "I haven't any tights with me. You'll have to allow me my pants."

Stephenson nodded from his throne.

Muldoon slipped off his shoes. Suddenly he spun about and slammed his hand down on the bar next to his gear. "Touch nothing!" he said. "If anything goes missing, this place will be closed down. But not before the B'hoys come through."

The bartender nodded, his eyes growing large. He seemed to have momentarily forgotten the bludgeon in his hand.

Calls of "George! George Army!" filled the room as the big African strode forward to meet Muldoon in the center of the cleared floor. Men scrambled from the space, drawing chairs and tables with them. The two squared off, placed their feet for balance, and grasped one another, heads close together. Although they began with a semblance of formality, Muldoon knew this would be no Greco-Roman bout. It would be quick moving, the rough-and-tumble fighting of the poorer classes. He'd learned the classic style in the war, but he knew it held little attraction for this crowd. He gauged his opponent and found them roughly equal in size and weight, though his skill was still unknown.

High atop his chair, Stephenson nodded. A small wiry man pulled the hat off his tightly curled hair and held it high, where both contestants could see. Again, Stephenson nodded, and the hat was dropped. The little man snatched back his hat and scooted quickly away as the wrestling began, fast and furious. The African put him on the defensive immediately, working hard, and Muldoon regretted his meal.

"Lookout, William!" Kelly yelled above the roar of the crowd.

George Army tried for the first throw, turned swiftly and grabbed for Muldoon's waist. But he countered, slipped over him and tried to draw him to the ground. They struggled hard for a time, but Army got away.

They came together again, on their feet for several minutes, when suddenly Army dove for Muldoon's leg, lifting him. He struggled out of the hold and held an arm out, fending him off long enough to catch his breath a bit. They locked together again, and then Muldoon took his turn, going for the leg.

"Oomph," grunted Army as he fell hard to the ground. Muldoon followed him quickly, getting a half-nelson. But Army spun about, breaking loose to an appreciative roar from the crowd. Muldoon reached forward and grabbed the man's foot.

"Ahhh," Muldoon grunted as Army's foot caught him square in the jaw and he yanked free.

Muldoon stood, wiped his sweating palms on his thighs and took his stance again. Once more Army went for his leg, lifted him despite his resistance, and threw him heavily to the ground. Army latched on with a half-nelson, and Muldoon arched his back, twisting free of the lock. Suddenly, they were both up again.

This time, Muldoon dropped Army and tried for a hammerlock once the two were on the ground. He switched tactics and tried for a half-nelson again, but Army's legs lifted suddenly, and he turned on his head. Strong, Muldoon thought. Strong enough to kill Schneider?

"Heh," Army half-laughed as he slipped over and behind Muldoon in a split-second.

"Yeah, Army!" roared the crowd. The room filled as word spread on the street of the impromptu match between Muldoon and the African.

They struggled for a bit, and then finally Army got a half-nelson and was able to work his other arm to a crotch hold. Muldoon struggled for a moment, bridged in a last effort to save himself, then dropped his shoulders to the floor and the fall was given to the African.

"Hey Muldoon! It's even money . . . want in on it?" called a voice from the crowd. The betting was furious, as money changed hands among the onlookers. Muldoon noticed the large number of Irish faces that now filled the room. He ignored the soldiers, trying not to wonder which were real.

Then they came back together, and Muldoon dropped Army almost immediately. He tried for a hammer, then a scissors, but couldn't quite get either. The pace was slower than it had been for the first throw, each man going on the offensive in turns. Suddenly Muldoon got his opponent in an arm-lock, and Army struggled fiercely to break free. Muldoon tightened his grip and forced the struggling man's shoulders to the mat.

There was one fall left. They stood again and squared off. Blood dripped from a deep gouge over Muldoon's brow. He reached up and cleared it from his eye.

"Woohoo, Champeen," called Mabel from the bar. "Can I tumble with you next, Irish-Boy?"

He grinned at her, blew her a kiss, and then turned to Army as they came together again.

Muldoon knew he had him as he reached for his opponent. He quickly secured a crotch and a half-nelson, and forced Army's shoulders to the floor for the final throw.

The crowd went wild. He hadn't failed his fans, and even among the Africans, there was a grudging respect. He had beaten their champ, but the disappointed brawl Muldoon expected didn't happen. Instead, the men crowded around him, and patted him on the shoulder or shook his hand in congratulations. He turned to Kelly McAllister, who had left his seat when the long match had begun, forgetting his injuries in the excitement of the bout. The younger man smiled broadly and grabbed Muldoon by the arm.

"What a match!" he said. "When you lost that first fall I was afraid you couldn't come back. It was amazing."

"Thanks," Muldoon said as he walked to the bar where he'd left his gear. Over aching muscles, he drew on his jacket, hooked the belt about his waist, and stowed his equipment.

The bartender handed him ten dollars, his share of the bout's take, and set aside two dollars for the loser. Army made his way to Muldoon's side and offered his hand.

"Fine job," he said in a Deep South patois. "They said you were good, but I didn't know how so. You are good. You need something, you come here. You ask for George Army."

They shook hands. Muldoon turned to leave, but a thought came to him. "Army," he said. "Have you seen a man . . . " He paused. "A man with crimson eyes?"

The man didn't respond at first, then shook his head. "No. No sir, I never seen anyone like that."

"Okay," he said, then turned to Kelly. "Come on. We need to get out of here." He placed the flat policeman's hat on his head and hooked elbows with the younger man. McAllister leaned heavily against him. He looked back at Army as the wrestler pushed his way through the crowd, heading for the back room. Had he seen something in the man's eyes? A hint of recognition when he'd mentioned the crimson-eyed man? Maybe even fear?

He turned his mind from the African champ. "I've got to tell you something Kelly," he said. "You've got a great big problem, and it's not gonna go away too easily."

Muldoon glanced about warily, looking for policemen in the crowd, but there were none he could see. He continued quietly, "Well, you know now, this is the way it is. Karl Schneider found himself a one-way trip to the coal cellar. And he isn't ever coming out again, if you know what I mean."

"He's dead?" McAllister asked. "Who could have killed a big mug like him?"

"Here's the thing, now," Muldoon answered. "They think you did."

"Me?"

"I'm sorry, Kelly. But I'm gonna have to take you in."

"Take me in? Take me in?" he repeated as if dumbfounded. Suddenly he began struggling, trying hard to pull away from Muldoon.

"No, I'm not going to let you run. If you do, there's others that'll come after you. And they're not on your side. They won't treat you so well . . . you might even end up dead."

"They'll never find me, William! I'll hide out. Nobody knows the Points better than me."

"They'll find you. There's plenty of folks who'd turn in their own brother for a coin, let alone you."

"But they'll hang me, that's certain. I don't wanna swing!" Kelly turned to face Muldoon, pleading with him. "I've got to get away."

"I'm not going to let you hang. I'll find out who really killed Schneider. But you have to come with me now. It's the only way you'll be safe. With those ribs, a bit of rough handling could do you in."

Kelly loosened his grip on Muldoon's arm. "Okay," he said, deflated. "I'll come with you. But you've got to take care of Ma for me. She's gonna be worried."

"I know." Muldoon half-carried the younger man until he was able to catch a cab. They climbed into the buggy and settled heavily into the seat. The cabbie flicked his whip and the horse trotted slowly toward police headquarters. Even its leisurely pace seemed too quick for his friend. He helped Kelly from the buggy, and paid the cabbie. The young man stood beside him—head hung down and shoulders drooped. Then he held out his wrists, and Muldoon lightly secured them with his come-along, the leather-covered wire held Kelly's hands together. Grasping the ends, he led his prisoner into the building.

"Well done, Muldoon!" Captain Hayle said. He was just leaving for the day, and had paused at the door. The entrance hall behind him filled with policemen.

"McAllister's not so big," one patrolman said as he stood on the steps to see over the crowd.

"That's just an illusion," said another. "If he weren't standing next to Muldoon, he'd look his true size."

Quiet voices expressed their disbelief. Many of the cops didn't think Kelly McAllister could be the murderer, and they argued with those who did. Captain Hayle seemed to ignore their remarks.

"It looks like he gave you a struggle," Hayle said motioning toward Muldoon's filthy pants.

"Aye, sir. But I saved the jacket."

Twitters from the crowd brought a slight pink to the Captain's face. "Take your prisoner in and book him. He'll be spending his nights in the Tombs."

Blood seemed to drain from Kelly's already pale face. "Why do they call it the Tombs?" he whispered to Muldoon as he began shivering.

Muldoon nodded at the Captain and walked past. "Don't worry," he said in a low murmur. "It's not because it's filled with dead folk. The prison's just called the Tombs because it was built after a picture of an Egyptian mausoleum somebody saw in a book once."

Knowing that fact probably wouldn't make Kelly feel any better. He'd been accused of a murder he hadn't committed. Muldoon knew that now . . . with certainty. He couldn't possibly have killed Schneider in his current condition. And with the weight of police headquarters against him, it would be an uphill climb getting him out again.

CHAPTER 5

H E paused in the doorway. It always took Muldoon a moment before he entered the catacombs of death. The city morgue had a smell about it he couldn't really define. Just the smell of death, he supposed, mixed with the chemical scent of formaldehyde. The floors were swept clean down here, like the dead really cared about cleanliness. A derisive snort escaped his lips. The morgue was the cleanest spot in the city, he thought. But he still couldn't get used to the smell.

He shoved through the door. It had taken him all day to get here, when he'd planned on coming first thing.

"Hello, Danny," he greeted the desk clerk. "You're working late."

Young Danny O'Leary straightened abruptly, hiding a dime novel under the counter, a bright scene of cowboys on horses splashed across the cover. "Hello, Sergeant Muldoon. It's been a busy day. You here about the big guy? Real big one came in during the night. Doc's got him out right now."

The clerk almost skipped alongside Muldoon as he strode past the desk and into the inner recesses of the cellar morgue. He nearly smiled at the eleven-year-old's energy, the corner of his mouth turned up slightly, lifting the right side of his bushy red mustache. The boy gazed eagerly at Muldoon, hanging onto his every word and action.

"Yeah, it's my case," he lied.

"They didn't assign this one to a detective?" Danny asked. "They kept you on it? How come? I'd have thought Detective Benson or Graham would've come this morning."

"You know, Danny-boy, I'd have thought so, too, but sometimes a sergeant can figure things out that the best detectives in the ward can't see for nothing. And I suppose it's got something to do with his being a wrestler. Maybe the Captain figures I have more connections. You think I do, Danny?"

The youth laughed aloud, a high little boy's giggle. "Aye, that I do," he said. "I'd say you know all the right folks. You being the champ and all."

The boy's enthusiasm was infectious. Muldoon reached around the boy's shoulders squeezing playfully, tousling his hair with his other hand. He slid his arm down around Danny's neck, holding him in a light headlock. Danny giggled again and pushed free.

"You coming in?" Muldoon asked as they stepped into the far room.

Danny jerked away, backing nervously through the door. "Uh, no, I . . . I got some work to do in the front. Wash the floor . . . or something." The boy's big eyes opened wider, spooked, as he whispered, just loud enough for Muldoon to hear, "This one's different, nothing natural could have killed him."

The boy scrambled quickly from the room, imaginary shadows of ghouls and beasties chasing him out, mixing in with the gray corners of the dimly lit hall. He couldn't blame Danny. He wouldn't be in here if he didn't have to be, either. He pitied the boy when his duties brought him into this back room full of dead flesh. An image flickered into his mind, of severed arms and legs piled high, of battlefield doctors sawing, while other soldiers held screaming men down. With an effort, he pushed the thought aside, and turned about, ready to see what tales Schneider's body had to tell.

Muldoon stifled a shiver, whether from the chill of the room or the sight of yet another dead body, he wasn't sure. Death is a hard task-master, one he'd never truly got used to. It wasn't like death was new to him. He'd fought in the war, where dying was arbitrary . . . the man next to you, the one behind . . . yet the reaper left you standing. Now, as a policeman in New York, he saw the violent results of gang clashes and crime on a daily basis. He nodded in greeting and stepped toward the tall, dark-haired man leaning over the body on its slab. An oil lamp sputtered above him, casting dark shadows about the room.

"Hello, Doc," Muldoon said.

Bob Gamble, the coroner, glanced up from the rigid body, smiling with welcome. "Hello, Muldoon, I thought it would be you."

"So?" asked Muldoon, his light brogue stark next to the doctor's cultured English. "Have you learned anything I didn't already know?"

"Besides the lack of hair?" The doctor smiled broadly and leaned back on his heels. "The man was strangled."

The doctor pointed, tracing a dark bruise against the pallid flesh. "Look here," he continued. "You can see where the perpetrator held him. I'd say he was attacked from behind. This is the mark of an arm, not hands around his throat. You can see the way his elbow hooked around the neck, pulling back, pressing into the flesh. And here on the left arm, you can see where fingers dug into his forearm, pinning the arm down. Now, this had to be one strong fellow. He couldn't have easily killed a man the size of Karl Schneider."

"Just one man . . . " said Muldoon. How the hell could one man, alone, strangle a good wrestler? It would be a tough enough job for Muldoon, and he was the best wrestler in town. "Right handed?"

"It's probable. Right arm around the neck, the weaker, left hand leaving the finger marks."

Muldoon studied the cadaver, noting its complete lack of hair. He passed his hand over the scalp, where the stubble was just beginning to show. Even after death, Gamble had told him, hair and fingernails seemed to grow. Schneider hadn't shaved himself, he felt certain, but every last strand had been sheared clean. Why? He couldn't even begin to guess. He raised his eyebrows inquiringly, but Gamble simply shrugged.

"So, how did he do it?" asked Muldoon. "Came up behind him real quick, grabbed him in a headlock, and . . . is his neck broken?"

"No. That's the first thing I checked. There's no break."

"What is it, then? He had to have passed out quickly, before he had a chance to react. Is his windpipe crushed?"

"I think so, yes. That's what I'm about to check now." The doctor slipped his knife easily through the skin of the throat, baring the broken trachea. Science, Gamble had told him the first time Muldoon had come down here. Science can reveal the darkest secrets, simply by opening the dead. "He's got a thick neck. It took a tremendously strong arm to do this."

Muldoon nodded. "Alcohol?" he asked suddenly.

"Not much," answered the doctor. "There wasn't a smell of it, and none in his stomach. Just the remains of his dinner—pork, peas, carrots. I'd say a meat pie."

One arm across his waist, Muldoon rested his right elbow on the other fist, raising his hand to his face. He stroked his mustache with his index and thumb. "So, it was fast," he said at last. "From behind. And he didn't fight. He might have known his killer . . . but he was moved, so we can't tell. I don't think he died where we found him. He was brought there."

The coroner nodded in agreement. "That's about the gist of it. Oh, there's a little stab wound. There, in his rib." He pointed, and Muldoon picked up the dead man's left arm. A tight purple mark marred the flesh.

"Doesn't look like much," Muldoon said, but he knew it was the length of the blade, not the width that counted. "How deep?"

"Not very."

"Hmmm." The small instrument's use hadn't played a significant part in the man's demise, except perhaps, to prompt him toward it. It also meant that more than one man might have been present. One wielding the knife, the other strangling the victim.

As he dropped the arm, he noticed a ragged purple line at the wrist. He turned over the hand, studying a scrape on the inside of the wrist. Not a scrape, really, it seemed more like carefully removed skin. He looked questioningly at the coroner.

"That happened after he was dead," said the doctor. "I don't know why, I can't tell from what's left."

"Looks like he was skinned. I wonder what was there. Maybe a tattoo or a scar. Something the killer doesn't want anyone else to see."

"What do you think of the bruising?"

"Nothing," Muldoon replied. "The old stuff's from wrestling. The purple star? It's a bruise. Maybe meant to confuse us . . . maybe cause fear. Or send a message."

Muldoon grunted his thanks and passed back through the corridor and outer room. As he expected, Danny straightened quickly and dropped his book below the counter. He nodded to the youth. "See you, Danny-boy. Don't strain your eyes with all that heavy working, now." He knew the book would quickly reappear, its flashy red cover vivid in the drab gray room. He thought of the crimson-eyed man. Was it he who sent a message?

Depression dogged him as Muldoon headed home. His head pounded from the strain of taking his foster brother into custody, and he ached for a drink. The soldiers in his head crowded in on him, pacing him, staring at him . . . accusing him. As he passed a dark alley, a hand reached out and grabbed his forearm. He spun about and raised his hands defensively, but dropped them again as he recognized Detective Graham.

"McAllister was my catch." The Detective curled his lip into a snarl. "I sent my men to arrest him."

"Apparently, they weren't able to find him," Muldoon said. "He spent the afternoon sitting in a saloon, sipping cool drinks. Shouldn't have been too hard to spot him."

"You know they were supposed to pick him up. You beat them to him."

"And you think I'm supposed to do your work for you? Sending your man after me? I lost him in Mulberry Bend. It wasn't too hard. He couldn't even follow me through one alley and a ramshackle tenement. And now McAllister's safe in the Tombs where you can't touch him."

"Who says I want to harm him?" Graham narrowed his eyes. "He murdered a man, and now he has to pay. It's not me that wants him dead . . . it's the law."

"Says you! I say he did no such thing. And I'm going to prove it. The last thing that's gonna happen is the hanging of Kelly McAllister."

"That's right, Muldoon. He'll be swinging. I'll make sure of that."

"How will you do that? You have no proof. Just speculation."

"Whoa!" Graham said. "Big words there. Especially for a mug from the Points."

"I live in the Bowery," corrected Muldoon. "And I didn't come out of the city. I'm from Belfast . . . New York, not Ireland."

"Isn't that a Mick town?"

"Sure, it is."

"Irishmen," Graham spat on the sidewalk. "You Micks, where were you when the country needed help? Whining and crying like little children, complaining you didn't have a few hundred dollars to buy off the draft. You should have been proud to go to war. No, you got off the boat, claiming America as your new country. What do you Irish want? A new Ireland? Well, you can't have it. This is America."

"I fought in that war," Muldoon said, low and dangerous. "I'm proud of that. A lot of other Irishmen did, too, and died. What about you? Did you fight?"

He already knew the answer. Graham hadn't volunteered, and he hadn't been drafted. He wasn't Irish, so his number hadn't been called. Only Irishmen were called up when the draft started. What a foolish thing, he thought, to implement the new draft in New York City, something never done before in this country. And then not just anywhere, but smack in the middle of the Irish slums. Maybe if they'd included everyone in the draft equally, it would have been all right, but they hadn't. It was only for the Irish. The gangs fought each other most of the time, but just this once, they fought together . . . against those who tried to take away the one thing they had—their freedom.

Muldoon snorted. "Don't talk about war when you didn't have the guts to go."

Graham stood still and glared at him. "And one more thing," the detective said after a long pause. "Clean up your pants. You look like you've been wrestling in the street. I don't want to see you like this again."

Muldoon laughed aloud as Detective Graham stalked away.

He walked slowly toward his rooms on Elizabeth Street and thought about the war. They called it the "Civil War" now. He had volunteered for the 6th New York Infantry. Nobody had to ask him, he'd just gone.

Graham didn't know what he was talking about when he spoke about the Irish with such contempt. They'd stood up under pressure, and proved good enough for their adopted country. Of course, he was second generation Irish. It was as much his country as Graham's, or any Nativist English. He sighed as he trudged the long route from the morgue. He was past ready to end the day.

As he turned up the steps to his rooming house in Elizabeth Street, Muldoon clenched his jaw. Damn Detective Graham, he thought. He doesn't have the least idea what real death is like . . . what real sacrifice is. He rubbed his forehead, just above the eyes. This was going to be one hell of a headache. He was bone tired. Hadn't slept well. The dreams plagued him. He wanted a drink so badly, he could taste it.

CHAPTER 6

HE couldn't get away from the war. Memories of battles, snatch-es of conversations with men long dead, and hellish images of torn bodies in the aftermath of an engagement haunted Muldoon. Even in the middle of the day some minor event could trigger a flashback. Nights were the worst. He had to make it through the dark hours, and talk like Graham's brought raw memories to the surface. His dream began as they often did. Abrupt. Taking Muldoon back to the war—different times and places, but always locked in a helpless struggle with death. This time it took him back to October 9, 1861, and his first taste of war. He was back on Santa Rosa Island, Florida . . .

A hollow thud dragged him out of one kind of darkness, and dropped him into another. For a moment, he couldn't remember where he was, then with a swift movement William Muldoon grabbed his pistol. He rolled to the side as a lead ball ripped through his blanket. Half-kneeling on the sand floor of his tent, he pulled the trigger and the gun leapt in his hand. Its sudden flash lit the surprised face of the Rebel as his throat burst and he crumpled to the ground. The darkness was complete in the tent, and Muldoon figured it about two-thirty, maybe three in the morning. He couldn't have been off watch long. Patrick Ryan sat upright, the gray woolen blanket twisted around him. Ten other men stirred in the tight confines of the Sibley tent.

"Come on," Muldoon said. "Johnny-Reb's come to call." He was glad he slept fully clothed, only pausing to take hold of his Minnie rifle and check for his Bowie knife in its sheath. The Regulars hated the Irish sleeping with their guns close to hand, but they didn't trust Yanks much more than Rebs. Chaos engulfed him as he opened the tent flap.

Night's darkness tried to hide the running figures from his sight, but burning tents fought the shadows as men battled one another. It was oddly quiet, the sounds of fighting muffled in the night air. His tent was at the edge of camp, one of the first to be attacked. They would have to try to hold the Rebels back as the rest of the troops awoke. A gray-clad shoulder slammed into him, nearly knocking his feet out from under him. Friends and foes, both wore gray. He cursed with the realization as he wrapped his free arm around the man who'd run into him. The man screamed and shuddered as Patrick's bayonet speared him. Letting him drop, Muldoon moved into the fray, and his tent-mates spilled out behind him.

He didn't have time to look into faces as he stabbed, but he tried to recognize the plain gray broadcloth of the 6th New York uniforms. They weren't much different from the Rebel's, and as blood poured freely the men looked more and more alike, clothed in red spattered gray. He and Patrick fought back to back. For all Paddy's short size, there was no man Muldoon would rather have beside him. Raised on adjoining farms, they'd been friends all their lives. They'd tracked coyotes, and badgers, fox and bear. They'd hunted and adventured together. Now, they fought against the Rebs together. If he made it home, he'd ask Sarah Ryan to marry him, and then they'd be brothers.

Shadows flashed eerily against the backdrop of fighting men. Out of that sea, Muldoon picked out a figure he didn't recognize and squeezed the trigger of his Minnie. Its reassuring weight recoiled in his hands, and its bark filled his ear, temporarily blocking the higher pitched screams of men sounding their last cries. Instantly, he turned to deflect a thrust from a bayonet with the stock of his rifle. The blade slid past, lightly grazing his forearm, and his own red blood joined the mess on the battlefield. He stepped close and kneed the man in the groin, brought his own rifle around, and slid the bayonet in through the stained shirt.

Each new kill brought an exhilaration he hadn't expected. Red hot anxiety pumped through his veins as he engaged in the kill, or get killed, game. As each man fell before him, he felt a surge of triumph. In some detached corner of his mind he knew he ended the life of a brother, a son, a husband. But with certainty, he knew that man would just as easily have killed him. He didn't have time to think about them. He could only parry and swing the deadly bayonet on the end of his rifle as if it were a scythe, harvesting a field of men.

Muldoon couldn't figure how the Rebs had made it past the sentries without an alarm. Yet, here they were. The camp was filled with them, more than their small contingent could begin to handle. Unfamiliar gray began to outnumber the familiar as the Rebels continued up the trail.

Somewhere behind him the drum beat, and he knew Colonel Wilson had men formed up, waiting for the skirmish to reach them. They couldn't hold the larger force, and slowly he dropped back to the Colonel's line. Even then, Muldoon knew, the Rebels vastly outnumbered them. The 6th had been divided, some companies to the Keys, others to man Fort Pickens and its surrounding Batteries. Only three companies occupied their camp, two hundred some odd men against what seemed like a thousand.

"Fall back!" Colonel Wilson commanded as Muldoon stumbled backward through the sand, parrying and stabbing, and then another step back. Fort Pickens loomed behind them. If they could just make it to the Gulf side, the cannons could let loose and break the Rebel onslaught.

The Rebs didn't follow them as they rounded a bend in the path. His opponent suddenly disengaged, spun around, and ran down the trail. They all just turned and went back the way they had come. Out toward the gulf, the popping of guns sounded. It wasn't his battle over there, and he started to breathe easier.

They halted in an open area between dunes. A man vomited, unable to contain the horror of the battle. Others stood dumb with relief, or bent over gasping for air. Muldoon collapsed on the sand and looked up at the sky. A thin veil of smoke muted the stars. The metallic smell of blood, mixed with the sharp scent of burnt powder filled his nose. He gulped the air, wondering if it would ever be fresh again.

"William." Patrick flopped down beside him, laughed shrilly. "Heh, do I look as bad as you?"

"Worse." Muldoon looked at his friend, who'd begun wiping blood from his bayonet.

"You know, it's just gonna get dirty again. Probably before it even gets a chance to start drying."

Patrick continued cleaning, swabbing the blade over and over, trying to clear away the red with a blood-soaked bit of cloth. He dropped the rifle and rag and stared at his hands. He began rubbing them, trying to get rid of the blood. And then he began to shake.

Muldoon wasn't sure what he was supposed to feel. He only felt a kind of elation, a sort of excitement from the battle, and an eagerness to get back into the fray. He looked at his friend, who sat shaking and staring wide-eyed at his bloody hands. He glanced down at his own hands, noticed the blood oozing slowly from the wound on his arm. He didn't feel it. Later it would hurt, and maybe then he'd feel the emotions Patrick showed so plainly. 'Maybe he's a better man than I am,' he thought.

The sounds of battle echoed across the dunes. The distant popping of firearms reminded Muldoon of an autumn hunt. They'd flush the birds out of the brush, every gun would start blasting, and birds would rain out of the sky. But they weren't shooting fowl, they were killing men.

"They might be leaving. They didn't follow us," Patrick said.

"Knock on wood for that one." Muldoon tapped the butt of his rifle.

"You letting your Irish show?" Jimmy Dolan sank down beside them. New York City born and raised, the man was proud to hail from Hell's Kitchen, and he made sure everyone knew it. His small size belied his strength. Back home, he was a bricklayer and a fireman. Either place, he was one hell of a fighter. "I can't tell what's redder. Your hair, or the blood on your face."

"Long as it's not mine," Muldoon muttered and leaned back on his elbows, his Minnie resting across his knees. He'd reloaded, and she was in easy reach.

"You make a good target, Muldoon," Jimmy said. "Big guy like you should be the first shot."

"Damn you!" Patrick leaped toward the man. Muldoon grabbed him, and noticed the shaking hadn't subsided.

"Save it for the Rebs," he said.

"No, that's a jinx, William! He's gone and jinxed you!"

"I didn't mean nothing by it," Jimmy said. "Son of a bitch . . . looks like we're going back into it." He gestured toward the Colonel, who was quarreling with Major Vogdes and Captain Hildt. They'd brought up a few companies of regulars, and if push came to shove, the regulars always won.

" . . . we lure them into cannon range . . . " Colonel Wilson argued. "We could win this damn campaign in one go round."

Captain Hildt had drawn his saber, and shook it, pointing toward camp, his face red with anger. Muldoon couldn't hear his words, but knew he'd win the disagreement. Colonel Wilson might outrank the man, but he and his 6th New York Infantry were volunteers. The Regulars always won out. He dragged himself up from the sand. Within minutes, they had formed up again. Guns were loaded, and bayonets fixed. He felt a twinge of anxiety as they trotted toward the Rebel line. Not down the path, but straight across the snake and gator infested dunes.

"AAAHHHRRRR," he yelled, his voice mixing with the roar of his fellow Yanks as they charged through the ragged underbrush. Rattlers, Copperheads, Cottonmouth, he didn't think of them as he ran, but almost stopped short at sight of the odd square the Rebels had formed up in. Like walls made of men. Shots came from the darkness beyond their formation, and some of the Rebs dropped dead. As the 6th approached their shouts seemed to grow louder. From somewhere deep inside, his anger swelled, poured out, and he wanted nothing more than to feel the dull slip of his bayonet into Rebel hide. His vision clouded red, and his sense of time blurred. Bodies dropped before him, and the enemy turned and ran from their onslaught. He followed, butchering anyone unlucky enough to cross his path. The Rebels ran for their boats, and safety across the short stretch to the mainland. He stood, roaring angrily at them from the beach, frustrated to lose them so quickly, yet joyous in the victory.

As his rage subsided Muldoon looked at his fellows and recognized the ugliness. Battle lust distorted their features, their lips twisted with anger and eyes thinned to steely slits. He scanned their faces as he looked around for Patrick, but didn't see him.

The drums beat again, and he joined the mass of soldiers sorting themselves into their respective companies. The sergeant began calling names, marking them as present, injured, or dead. "Patrick Ryan!" he said. No answer. "Ryan! Anyone see what happened to Ryan?"

Muldoon's blood ran cold.

He growled savagely as he kicked off the blankets. The blood froze in his veins as he threw himself to the floor. Push-up after push-up, he couldn't drown the sounds of bullets whizzing, cannons roaring, and men screaming. The echoes of death filled him, drew him to the bottle, so he could finally drown the sounds in a black stupor. But he couldn't give in to the darkness, he wouldn't allow himself. With shaking hands, he drew on a pair of ragged pants, flannel shirt, and shoes. Outside he could run, like he did so many nights, trying to outpace the hounds of his own hell. Hours later, exhausted, he could return to his bed. Tonight, consumed with visions of the war, he thought of Kelly McAllister. He couldn't lose another friend . . . a brother . . . not like this.

CHAPTER 7

April 17

MULDOON snatched a few hours of exhausted sleep after his midnight run. He was bleary-eyed and sore, but not as bad as some days. He could deal with tired, but forget hangovers. He was done with them. The hard stuff called to him, but he hadn't had a drink in months. The few hours of rest a bender could give him wasn't worth the price. He couldn't get drunk enough to forget the war, and his dulled senses made him feel sluggish and dumb. So, when the liquor beckoned, he lost himself in exercise instead, a hard run, push-ups past the edge of endurance, or pull-ups at the bar he'd installed in his bedroom doorway. And then he'd wrestle, working out his anger and aggression on the mat.

He checked the clock on the mantle . . . it was too quiet. He couldn't hear the familiar sound of a baby crying, or Bonnie Nolan yelling at her husband in the next room. They'd never been ideal neighbors, and once they had the baby, their fights got worse. The infant's constant cry made the husband mad, and he'd demand that she shut the kid up. Then she would scream back, and finally start throwing things. Muldoon couldn't tell whether he hit her. Mrs. Dunn, the landlady, must have given them the boot. She'd threatened to ever since the child came.

Despite the Nolan's, the boardinghouse was better than most, and he could overlook the clamor. The building was a good one, not like the ones farther south in the Bowery where he used to live. This place was almost to German Village. Many of the buildings here were newer and better kept. The streets were cleaner, and spring flowers had just begun to bloom in pots set out on windowsills. Pretty Irish lace curtains flapped in the breeze, windows open to let in the air. The distance wasn't much, but it was a far cry from the squalor and filth he'd lived in since he'd returned from the war. He'd gone home to the farm first, but only ashes and burnt timbers marked the spot where the house had stood. His parents died in the blaze, and his brother hadn't come back from the war. With nothing left to his name, he couldn't support a wife and family, and he couldn't bring himself to face Sarah Ryan. Not after losing Patrick. So, he left Belfast and joined the masses of poor, struggling Irish in New York's slums.

His stomach growled, pulling him back from his thoughts. Mrs. Dunn charged for breakfast and dinner, whether her tenants ate it or not. If he didn't hurry, he'd miss it. He tossed the blanket up over his bed but didn't smooth it, leaving it for the maid. The room had come furnished, but all the little things were his. The bedclothes and spread, the linens, things most men took little notice of. Green dominated the room, his mother's favorite color. She would have said it was the color of Erin, but for him it was the color of his youth. He wanted the best of everything, and took care of what he owned.

Several people were already seated at the dining table when he entered. Danny and Margaret Flannigan sat across the table, by the front window. Danny's chair was pushed up against the heavy gold brocade curtains. Casper Biggs sat in the first chair, near the head of the table, and glowered at Muldoon as he came in. As the oldest man in the house, he made it clear that he felt the seat at the foot of the table was his due position. Mrs. Dunn had pointed out that her dining table was simply too small to seat Muldoon and two other people comfortably on one side. Biggs had acquiesced, but at each meal he would glare at him, and try to goad him with his conversation topics. Muldoon's gaze slid over the man, and then noted the empty seat across from Biggs. Don Hardin hadn't come down yet. Two empty chairs marked the absence of the young couple and baby. Mrs. Dunn's seat at the head of the table was also empty—at least for the moment.

"So where were you last night?" asked Mrs. Flannigan, as she turned to Muldoon.

"I had a case," he said. She moved almost imperceptibly closer and leaned one elbow on the table.

"Can you speak about it?" she asked and winked conspiratorially.

"Don't be silly, Margaret," ordered Mrs. Dunn as she swept into the room, a dish in her hands. The small figure of Betsy, the maid, peeked from behind her, a loaded tray held precariously in her arms. "We aren't interested in what dismal goings on Sergeant Muldoon must be involved with! Scandalous behavior is not fit conversation at my table. It is unfortunate enough that the dear man must clean the gutters for us, but after all, it must be done. One simply doesn't want to hear about it." She lay the dish on the table, and then took her seat, back ramrod straight, and watched as the nervous servant girl placed dishes on the sideboard.

"Well," replied Mrs. Flannigan as she quickly removed her elbow from the table. "It's not like we get any news here."

"No, we don't," Mrs. Dunn said. "Now that is enough of that. If you must have conversation with your meals, at least make it pleasant."

Mr. Biggs tried to hide his snide smile. He was an unpleasant fellow, thin and waspish. He kept the books at Lloyd's Pharmaceuticals. Muldoon imagined that sitting behind a ledger all day had turned the man sour. He almost wished Biggs had killed Schneider. He'd love to bring the man in. He could never have pulled it off alone, of course, but perhaps if he'd acted as part of a larger group? Muldoon had seen Biggs at wrestling and boxing matches. He, and his cronies, always backed fighters from New England. There was one in particular, a large boxer from Boston, he thought, but wasn't sure of the man's name. He looked across the table again with a new shadow of suspicion. After all, he thought, the man is blatantly Nativist. He shrugged off the feeling. What were the odds a tenant of his own boardinghouse could be involved in this murder?

Mrs. Flannigan nudged her husband. Muldoon could see the tiny movement of her body as her foot swung toward the man, her up-swept auburn hair bobbed as she motioned toward his chair. The man's face grew pink as he tried, quietly, to move his seat away from the curtain. It was no use, the back leg was lodged on the brocade, and the fabric pulled forward as he moved.

All eyes shifted to Mrs. Dunn.

"If you would like to pay for that, Mr. Flannigan," she said, "I would gladly refit the fabric to your bed. I'm sure the gold would do wonders to liven your room."

His complexion burned even brighter as the man turned his mild face toward the landlady. "Thank you, Mrs. Dunn. I'm sure I would love a new bedcover, but it does look so beautiful in here. Your decorating touch is superb. I know my wife would appreciate any suggestions you would care to provide as to the decoration of our room."

Muldoon glanced again at Mrs. Dunn across the table. She graciously nodded at the unfortunate offender, and then asked Biggs to say the prayer. The little man's gaze slid across to Muldoon as though he expected a challenge to this responsibility, too. But he was Protestant, as was Mrs. Dunn. Like the Flannigan's, Muldoon was not. Any prayer at her table wouldn't be led by a Catholic. Surreptitiously the husband and wife quickly crossed themselves, their own prayers silent. Finally, the dishes were passed, and Muldoon took his double share. He paid extra for it, along with his rent, so Mrs. Dunn didn't object.

"The Nolan's aren't with us, I see," said Mr. Biggs suddenly and his wicked smile spread slowly across his face. Mrs. Flannigan almost choked on her eggs.

"They've found other rooms," Mrs. Dunn said. "In an establishment that allows children."

Muldoon controlled his surprise. He thought they had been turned out because of the fighting. He hadn't realized it was the child. For a moment, he wondered if she'd have turned them out if they hadn't been Irish and Catholic. His eyes shifted toward Biggs. That man would have none of them here, not Muldoon, not the Flannigan's. He was an unabashed Nativist, and had been a Know-Nothing before that party had been swallowed up by the new Republicans. They were called that because of their refusal to speak about the issues . . . they 'knew nothing' . . . they were anti-slavery, anti-alcohol, and anti-immigrant, and brought their prejudices into their new fold. But, mostly, they were anti-Irish.

He took a sip of coffee, then asked Mrs. Dunn, "Have you any prospects?"

"I'm certain we shall have several inquiries. I've put a notice in the Times." Her expression softened as she turned to look at him from her end of the table. "I'm sure you would be interested in who will be on the other side of your wall, Sergeant Muldoon. I shall inform you before I make a decision."

"I hope you would let me help you with this decision, Mrs. Dunn." Biggs stared at Muldoon, raw dislike filling his expression. "We must be certain to keep the wrong element out. Too many of them have forgotten their places in society. They scrabble out of their filthy lairs, trying to dislodge us from our rightful places."

Muldoon barely controlled the snort that rose to his lips, but he knew that dislike sparked in his own eyes.

CHAPTER 8

MULDOON turned up his collar against the cold rain. He strode quickly toward Police Headquarters, and wondered where Casper Biggs had been the night Schneider had been killed. The wrestler was exactly the type the man railed against. The neighborhood, once all English, had become a mixed district with an ever growing Irish and German population. As a patrolman, he hadn't made enough to live in a neighborhood like this, but once he made Sergeant, he was able to put aside a bit . . . just a little at a time. Then he hit pay dirt after he became the city's wrestling champ, and he could easily afford to live in Mrs. Dunn's boardinghouse.

Wrestling was the one thing he had left. His only inheritance. With it he improved his lot, and hoped to regain the wealth his family once had.

"Collar-and-elbow," his father had said. "Now that's a gentleman's type of wrestling." Muldoon had learned to grasp his opponent's collar with one hand and his elbow with the other, and then try to force the other man off his feet.

Once he'd gotten pretty good, his father decided he was ready for Lancashire style. It was the less skillful of the two techniques, really a rough and tumble affair. Two men wrestled wildly, no holds barred. They tried to break bones, or gouge eyes. They stopped at nothing, intent only to win. There simply weren't many rules. Muldoon had thought he should have learned this style first, but soon realized his father was right. With collar-and-elbow, he'd developed his muscles, and gained balance and flexibility while learning how to withstand his opponent's methodical assault. When he got into his first real Lancashire match he thought he was prepared for the violent onslaught, but he lost, with a dislocated shoulder and a deep gash on his cheekbone where his opponent had tried for his eye.

During the war, he continued to wrestle. It was something soldiers did in their free time. It didn't cost the army anything. All it took was two men with a little time on their hands and someone to referee, so the officers encouraged it. It kept the boys busy. He learned the most formal type of wrestling, Greco-Roman, during the war. But mostly, the troops liked Lancashire. Muldoon won nearly every match, and became his regiment champion. Soon, he was wrestling the champions from other regiments, usually winning, as they moved about the South.

After the war, he wrestled in impromptu back street matches until his prowess drew the attention of Harry Hill, whose saloon on Houston Street was the premier fighting venue. Within a week, his first match had been arranged, a boxing match. Harry Hill and his patrons preferred the danger and excitement of a heavyweight bare-knuckle brawl. Muldoon was good, but he liked the studied science of Greco-Roman wrestling. A few weeks later, his burly size and fighting skills drew the attention of State Representative William Tweed. Muldoon had taken down one of Tweed's henchmen in a mixed match, wrestling for the first and second falls, and boxing to end the match. He got one of the two falls, and knocked the guy out in the third round.

"Get rid of him," Tweed had said, waving toward his fallen man. A couple men grabbed the fighter under the arms and dragged him away. The fat politician walked slowly toward Muldoon, tipped his head to the side, and surveyed his physique. "You're a good fighter. And, it looks like I'm in need of a new man. Show up at police headquarters tomorrow morning. Tell them the Boss sent you." As head of the Democratic machine, Tweed had influence, and liked to put men in places where he could use them.

As Muldoon climbed the steps to the big building on Mulberry Street, Detective Benson emerged, a look of concern on his face. "Muldoon!" he said, grabbed his arm and pulled him back down the steps. "Come on. I've left word you're working with me today. We've got to move quickly, or it'll be too late."

Muldoon let the detective lead him down the street. Benson was a tall, slender man . . . nearly as tall as Muldoon . . . and rather handsome, with dark hair and flashing eyes. He had a trace of something indefinable about him, something Muldoon attributed to loneliness. Like so many people, he'd lost his family during the war. As a detective, he wore civilian clothing instead of the blue uniform Muldoon had on. His clothes were rumpled, as though he'd slept in them. When they'd gone a short distance, Benson spoke again.

"I heard about your friend. I mean, I didn't know he was your friend at first. Graham was so smug, acting like the cat that's caught the rat. All he could talk about back there was how he captured the man who killed Schneider." He glanced at Muldoon. "And then, I found out you brought him in. He was gloating like it was his collar, and he didn't have anything to do with it at all."

"I didn't want to. I was afraid if I didn't bring Kelly in first . . . well, you know." Muldoon studied the tips of his shoes, then took off his hat and ran a hand through his thick red hair.

"Yes, I do know," Benson said. "You were afraid he'd be killed. That's Graham's way, all right. Bring them in on their feet, or off."

Muldoon nodded. He'd seen plenty of men, innocent or not, who never got their day in court thanks to Detective Graham. "So, if we're going to investigate, we're going to have to do it quickly," he said.

"That's about the size of it," Benson said.

"I want to take a look at Schneider's stuff. I didn't have a chance to before. Hayle and Graham jumped so quick on McAllister, I thought I'd better find him first."

"You did what you needed to do." Benson patted Muldoon's shoulder. "Do you know where Schneider lived?"

"Aye. Up in the Village, in the German section."

The two turned north up Mulberry, and went back past headquarters. The street got increasingly nicer as they headed away. Windows were clean, doors propped open, even in the drizzle, to let fresh spring air into well-tended shops. Karl Schneider had lived in a narrow, three-story building. It was a corner structure with a bakery on the ground floor, which opened out to the street. Big glass panes provided passers-by a glimpse of hearty breads and sugar-powdered cakes. Muldoon breathed in the warm scent of yeasty bread, and for just a moment, he pictured his mother in her bright kitchen, pulling a loaf out of a black cast-iron oven.

As he turned the corner, Muldoon opened a side door and entered the dark stairwell. A door behind the steps led into the baker's apartment in the back of the storefront. He climbed the steep stairs, passed a lone door on the second floor and went on up to the room at the top. The building was well kept. Unlike the McAllisters' tenement, you weren't likely to find rat droppings on these stairs.

Detective Benson ran lightly up the steps behind him, with a key the baker had given him. Reaching forward, he unlocked the door, and pushed it open. They stepped carefully into the dark room. Tightly-closed curtains blocked the day's damp light, not the airy open-lace type of the Irish, but a heavy jacquard print. As Muldoon's eyes adjusted to the gloom, he realized this was a large outer chamber. Several worn chairs and a settee were arranged by the window, a large desk against the far wall. A door, just to the left, stood slightly ajar. A light noise came from the other room, and Muldoon pulled out his nightstick as he nodded toward the door. Benson returned the motion.

Quietly, he crossed the open space and stood to the side of the door. He didn't own a gun, and the department didn't supply them, but Benson did. The detective came up just behind him, pointing the barrel at the door. With a swift motion, Muldoon opened it and looked inside. The room was empty. The furniture was sparse, the bed shoved up under an open window. The curtain billowed inward as it caught the breeze then rattled against the pane as it sucked back against the glass with the retreating wind. A short chest of drawers sat against the opposite wall. At the far end of the room, a single, ladder-back chair stood, turned slightly toward the window as though an unseen figure sat there and watched the street below. Rain ran down the window glass, dripped from the partially open window, and soaked the drab wool blanket a deeper shade of gray.

"You can look around in here," Benson said. "I'll look in the other room. But I doubt there's much here."

"I don't think so, either," Muldoon said. He turned to the chest and slid open the top drawer. He removed each article, and placed them on the dresser top next to a wash basin and pitcher. The drawer held underclothes and socks, a shaving cup and brush, and a straight razor. Its blade gleamed wickedly as Muldoon removed it from the drawer. Had it sheared every hair from Schneider's body? He pulled the drawer completely out, turned it upside down, and checked to see whether something had been attached to the bottom. Then, he looked inside the now-empty space where the drawer had been. Nothing.

The second drawer held extra shirts and two pair of gloves. Several of the fingers on one set were nearly worn through. The second pair was brand new, of an impeccable cut. Muldoon held them for a moment and imagined them on his own hands. They would probably fit. He replaced them reluctantly.

The bottom drawer was the same, nothing except for several pairs of slacks. They were all exceptional quality. As before, the drawer and space held no hidden surprises. Muldoon stood up slowly, his left foot had gone to sleep while he was kneeling. He shook his leg as he felt around the edges of the mirror, then pulled it off the wall, looked behind then re-hung it. Nothing hid behind the dresser, either.

A peg on the wall held several jackets. Muldoon checked each one thoroughly, and admired their cut. He hadn't remembered Schneider as particularly well dressed. He must not have noticed, it hadn't really mattered before. A second peg held the man's wrestling tights. Again, there was nothing unusual about them. He picked up the chair, turned it over, and then replaced it where it had been. As an after-thought, he pushed it slightly askew, as Schneider had left it—a token superstition—as if the man's spirit occupied it still.

The only thing left in the room was the bed. He pulled back the blankets and set them on the chair. He felt the stripped mattress, but he couldn't feel anything through the ticking. He knelt down and looked underneath. At first glance, there was nothing. But just as he started to rise, something caught his attention, a sudden flash of blue as his gaze slid past. He lay down flat on the floor and looked up at the underside of the bed, the horsehair-filled mattress rested on woven straps. Near the head of the bed, he spied the bit of blue. Pulling it from its hiding place, he brought it out from under the bed.

"Now why would anybody want to hide a Bible?" asked Detective Benson from the door.

"I don't know," Muldoon said. He flipped through the small book, a King James version. It was printed in English, not in German. Muldoon wondered about that, since German was Schneider's native tongue.

"Maybe it's how he learned English," Benson said.

"Didn't do him much good," Muldoon said, remembering the man's stilted speech.

"Keep it," Benson said. "We might need it again. And if not, you've got a Protestant Bible."

"Just what I need, I think my Ma would turn over in her grave!" Not a German Bible, he thought, but English. Why would he hide an English Bible?

Benson laughed heartily and wiped tears from his eyes. "I didn't know you were so religious," he said at last. "Old 'Father' Muldoon . . . he wrestles with the devil."

"All right, all right, not funny," Muldoon said. "Did you find anything? Or am I the only one to win a prize this morning?"

"Nothing out here," Benson said. "But the man had some expensive taste. That's good tobacco in the humidor. And he has a couple of bottles of expensive wine under the table over there." He pointed in the general direction.

"What's that?" A small piece of wood, about six inches long, lay on the table between settee and chair. Picking it up, he turned it over in his hand. It looked something like a stake and was splintered at each end, as if broken from a larger piece. The initials A.R. were carved on one side.

"I don't know."

Muldoon pocketed it, along with the small Bible.

"We should take along those bottles of wine, too," said Benson.

Muldoon picked up the two glass bottles.

"I'll take those for now," Benson said.

Muldoon gazed longingly at the bottles. He wasn't sure whose problem was worse—his or Benson's. Both craved the magic elixir to help them forget. But he'd sworn off the stuff and Benson hadn't.

"Did you find anything else in here?" Muldoon shook off his momentary weakness.

"Just this." Benson handed Muldoon a small photograph. It was a grainy, sepia-toned picture of a sergeant in the Union Army. Muldoon looked closely at the small face of Karl Schneider. Not that it was unusual, since so many men had taken part in the war. Still, Muldoon slipped the little picture between the pages of the blue Bible.

As they left the building, Muldoon and the detective stopped in at the bakery. "Did you get what you want?" the German baker asked them as he handed a diminutive elderly woman her change.

"Aye, we did. But we're taking some things, might be evidence. Do you have something I can put them in?" Muldoon showed him the wine bottles.

"Certainly. If you have a nickel, I can give you a flour sack."

Muldoon dug a five-cent coin out of his pocket and offered it to the man. The fabric was valuable. After washing it, a woman could carefully remove the seams and remake it into a dress, a shirt, or an apron. The baker rummaged through a pile of sacks behind the counter.

"Any particular pattern?" he asked with a grin. "If they wouldn't stamp their name so big, and maybe use flowers instead of always stripes, or plain, the women would pay even more."

Muldoon shrugged, it didn't really matter to him. He wasn't going to do anything with it besides store Schneider's paltry belongings.

"Has anyone come by?" Muldoon asked suddenly. "Besides us?"

"*Nein*. Not a soul."

"Does Schneider have any relatives? Someone who can claim his things?"

"I believe he has a sister. But I've never seen her."

"Then, pack his stuff up before you rent out the place. Don't get rid of it. If I find the sister, I'll send her your way." Muldoon knew the man would sell the items as easily as store them. Backed by the authority of his uniform, he hoped the baker would do as he said. Still, there wasn't much respect for New York City's finest.

The baker handed Muldoon a gold striped sack. It was relatively clean and neatly folded. He glanced at the policeman with a sheepish expression. "The women pay a few cents more when the sacks look good."

"Listen," Muldoon said. "If anybody comes by, or anything strange happens, you let me know, okay? Send someone down to Police

Headquarters on Mulberry Street. I work out of there, not one of the precinct houses. Ask for Muldoon."

"Yah, I'll do that." He looked carefully around, and then leaned closer to Muldoon, his voice low. "He said he was haunted by something bad. Because of something he had done. Do you . . . do you think he was killed by the devil?" Fear marked the man's voice.

"No, no witches, no devils. Just a man."

"Then, a strong man—like you," said the baker. "Nobody else could do that, to kill Schneider without the help of the devil."

Muldoon shook his head. Here again was the troubling rumor, and it brought the crimson-eyed man back to his thoughts. "Have you . . . " He paused. He didn't want to contribute to the superstitious alarm on the street, but somehow, he thought it important. "Have you seen a man with reddish-colored eyes?"

Fear flickered across the baker's face. "To see Schneider? *Nein.*" He turned away. "That's all I know," he said. "Nothing more. Please, no more questions."

Muldoon thanked the man for the bag, and carefully stowed the wine bottles inside. He wasn't sure why, but he kept the Bible in his pocket. He turned, and went outside, where Detective Benson waited. Curious, he thought. Does the baker know something, or is he afraid a devil actually killed the wrestler? They walked with long strides and swiftly reached Headquarters.

"Muldoon! Benson!" roared a voice as they entered the building. Benson glanced over at Muldoon and rolled his eyes. They turned toward the stairs where the Captain stood waiting. "I want to see you both up here, immediately!"

CHAPTER 9

M ULDOON stopped at the front desk and handed the Sergeant the bag. "Here, Foley, make sure this gets locked up. It's some of Schneider's personal effects. There's a couple of bottles in there . . . and I'd prefer if they're full when I see them again."

Foley pushed aside the papers he was working on. "You both know you're in for it. He's been stalking around all morning, wondering where you been. I got you on my list, Muldoon. Says you're working with Benson, so you're covered. But I couldn't tell him what you two are working on."

"The Schneider case," Benson said, then he nudged Muldoon. "Let's get upstairs."

Captain Hayle leaned back in his chair as the Detective and Sergeant entered. He glared at Muldoon. "Can you tell me what you've been doing all morning?"

"Detective Benson has been searching Karl Schneider's apartment. Of course, he required another officer's assistance. Since I was available, he asked that I accompany him. Sir."

"What were you looking for?"

"Evidence of his murder. Since he hadn't been killed where he was found, the Detective wanted to see if the crime took place in the victim's rooms." He carefully framed his answers to avoid mentioning Kelly McAllister.

"And did you find any evidence?" the Captain continued.

Muldoon wasn't deceived. The Captain didn't like him. He'd fire him in a heartbeat if he could, but he couldn't. His was an appointed position, and by Boss Tweed, no less. Hayle was stuck with him, and he knew it. Muldoon knew the Captain wondered what connection he had with Tweed—whether he was an informant, or not. If the Captain was caught looking into it too deeply he might be out of a job himself. For the time being, he continued to push the edges, feeling out how much influence Muldoon had.

"No, nothing important," Muldoon answered the man, guardedly. "Nothing to point to a murderer and nothing to prove motive."

"We don't need to prove motive!" said Hayle as he slammed his hand down hard on the desk. "We know why McAllister killed him! We have motive. We even know how he killed him. The only thing we don't know is where the murder took place."

"Aye, Sir," Muldoon said. "So you said yesterday."

The Captain glared up at Muldoon, maintaining eye contact even while he addressed the detective. "Benson, this case is wrapped up. McAllister was sentenced this morning, and he'll be strung up on Hanging Day. There's been a theft I need you to handle. And Muldoon . . . you can go walk the beat with Sergeant O'Malley. I'm certain Benson can handle this one on his own."

The Captain's words numbed him, and he nearly stumbled as Benson pressed a hand against his chest pushing him backwards out the door. How could he have been tried so quickly? And on so little evidence? He thought quickly . . . ten days. That's all he had. Ten days until hanging day, and he had nowhere to start.

"Connect the dots," Benson breathed as they left the office. "Do it quickly or your friend will swing on the 27th." The words echoed in his head as Muldoon made his way to Paradise Park to find Sergeant O'Malley.

CHAPTER 10

Sergeant O'Malley grinned broadly as Muldoon entered the Park. "The Captain finally found you, did he?"

"Aye. Made the mistake of stopping by to drop off evidence."

"Too bad, if I'd seen you, I'd have warned you. He was raging this morning. Then, when you and Benson didn't show up, he was right mad."

The rain had let up, but dark clouds hung low and threatening. Muldoon leaned against a ramshackle sentry box, swinging his short daystick. The building groaned with his weight. Like the rest of this part of the city, it was bare of paint, the color long since peeled away. Its timbers were warped and slowly rotting. The building had stood nearly sixty years, a remnant of better times in this quarter, when policemen had been called Leatherheads because of the odd, tight-fitting hats they had worn. The dilapidated building wasn't really much more in size than an outhouse, tall and thin, barely wider than the width of a door on all four sides. A round hole had been cut on each side at about head-height so a man could stand inside and still see out. The policemen rarely sat inside. It was easier to walk, especially when winter's frigid cold set in. A man might be found frozen in his box the next morning if he wasn't careful.

Muldoon pushed off from the shack and walked slowly down the street. Two cops standing by their box very long looked like idlers, gossiping rather than preventing crimes. O'Malley stepped in alongside him. Muldoon watched the people as he strolled past. This district was rife with transgressions, all he had to do was point in some random direction and he could arrest any man or woman in his sight. But that would be pointless, he knew. There wasn't enough room in the Tombs and all the other jails and prisons in the city combined to hold all the criminals from this one district.

Still, it was a lively place, a beat Muldoon loved. He could stand in the middle of the Park and facing any direction, he could look up two streets. The five points, as they were called: Cross to the northeast, lower Orange to the southeast, Cross again southwest, Anthony due west, and Orange again to the northwest; this was home to a multitude of Irish immigrants. Nearly everyone was on foot, walking from place to place. The tall, once-stately buildings—most constructed a century ago or more—had fallen into ruin. But the streets were long and straight, packed with vibrant humanity. Walk up any of those streets, and it would lead a man to the future of the city.

All around him, Muldoon could hear the people. In this district, the sounds were Irish, the particular lilt to their voices familiar and somehow comforting. Children dodged between passers-by, but he knew most of them weren't playing. It just appeared as if they were. They were pickpockets, messengers, or match girls. Each had a job to do, and did it as well as they could, or they wouldn't survive. They were clothed in rags. Secondhand cloth was remade into ever smaller items, children's clothing being last, before the material became patchwork bedding or was discarded. And even then, somebody else would find a use for it. Although the place was filthy and vermin-filled, nearly everything was recycled. Only human and animal waste was not used again and again. The piles of rot thrown from windows were excrement, not trash.

Muldoon watched as a young boy with a heavy bat in his hand chased off another kid, and then returned to his vigil at the tall iron fence that bordered the park. His brother stood nearby, at the other end of a row of rags hanging from the bars. When their mother had finished washing, she had carried the clothes out here and hung them on the fence to take advantage of the break in the rain. If they were left alone to dry, they'd be gone within seconds; people would swarm down on the unguarded rags like buzzards to a dying dog. All along the fence, other boys watched laundry, too. But if they could pinch something off the next kid's wash, they'd do it quick as a breath of air.

Men and women alike filled the streets. Most looked as though they loitered. But ragged people had places to go, every bit as much as wealthier folk uptown. Women carried baskets of vegetables for the evening's meal. Potatoes and cabbages, beans and peas were all past their prime and wouldn't last long, but they couldn't afford to buy better quality foods. Men pushed carts full of rags, or dented pots and pans, or some other item that still had some useful life left in it, hoping to sell them for the pittance they could receive in this depressed sector of the city.

The two policemen strolled slowly through the crowd. They were well known in the Park. O'Malley was here more often than Muldoon these days, since Detective Benson had started using him in his investigations. Sometimes brawn was needed if things went bad, but Muldoon was also smart and the two made a good team. Now, Muldoon chafed at the bit that Captain Hayle controlled.

"It's too bad the Captain is taking Detective Graham's side," O'Malley said. "That Kelly McAllister, he's a nice fella, now."

"Aye," Muldoon said. "He's a good man. I don't think he did it. He couldn't have. He took a real licking from Schneider. Got busted up bad."

"I seen that fight." O'Malley nodded. "He took a pounding. I thought, right at the end there, that he was dead his-self."

"I know. He was bent near double for that final fall. Broke some ribs. He's lucky his back didn't break, too." Muldoon shook his head dismally. "I shouldn't have let him fight Schneider. Didn't really think he was ready, but he's such a scrapper. He wanted his big shot."

"Don't go blaming yourself, now. You had no way of knowing someone would kill Karl Schneider that way. I don't know of anyone so strong as could strangle a guy like him. Excepting you, of course."

"Schneider was a good wrestler. He had a thick neck, and could break out of near any hold . . . and quick."

"Course, he wasn't up to your caliber. I can't think of a man in town who is."

Muldoon considered the various wrestlers in the city. There were few men left in town willing to fight him. Harry Hill had to issue challenges to outsiders now. He didn't have a match every Saturday any longer. But the pay was better. The local champ from some distant locale would arrive in town, fresh-faced and unsuspecting, eager to prove his skill against the New York City man. He would come with a reputation of his own, and an ego to match. And then he'd get in the ring with Muldoon. Harry Hill's back room would be filled with fans, drinks in hand, thick tobacco smoke curling toward the ceiling. Clutching fistfuls of cash, they'd bet heavily, the regulars for Muldoon, newcomers for their man. But Muldoon always won.

"You don't put any stock on these rumors about the devil, do you?" O'Malley crossed himself quickly. "What with that star marked on him. I heard there's devil-worshiping witches on the prowl. They come out at night, like rats."

"I don't think it's got anything to do with the devil," answered Muldoon. He'd heard the troubling rumors, too, about men who gathered at night and held secret meetings. Even in New York City, not everyone was happy with the outcome of the war, and he suspected there were still some rebellious souls holding the meetings. "Men make men's problems."

They turned a corner, heading back toward the shack. Muldoon looked sidelong at O'Malley. "You haven't heard of a man with crimson eyes, have you?"

"Crimson eyes . . . you mean . . . red?" O'Malley laughed. "Every night. Comes from staying too long at the bars."

Muldoon snorted.

"Well . . . " O'Malley dropped his voice. "Maybe I've heard of someone. Something. Word on the street says there's a beast. A devil. It's him, they think killed Schneider. Could be, he's the one you're asking about?"

A cold finger slid down Muldoon's spine. "Could be," he said, squelching the raw sensation. Men make men's problems. Whatever else he might be, he isn't a devil.

He stopped as they reached the policeman's shack. "You know," he said. "The Captain's stuck me down here on the beat, and he said the case is over. But he didn't tell me I couldn't do a little talking to folks while I'm here."

"Well now . . . I suppose he couldn't stop you from talking. You've got to do that to get your job done anyway."

"And we're right down here, near the scene of the crime."

The two spent the rest of the afternoon questioning people who might have seen something. They walked back over to the location where the body had been found, where Cross Street headed slightly northeast out of the Park. There wouldn't be any clues left . . . if there had been any at the start. Too many people crowded into this district, and every inch of ground was traveled, muck stirred up by passing feet.

At the spot, Muldoon glanced around, imagining the Park as it would have been when Schneider's body was dumped in the road. It would have been dark, as it was when Muldoon had last been here. But the area stayed lively until perhaps three in the morning, and even after that, some people would be on the streets. There might have been a nightwalker around. The prostitutes traversed the streets very late, some of them coming home from a better district where they had waited outside exclusive gaming halls and clubs, hoping to catch the eye of a willing customer.

Muldoon looked up at the buildings, their windows opening onto the street like blind eyes unable to see, or tell, what had occurred a few nights previous. Now, he had to move quickly to find out what they'd looked down on. He chose the first building, and entered its cool recess. On the ground floor was a grocery. In this district, it was mostly a front . . . to be a grocer. Men and women alike ran the various stores, but in the back rooms they sold liquor in squalid barrooms.

A short, round man worked behind the counter, pulling tins out of a crate and stacking them on a shelf along the back wall. Muldoon was impressed. This was probably the only legitimate grocery on the Park.

"Can I help you?" The proprietor turned as he heard the cop's feet scraping on the wooden floor.

"I hope you can. Two nights ago, a man was murdered. His body was dumped just outside your store."

The grocer quickly crossed himself. "Ah, and you'd be talking about that German fellow . . . Schneider was his name?"

"Aye. I'm looking into the case."

"I heard they've gone and charged one of our own. An Irishman. You trying to clear him . . . or hang him?"

"Clear him," Muldoon said.

"That's different, then. I'll talk to you, but I don't have much to say. I didn't see anything. It happened at night, you know."

"Are your rooms behind the store?" Muldoon asked.

"Aye, but the window's on the other side from where the bloke was dropped. Got a tenant rooming on that side. You might want to talk to him."

"That I would," Muldoon said. "Just a few more questions?"

The grocer nodded.

"You were home Sunday night?"

"Of course. I got my wife. She'd never abide it if I weren't in the sack all night alongside her."

"Right. And the front is locked up good and tight, you don't have anything else going on in here?"

The man's face reddened, more with anger than guilt Muldoon thought. He bit out his words. "If I did, I wouldn't have the wife I got now." Watching his own hands the grocer set the tin he'd been gripping onto the counter between them. He turned his gaze back on Muldoon, the flush fading from his skin. "No, we're quiet folk, sergeant. I know it's just your duty . . . to ask such a question. Let me show you, so as to set your mind at ease."

Muldoon nodded at O'Malley, where he stood leaning against the door. Turning back to the grocer, he assured him the small shop would be safely guarded by the man in blue. A door behind the counter opened to a short hall with two doors, one on each side. They entered the door on the left. Inside was a set of rooms, the large front room with an attached kitchen, and a small back bedroom. A third room, not more than a closet, was being redone for a child.

"It's for the babe," said the man, running a hand over his balding head. He swelled with pride. "He's getting big for the cradle. Going to need his own room soon."

Muldoon nodded, returning again to the main room.

"Where are your wife and child now?"

"She's at her Ma's. She goes over there to watch the wee ones so's the old lady can work. The babes don't do too well over here, what with the grocery."

"Get into trouble, I suppose?"

"That's about it. Now, do you want to see the other side?"

Muldoon nodded, following through to the other apartment. The grocer fumbled with his keys, finally unlocking the heavy door.

Nobody was inside. "Mr. Kavanagh's a good tenant. Comes in early, so I can lock up. And he don't go out again 'til morning."

"Good. Then, he might have something to tell."

"If you'd come back again, around six this evening, he should be in."

Muldoon strode over to the window, pulling back the curtain. On the sill, a nearly empty whiskey bottle sat on a cloth, a glass at its side. His stomach knotted. The longing was as strong as it had been the first day he'd gone without a drink. He pulled his gaze away. Next to the glass lay three dice. Muldoon fingered the curtain. It was Irish lace. Good stuff. Like his parents had when he was growing up. He turned to the grocer. "Did your wife make these?" he asked.

"Sure, and she did. She's good at that sort of thing. It's her gift . . . learned it from her ma, though the poor woman's working in the shirtwaist factory now. Sewing. Waste of a good talent, as I say."

Pulling the curtain further aside, Muldoon looked out the window. Kavanagh had a clear view of the crime scene. He'd be very interested to see what the man had to say this evening.

He spent the rest of the afternoon making little progress. Most of the apartments lining the street were empty this time of day. Still, he climbed stairs and knocked on doors. Those women he found home had little to say. Many, he suspected, weren't home the night of the murder, Sunday night or not. They had to make money somehow, and much of it was got during the night. By the end of the day, he had little to show for his trouble, but he'd begun building a picture of who lived along the block, near enough to have seen the dumping of the body. He'd have to return after work and see if more folks were home then. Others, he might have to hunt down in the saloons and gaming halls around town.

At five, the two policemen began the walk back to headquarters. It was hard to believe, but the neighborhoods actually got worse before they got better again, going north along Mulberry. They checked in with the Sergeant and headed home, each going his separate way. Muldoon had hoped he'd see Detective Benson, but he hadn't. He wanted to go over with him the few things he'd learned, and the possibilities that were forming in his head. But he suspected the detective could be found in any one of the city's many saloons. Muldoon's thoughts turned back to Kavanagh and his perfect view.

CHAPTER 11

MULDOON slipped quietly into the boarding house when he arrived home. The parlor door was open just a bit, and he could hear voices inside. He didn't recognize the tone and wondered if it were an applicant for the recently vacated rooms. He passed by the door quickly, catching only a glimpse of a woman in a pale dress sitting carefully on a chair. From the angle, he didn't think he knew her.

He emerged from his room a short time later, washed and changed. Mrs. Dunn placed a full pitcher of water on his dresser each evening, knowing he needed to clean up after a hard day's job. If he was too much of a mess when he got home, either from his duties or from wrestling, the pitcher and basin wouldn't be enough. Instead, he went to the outside pump, which had been installed for the use of tenants in the boarding house. He appreciated this luxury, since most folks had to use the common one further up the block. He'd fill several buckets and carry them into the kitchen, where Betsy would heat them on the stove. She'd pour them into the big washtub, and after she left the room, he would prop himself up over the tub and wash the sweat, blood, and dirt from his body. Tonight, a good washing in his room with the carefully laid out towel and washcloth, a bar of soap and water from the pitcher, was enough. He hung his uniform from a peg, ready to be worn again the next day. He might even ask Betsy to give it a good brushing. Once it got too soiled, he'd pay to get it washed, switching to the extra uniform hanging in his wardrobe.

He donned his most worn-out pants and shirt, pulling suspenders over his shoulders. His shoes were good, but old. Normally, he liked to be well-turned-out. It was a symbol of his success, not just as a wrestler, but as a New Yorker. This night, though, he was going back to the Points. He had two things he needed to do. First, he needed to see Kavanagh, and second, he wanted to check up on Meg McAllister. He hadn't seen her since he'd arrested her son.

The evening grew dark as the rain started again. Muldoon walked swiftly toward the Points, turning up his collar. Mrs. Dunn had been thrilled when he told her he wanted the front rooms as he'd headed out the door. She had interviewed several people during the day and found nobody suitable. With the smaller, back apartment vacant, she could afford to wait for the right tenant. The larger front rooms nearly doubled his rent. Figuring his finances, he'd realized he could easily afford the change . . . so long as he continued to wrestle. It would be nice to sleep in the big double bed in the front apartment. A bigger place, nice things, and expensive clothes—he wanted to stand on an equal footing with Harry Hill, or even with Boss Tweed himself—and the things he gathered around himself gave him a sense of satisfaction.

The muddy streets were still crowded as he headed south. That was one of the things he liked so much about the City. People constantly moved through the streets, going about their business. Noise filled the air as people called out their wares, pushing a cart, or carrying a basket full of some item or another. Wagons and buggies rushed by, horses clip-clopping at a fast pace.

As he reached the grocery, he could see the proprietor through the window. The man pushed a broom, carefully cleaning his store of the grime tracked in during the day. Somehow it seemed out of place in this district, a gleaming nickel in a jar of darkened pennies. Muldoon tapped on the window. The grocer waved when he saw the policeman, pausing only a moment before he bustled over to the door and let him in.

"I almost didn't recognize you," he said. "But I thought you might be back this evening. As how you wanted to see Mr. Kavanagh, that is. He came in a short time ago. If you'd follow me?"

Muldoon shrugged. "Don't worry, I know the way. You keep on cleaning up."

"The quicker I'm done, the quicker I get my supper." The man grinned widely.

Muldoon nodded, then passed through the store and into the back hall. He turned to the door on the right and rapped lightly. On the other side, a chair scraped across the floor, papers rattled, and a drawer slid shut. The door swung open, a man standing just inside. Short brown hair curled tightly against his neck, and dark lashes framed pale blue eyes. Muldoon noted the clean brown slacks, suspenders, and white shirt. Spectacles barely peeked out the top of his chest pocket. He looked young.

"You must be the policeman Mr. Connolly said was coming?" The man smiled, bringing a twinkle to his eye.

"That's me. And you'll be Sean Kavanagh?"

"Aye. You've been inside already. But you can come in and look around again, if you wish." He smiled again. His actions and appearance seemed devoid of any fear or guilt.

Muldoon followed him into the apartment. He glanced about as they walked through the sparsely furnished front sitting room, and through to the bedroom in back. Nothing had changed from his earlier visit. He hadn't expected it to. What he was interested in was Kavanagh.

"You don't have any other folks living here, do you?" Muldoon asked. It was unusual, a man in the Points living in such a large space alone. It should be filled to the brim with humanity, mother, father, children, aunts and uncles, even grandparents. When a man could afford this much, he moved to a better part of the city.

"No, just me. I'm only living here for a while. Until I get my affairs straightened out."

"What affairs?" Muldoon pulled aside the curtain and looked out into the street.

"I lost my job," Kavanagh said. "At the bank. I'm . . . I was . . . a clerk."

"I'm sorry to hear that. What happened, if you don't mind me asking?"

"Nothing, really. Certainly, nothing I did, that is. I was just told, that . . . well, the bank didn't have a need for me anymore. I went back the next day, because I have an account there . . . and another man, a new boy, was at my usual seat."

"Let me guess," Muldoon said, barely hiding the irritation in his tone. "He was a native?"

"Aye, he was English. And now the money's tight, so I've moved back down here to the Points. I can afford a place down here."

Muldoon raised his eyebrows.

"I had some savings." Kavanagh shifted his weight from one foot, to the other, and then back again.

"I see." Muldoon gazed long at the younger man, then pointed out the window. "You know the dead man was found right out your window here?"

"So I've heard. But I didn't see anything."

Muldoon looked down the road toward the park. The street light had been lit, and glowed dimly through smoky glass. It wasn't quite dark yet, but Muldoon remembered the lamp hadn't shed much more than a slight pool of light, barely reaching the ground beneath it. Its glow didn't illuminate this stretch of the road.

"You didn't wake up? Maybe look out the window?" Muldoon dropped the curtain and turned to glance around the room again.

"No. I didn't see a thing."

"Okay, then. If you think of anything, you can leave a message for me at the front desk at Police Headquarters. Or I'll be walking the beat in the Park." Muldoon headed back across to the door, turned the knob, and stepped out into the hall.

"Sure, if I think of anything," Kavanagh said.

Muldoon turned suddenly, head tipped just a bit to the side. "You didn't see anything, but did you hear anything?" he asked.

Kavanagh thought for a moment. "You know . . . maybe I did. I'm pretty sure it was Sunday night." He reflected, tipping his own head, his ear cocked toward the window. "I think I might have been woken up. But I don't know what it was that woke me. A sound, maybe. Or, no! I know . . . it might have been wheels. And a horse. I think a wagon came by just there . . . outside my window."

"Thank you," Muldoon said. "That might be very helpful." He pulled out a stub of pencil and scribbled on a small pad from his pocket. Pushing it back into the recesses of his jacket, he nodded and took his leave.

CHAPTER 12

O NE more place to go, Muldoon thought as he headed deeper into the Points. He had to get over and see Kelly McAllister's mother. She didn't live far, just the other side of the Park. He picked up the pace, turning his collar up against the damp evening mist. It wasn't particularly safe in this district after dark. Still, the streets would be active for hours yet; then slowly they'd thin out. First, the mothers and children would disappear from the streets, then the fathers heading home from a day's work in distant parts of town. The less respectable folk would remain on the streets, moving from saloon to saloon . . . shady women, gamblers, and thieves.

As Muldoon crossed the Park, he passed the two night policemen who quietly whiled away the time. They swung heavy nightsticks rhythmically, holding them ready just in case. They were both patrolmen, though he'd heard Mickey O'Brien might get promoted soon.

"Hullo, O'Brien, Denehey." Muldoon called out as he passed.

"Hey there, Muldoon," they responded almost in unison, and fell in beside him.

"Quiet evening?" Muldoon asked.

"So far," O'Brien said. "Den and I've just been having a talk about the man that killed that wrestler-fella. Talk on the street says he's some sort of devil worshipper . . . called up the devil his-self to do him in."

"He's not." Muldoon growled. "He's a man, same as me or you."

"Don't get me wrong none," said O'Brien. "It ain't for nothing. There's talk of strange symbols where he died. And on the body. Stars and the like . . . and a circle drawn in the dirt around him. That's unholy stuff, Muldoon!"

"Aye," put in Denehey, crossing himself quickly. "They say he was shaved clean and drained of blood."

"He was shaved. But not drained," Muldoon said. The cold finger ran down his spine again. He shrugged it off. "He wasn't a sacrifice, if that's what you're thinking."

The two cops reached the end of their beat, and turned to head back to the police shack. Muldoon moved on to the McAllister's place on Cross Street. By now it was full dark, and he knew it would be even darker inside. He remembered the garbage-strewn hallway, his lip curling at the thought. Still, he needed to see to Meg McAllister.

He climbed the stairs inside the dark hall carefully. His eyes adjusted quickly to the gloom. Muldoon avoided touching the greasy banister, instead running the back of his hand lightly against the wall, not really for support, but to help keep his bearings. As he reached the top floor, he rapped on the door. He waited a moment, and then knocked again, this time a bit louder. Cocking his head, he listened intently to the darkness. The loosely hanging door stood still, no step came to greet him. No light filtered through the cracks at its sides. Somewhere beyond the door, a slight creak of the floor alerted him.

Muldoon could picture the marks along the wooden boards, dug in from years of scraping, he knew them well. Why hadn't Kelly ever fixed that? But of course, the boy was raised in this world. He didn't know any better. He slid his fingers between the door and the jamb, where the crack was largest, and pulled, guiding its movement with the loose knob. It scraped hard along the floor. So much for a quiet entry, he thought.

Muldoon stepped inside. He didn't bother pulling the door shut behind him. He didn't know what waited for him in the dark. His policeman's instinct kicked in and he moved forward cautiously, standing low, akin to a wrestler's stance. The place felt wrong. Heavy silence weighed in on him. A chair lay on its side just inside the door, one leg hanging crazily.

Muldoon inched forward, his head cocked. He stood at the ready. In the deep silence, he heard a sound—just a light noise—a breath. He tried to see through the blackness. Turning his head slightly, he tried to peer into the darkness of the corners. He couldn't see a thing. Nothing moved.

"Ma?" he finally whispered.

No answer came. A touch of light filtered in the window. The pane, ancient and waved, the glass thicker at the bottom than top, was filth-encrusted from years of dust and dirt build-up. A slight movement drew his attention, not toward the bed, but the far corner, in the shadows next to the window.

"Ma?" he asked again. He could just make out her pitiful form squatting in the corner. "Are you alright? What happened here?"

His foot brushed something that rolled unevenly away. He reached down and grabbed the stub of wax. Pulling a box of matches out of his pocket, he struck a small wooden stick and lit the painfully small candle. Light sputtered from its wick, its tiny flame trying to illuminate the room.

Muldoon held up the candle. The place had been laid bare. Nothing of value remained, not like there had much to begin with. Anything left had been smashed and broken.

Meg didn't respond at first. Then she reached one hand toward him. For a moment she seemed to be a shadow of his own mother, lost so many years before.

"Can she bake a cherry pie? Billy-boy, Billy-boy," she sang quietly, then rising up in her corner. She took a few steps toward him, and collapsed into a heap on the floor.

"Ma!" Muldoon rushed to her side. She moaned, and he laid his palm over her forehead. She was hot. He pulled his hand away as her flesh burned his and she began to shake. Her tremors grew violent, and he tried to hold her down. He'd never seen her like this, and he didn't know what to do. He didn't like being helpless.

"Billy-boy," she whispered again. With an abrupt lurch, her chest arched toward the ceiling, as if pulled by a thread attached to the center of her breastbone. She collapsed in a sudden movement, her arms and legs limp and head lolling back. Muldoon knelt beside her, and gathered her into his arms. She'd had some sort of a fit and she needed a doctor. But, he knew people who had fits like the one she'd just had were considered insane. He wasn't about to send her son to the Tombs and then send her to the asylum. As she regained consciousness her head tilted slightly upward. Dark eyes, pupils grown unnaturally huge, stared into his.

"There's a darkness within you," she whispered hoarsely. "And a darker one outside. It seeks a lamb for its altar. It will have five. Four are yours, two by your own hand. But in the end, it is six-sided."

She laughed, a low sound in her throat. Then, with a sudden movement, Meg McAllister pushed out of his arms.

She sat up and looked toward him again. The corners of her lips turned up slightly in a tiny smile.

"It's been so long since I've been able to see," she said, and then broke into tears.

CHAPTER 13

HIS mother read tea leaves. She used to collect sprigs of mint and make a mild herbal tea. After the last bit was drank she'd flip the cup quickly to drain the dregs. Turning the cup back over, she'd gaze into it and try to make sense of the shapes formed by small pieces of soggy herbs. Muldoon didn't believe in prophecies. But Irish women-folk did. He guessed it was their way of trying to understand the world around them.

Meg's sobbing eased. When ready, she would speak, but he wasn't sure he wanted to know what had happened in her flat. He helped her over to the broken bed and she perched on its edge.

"Now, tell me what happened," Muldoon said.

"Tell me," he said again, motioning toward the room in general.

"They came . . . " she whispered at last.

"Who? Who did this?" Muldoon could barely control his rage.

"The men who took Kelly."

"I took Kelly." He admitted it grudgingly, apologetically.

"No." She covered his hand with hers. "You just think you did. They told you to. The Natives."

Muldoon closed his eyes. "You mean, coppers did this?"

"Aye."

"Detective Graham."

"I think that's the name they called him by. He said he needed my things for evidence. I told him I don't have anything for him to take. Still . . . he took everything anyway."

Muldoon shook with rage. They took everything from her. More than was needed for any kind of evidence. Her small supply of dishes, the few extra rags she called clothes . . . even the blankets off the bed. And she wouldn't be getting any of it back. Graham and Collins would pawn the stuff to supplement their own incomes. Benefits of the trade, they'd call it. Muldoon pulled her slowly to her feet. Her hands clutched something close to her breast, something he hadn't noticed before. Pulling her hands loose, he eased the fingers of her left hand open. She cried out at their movement, and he apologized for hurting her. Her fingers had become stiff and cramped, so long had she held the small wooden frame. He gently took the picture from her, turning it around, though he knew what was there. It was the picture of a beautiful woman in Ireland, a woman of substance.

"Why did they take it all, William?" she asked. "It wasn't any of it worth anything to them."

Muldoon glanced away guiltily, though he knew he shouldn't feel that way. "I think it's because of me. They think they can get to me, by hurting you."

"But it's my son they have. Not you!"

"I know. And somehow, I think that's my fault, too."

"No. I won't have you blame yourself, now! I know you'll find a way out for my boy."

"I plan on it," he said. He looked around again at the empty room.

Suddenly, Meg McAllister broke into tears again. She turned her swollen eyes toward him. "They even took your dollar!" Big, wrenching sobs tore from her. "As if that was evidence."

Muldoon shook his head angrily, but what could he do? He was just a Sergeant, they were Detective and Captain. He was Irish . . . and they were Native—English stock. Though he was second-generation, they still looked on him as fresh off the boat, one of the newcomers bent on taking jobs and destroying the country. Muldoon shook his head slowly, deliberately. He held up the candle and looked intently at the room.

"Is there anything here you want?" he asked suddenly.

"No," she whispered, dropping her head with defeat. "There's nothing left. Nothing at all."

"It's not safe for you here. Not without Kelly. They might come back, or send somebody else next time. And nobody would be here to protect you. I want you to come with me."

Meg shook her head. "That's good of you, William, but I can't let you do that. You don't want to be saddled with an old woman . . . and one who isn't really your own mother."

Muldoon ran a hand through his hair, shoving a curl back from where it tickled his temple. "I can't leave you here, Ma. If you don't come with me, then I have to stay here." He dreaded that more than anything.

She shook her head, mumbling something he couldn't hear.

"You took care of me after the war, when I was sick. Nobody else would have." He paced across the small room and back again. He worried about her. She was ill, and had some sort of a fit. She clutched the picture close to her bosom, and he reached out to take her hand. She looked up at him, tears glimmering in her eyes.

"It won't be charity, Ma. I have more than I need now, and I'd like to share it with you, at least until Kelly gets home. It's safer for you that way. And you can keep working at the factory, or else . . . " he thought quickly. Keep my old rooms for her, and take the front place for me. At least for a while. Then, when Kelly's out of the Tombs, Mrs. Dunn can charge them a lesser rate, and I can pay the difference. But not charity. She'd never go for that. " . . . You can take care of my place. It's more than I can do myself." He didn't tell her that Mrs. Dunn, or her maid, came in to clean. If she thought he cleaned up the place himself, then maybe she'd think he could use the extra help.

"Like a maid?" She raised her head, sudden hope glimmering in her eyes.

"Yes. A live-in maid."

She gazed at him, then around her squalid apartment. "All right," she finally said. "I'll come. But you don't lift a single finger. I'll do all the work around your place."

"Aye, Ma." He almost smiled with satisfaction, but sobered quickly. He'd got her out of Paradise Park, but he wasn't sure if he could get Kelly out of the Tombs.

CHAPTER 14

April 18

Muldoon awoke with a start. He wasn't sure what disturbed his sleep. Not a dream, this time. It was dark. Still deep night. And then it came again. Not the popping of guns, but a sharp rap at the door that drew him from his slumber. The knocking came again, hard on the building's front door. He sat up in bed. It was probably for him . . . it always was. Glancing at the shadowed clock face, he read 3:42.

Within moments, a light knock sounded on his door. He slipped into a heavy robe and opened the door. Betsy, the maid, stood in the hall, her eyes large on a pale face. She'd only been at the house a few weeks and hadn't yet got used to his odd hours.

"It's a policeman . . . at the door for you, sir. Should I show him in?" The little Irish maid bobbed an awkward attempt at a curtsy. She pulled her shawl tight around her shoulders.

"Aye, show him in here and tell him to wait. I'll be out in a moment."

He left the outer door slightly ajar and slipped back into his bedroom to change. He kept four rooms now. The two front rooms for him, the back two for Meg McAllister. He crossed his new "front room" toward the bedroom. The place was oddly divided. The large sitting room occupied the center of the building. Its windows opened onto the side of the house, a thin walkway between buildings the only view. The bed-room was in the original parlor, at the front of the house. Big windows looked out on the wide front porch and gave him a view of the door. He pulled aside the curtain. The shadowy figure of a policeman waited there, then followed Betsy through the door. He couldn't tell who it was.

Muldoon dressed in his rumpled uniform of the previous day. He rubbed the stubbly growth on his chin as he headed back through his apartment toward his visitor, a young patrolman he didn't know. The man turned his hat round and round in his hands, and rocked onto his toes, then back on his heels, and began the incessant motions all over again.

"Hello, Mr. Muldoon, er . . . Champ, er . . . sir," he said.

"I'm just a sergeant, there's no 'mister' here," Muldoon said, try-ing to set the man at ease.

"Yes, sir, uh, there's another one, sir . . . and I was sent to get you."

"Another one?"

"Another murder, sir. At Paradise Park."

Muldoon placed his hand on the young policeman's back and steered him toward the door. A death or two in the Points was expected every night. "Call the coroner. The Captain will assign it to a detective in the morning, or the desk Sergeant will, if it's not too important a case."

"I . . . uh . . . I think . . . " The policeman cleared his throat and started again. "That is to say, me and Donny . . . uh . . . Patrolman Donovon, we think it's got to do with the other one. That wrestler fella. Only, this time it's not a man. It's . . . " He dropped his voice. "It's a woman."

Muldoon frowned. If there were a second murder, then it should rule out Kelly McAllister. But it also meant that somebody was on a kill-ing spree in the Points, or at least dumping their bodies there.

"Okay," Muldoon said. "Let's get out there and you can show me what you've found."

"It's pretty gruesome, Sergeant. You need to prepare yourself. We were mighty shocked."

They set off quickly. The maid shut the outer door tightly behind them. She wouldn't know when to expect Muldoon back, but he had a key so he could get in when he wanted. He had the only such key. Mrs. Dunn expected all her other tenants to obey her rules, and she was very strict about her curfew. Ten-thirty, she'd said, unless other arrangements were made in advance, and even then, it had to be for an approved purpose. She might allow an opera or some musical event, but she was wary about the playhouse, and definitely against any other sort of entertainment. She seemed barely tolerant toward what she called Muldoon's "habit" of wrestling in the poorer district. But he paid her, and she claimed it was comforting to have a large man, and a policeman at that, residing in her house. Not that policemen were particularly trustworthy themselves, she had told him, but she doubted the riffraff would try breaking down her door if they knew he lived there.

Muldoon and the young patrolman set a brisk pace, collars turned up against the persistent drizzle. Half an hour later, they stood over a sheet-draped object on the ground. Not too many nights ago, he had stood in this very spot—Karl Schneider under that sheet.

He glanced around, trying to get a solid picture in his mind. Was anything different tonight? Where were the people and landmarks? Who might have seen the crime from the safety of their window? Down here, he knew, folks were loath to tell what they'd seen. Partly it was because they didn't want to help anyone in blue, they saw the law as their greatest enemy. But also, because they feared for their own safety. It could as easily be them, next time.

At the end of the street, he could just make out Paradise Park in the dark where it opened into its triangular shaped "square." The streetlamp shed only a sickly glow of light, the ground at its base barely illuminated. The next lamp stood far off at the other end of the block, back the way he'd come. He turned again to the body under the sheet and prepared himself for the sight that had shocked the patrolman. The young man turned his face away.

"I sent for the coroner already," said Patrolman Donovan. He bent to grasp the edge of the sheet.

"This isn't your regular beat," Muldoon said. "You new?"

The young man shifted under his gaze. "Aye. My Da used to be a copper. Before he passed."

Muldoon pursed his lips in thought. "Sergeant Donovan, over in German Town?"

The boy nodded.

"I didn't know he passed. Not on duty?"

"No sir. Hit by a wagon."

"Sad way to go. I'm sorry, son. Now," He looked down at the sheet covered bundle nearly where Schneider had lain. "Detective Benson? He on the way?" He already knew the answer. That's why he was here. Benson was sleeping off the effects of alcohol somewhere, if he wasn't still on a binge. He shook his head, nearly imperceptibly. Nothing he could do for the detective. Benson had to want to leave the bottle.

"No, sir. The detective wasn't at home, so we got you. We haven't moved her. She's exactly as we found her." Donovan pulled back the sheet.

"What were you doing up here?" The two men should have been walking the park, not wandering up the side streets.

"We seen a wagon stop, didn't seem like it should have been here. When we got over here . . . well . . . we found her."

Muldoon squinted. If it was a woman, you couldn't tell from her scalp. She'd been shaved bald. He shook his head in disbelief as the body was revealed. Her damp alabaster skin shimmered as the moon's light momentarily broke through the overcast sky. Only a sick man could have done this, he thought. Like Karl Schneider, this woman was nude.

She'd been shaved of every bit of hair on her body, the white flesh pearlescent, except for a deep purple star-shaped bruise on her abdomen. She hadn't simply been dumped, as Schneider had been. Instead, her body had been set neatly on the ground, carefully arranged, knees bent obscenely.

He took the lantern from the young patrolman and cast its light on the ground nearby. There were definite wagon tracks. He could see how the dirt rose where the wheels had stopped. And then the wagon turned, and left the street the way it had come. On further lay a pile of fresh manure, not much more than an hour old, corroborating the policeman's story.

He walked back to the dead girl and began his examination. She couldn't be more than seventeen, he noted. He took her hand. Soft. No calluses marred the clear flesh. At her neck, he thought he could see bruising. He'd have to wait until morning and another visit to the coroner to be sure. He suspected that, like Karl Schneider, she had been strangled.

"Cover her back up," he said. He pulled her ankles, straightened her legs, and laid her feet together. She was already beginning to stiffen. He figured she'd been dead a while before she'd been placed here. He could see purplish bruising on her left side, a clear indication that her position had been changed as well. She'd lain on her side for some time after her murder. He didn't believe this was a rape, as it seemed to appear. No. It was a message. But to whom? And why?

He stood and peered at the window nearest to the body. How could a man live inside and be oblivious to the horrors just outside his walls? He'd have to visit Kavanagh again, and ask what he'd seen. His gaze dropped. Something had touched the edge of his vision. Something white. Looking straight on, he could see only darkness below the window, but when he turned, softened his focus he could just see it again. He stepped around the body and moved deeper into the shadows. He held the lantern forward so its light pierced the gloom, and then he saw it where it lay in the muck close to the wall . . . a wooden stake, similar in size and shape to the one he'd found in Schneider's front room. As he picked it up, he knew what he would find. The initials A.R. roughly scratched into one side. This piece was smoothly finished on one end and jagged on the other. The piece from Schneider's had been broken at both ends, and he suspected this section would fit neatly into one end of the other. He'd noticed something else, too. A roughly drawn circle had been traced in the mud around the girl's body. The star and the circle could be someone's attempt at a hex, or put there to exploit the public's mood. He was certain there hadn't been a circle drawn around Schneider . . . or had he missed it?

He looked around again. This time he peered into the darkness looking for the reflection of red eyes.

Muldoon waited beside the body until someone from the coroner's office came to pick her up. She seemed so sad, so lonely . . . but he knew she had no emotions left. He hitched a ride on the coroner's wagon as it headed north, then leaped out as the cart rumbled past the corner of Elizabeth Street. He headed back to his cold, dark room. He knew he wouldn't sleep much more this night.

CHAPTER 15

WHO is the alabaster woman? If Muldoon were to hazard a guess, she wasn't from the Points. She had the hands of a wealthy woman. She'd never done hard work in her life. He'd have to search for leads outside the Irish tenements. He had mixed emotions. At once, he felt sadness . . . for her and her family. But, he also felt excited. He could investigate Schneider's death again. Not openly, of course, but in connection with the girl. Where her murder took him, Schneider's would follow, and they would have to release Kelly McAllister.

He stopped at the morgue on his way to Police Headquarters the next morning. He descended the short flight of stairs and entered the dark recesses for the second time in so few days.

"Hullo, Danny," Muldoon said. "I see you've been 'washing the floor' real good lately. You still washing the same one?"

"No, I've got a new floor to clean." The boy smiled and flashed the cover of a 'penny dreadful' at Muldoon. "You can go on back. If you don't mind, I got some work to do. This new book is a real good job."

"Sounds like it, Boy-oh. Then, I'll be letting you get to your work."

Muldoon walked quietly through the outer room and down the hall. At the far end, he entered the cold room filled with the dead. Bob Gamble was at work, carefully dissecting the organs of a rather fat man. Looking up, he smiled quickly.

"Hello, Muldoon, I'll be right with you. No doubt, you're here for the woman from Five Points. It can't be this one, he's from uptown."

"Aye, Doc. It'll be the woman."

The doctor consulted a large text he'd set on a rolling table, and then carefully drew a likeness of the man's organs in a pad. Next to the picture, he wrote the details of his finding.

"It's amazing, all the things the body can tell us. Even after we've died, fingernails and hair seem to continue to grow. Different organs cool at different rates. Cancers blacken lungs. I think one day, the coroner's office will be able to solve murders without policemen." He laughed.

"Ah, but we'll still need policemen to catch the murderers," Muldoon said.

Some fifteen minutes later, Gamble finished his meticulous work and set his instruments on a tray. He wiped the blood from his hands and stepped out from behind the open body.

"Over here," he said, and moved toward a second, shroud-covered, figure.

Muldoon pulled back the sheet and looked down at the murdered girl's face.

"Was she strangled?"

"Mmhmm," answered the coroner. "Exactly like the first victim."

"The Captain won't like that."

"No, he won't . . . if he'll even listen. It seems as if he's made up his mind about the Karl Schneider murder."

"Aye," Muldoon said. "I'm not sure we should even mention Schneider, or else he might pull me off this case. You notice her hands?"

"Yes. She's not from the Points. She's a lady."

"Aye, that's what I gathered. Now to see if there's anyone missing."

"There's someone missing, all right," Gamble said. "The question is whether anyone has realized it . . . or cares enough to report it."

"You'll be noticing the bruising on her side?"

The coroner nodded.

"We found her on her back . . . knees up," Muldoon said.

"After she was killed, she lay on her side for a while," Gamble said. "You can tell from the pooling, the bruising where the blood settled. So, she was moved, too. Just like Schneider."

Muldoon agreed. He stepped closer to the body and bent over her to see the marks on her throat.

"The bruise around her neck . . . it's an elbow again, isn't it?"

"It looks like it. There aren't any finger marks, anyway. I suppose it might have been a thick cloth."

"I don't think so," Muldoon said. "See the way her skin seems to have been pinched, right at the center of her collarbone? I think that's from an elbow."

"That's my thought, too. You're looking for a man about your size? If you look at the bruising on her arm, you can see she was held tightly. The marks seem to be from a very large hand."

Muldoon nodded.

Who was about his size? He wondered as he set off toward Headquarters. He stood head and shoulders above most. He thought of George Army. The African definitely fit the bill, but he couldn't imagine what the black man had against these particular people. But it was worth looking into. Maybe he needed to hang out in the saloons for a while, as a patron instead of a wrestler. And he still needed to get back and question Kavanagh again. Something about him bothered Muldoon.

As he entered Headquarters, Sergeant Foley looked up from his work. "Hello, Muldoon," he said. "Detective Benson asked for you to go to his office when you got in. I expect it's about the Points Woman."

The Points Woman. Muldoon shook his head almost imperceptibly. So, they had given her a name.

"It's in the paper." Foley held up the Police Gazette. A huge headline screamed across the front page: HORRID MURDER! POINTS WOMAN STRANGLED! Muldoon snorted. Anything exciting for that paper. Yellow journalism at its finest. Its editors filled the pages with murders, crime, and blood sport.

He mumbled a reply as he crossed the room to the hallway. Halfway down the dark corridor, he stopped before Benson's office. Nothing like the Captain's a floor above, this room was tiny and cramped. The desk overflowed with files. Many were past cases long since solved. Muldoon grabbed the pile on the single visitor's chair and set them on top of a stack by the wall. Someday, Benson always said, he'd go through them, keep only the open cases, and send the rest to storage.

"So?" asked Benson between sips of coffee. "What was she like?"

Muldoon reflected. This was one thing he hated about the loose arrangement between him and Benson. He did the footwork, and then reported to the Detective. Someday, he hoped, an office like this would be his . . .

He passed on the coroner's report.

"She was obviously a woman of substance," he said. "The daughter of a wealthy man. I doubt she ever worked a day. Somebody brought her to the Points and left her there to make a statement."

He stood up and paced the confined space. "She was left in the exact spot as Schneider. And killed the same way. Her death is a message to somebody . . . but to whom?"

Benson leaned back in his chair, then spun about to gaze at the empty wall where a better office would have a window. A handful of pictures, carefully torn from newspapers, were tacked haphazardly across the space. They were Police Gazette illustrations of cases he'd once worked on. The cases that had got him into this office. Finally, he stood up and faced Muldoon.

"We have to find out who she was and why she was killed, without the Captain knowing we think the two murders are connected. He's going to want to see us about this one, maybe not today, but certainly tomorrow. It's already gotten too much publicity. We've got to hang on to it, figure it out before Graham comes charging in."

Muldoon nodded. "I'll check the precincts. See what they have for missing persons. She isn't on any reports that've come through here, yet. Maybe they've got some we haven't seen."

"And I'll check the papers," Benson said. "There may be an advertisement. Perhaps somebody asking about the whereabouts of a missing young lady."

They parted company. Benson headed for the corner newsstand and Muldoon went uptown, toward the nearest precinct house. His task kept him occupied nearly the whole day, but he came up empty-handed. At each precinct, it was the same. He found a long list of missing husbands, mainly immigrant men . . . and of them, mostly Irish. Few of them would ever be seen again, he knew. Some of them had probably been murdered, but most simply vanished, abandoning their wives and children, and the squalor of New York City for adventure out West. Each precinct also had a shorter list of women's names. Most of these were probably victims of foul play . . . kidnapped or murdered. Like the men, many of them would never come home. He wondered if some of them, too, had simply headed west in search of a new life. He scanned the lists of women's names and descriptions, and then turned to the longest lists in each precinct. The ones with children's names on them. He hated reading each name, each age, each date a child had gone missing . . . so many young ones, so many who had met violent ends.

As he scanned the lists of women and children, he looked for one that would match his unidentified body, but each time he came up empty. The girl in the morgue wouldn't end the uncertainty of some family whose daughter's name was already on the list, but marked the beginning of the terrible journey for yet another family.

The sun slanted low in the afternoon sky when he finally made his tired way back to Mulberry Street.

"I checked each of the papers," Benson said with frustration. "I thought maybe, possibly, there would be something already printed. But I scanned every damn rag in town. Nothing. So, I went to each of the newspaper's offices. I thought I'd get a jump on tomorrow's papers. But they hadn't taken any ads for a missing girl today."

"I didn't have any luck, either." Muldoon ran a hand through his hair, pushing the unruly waves back from his forehead.

"Well, we'll just have to try something else tomorrow. It seems to me a rich man would know his daughter is missing. He should have reported it." Benson paused for a moment and gazed up at the ceiling. "Maybe we're going at this from the wrong side. Maybe she's not a rich man's daughter. Maybe she's his whore."

Muldoon didn't believe that. There was something about her face, innocent in its final repose.

"Okay. Tomorrow, if I get a chance, I'll go see the seven sisters," he said.

Benson nodded. "I've still got my other cases, so you'll have to go alone. I've got to solve that damn theft the Captain stuck me with." He related the particulars of the case, a missing sapphire necklace. Muldoon commiserated, but couldn't get engaged in the conversation, couldn't really offer the help Benson looked for. Finally, he stood and took his leave. He needed to get back to the Points. One window overlooked both bodies. One man could have seen what happened. Even if he denied it. Kavanagh was next on his list.

CHAPTER 16

MULDOON leaned against the ramshackle building across the street from the grocery store. He turned his collar up against the relentless drizzle. He could see the grocer inside, his broom moving rhythmically as he cleaned up after a long day. Every inch of Five Points overflowed with dirt, dust, and filth. One man with a broom couldn't hope to make a dent in the mess. The streetlamp lighter walked along the street with his long pole. At the end a flame burned, and just below it, a shepherd's crook-like appendage protruded. The man pried open a lantern with the crook, turned the long shaft, and lit the wick. He pushed the glass closed and moved on to light the next one.

The evening settled in as Muldoon waited for Kavanagh. He had arrived at the corner store several hours earlier, and asked for the tenant.

"He isn't in," the grocer said. "Mr. Kavanagh hasn't been home since yesterday morning. It's not like him to be out all night."

Kavanagh had said he feared foul play. But Muldoon thought about the woman who'd been dumped just outside the man's window.

Shortly after dusk, a figure broke from the constant flow of passing people and stepped onto the stoop. He tapped on the door and the grocer stopped sweeping. As he opened the door, the proprietor glanced across the street at Muldoon where he leaned up against the building. He straightened and walked slowly toward the pair, the crowd parting around him. He held his heavy nightstick in one hand, just in case, though he rarely needed it.

"Hello," he said as he neared.

"Good evening," Kavanagh said. A nervous tick twitched above his right eye.

They stood outside silently a long moment and Muldoon gazed steadily at the man. Interesting, he thought, as Kavanagh paled.

"Aren't you going to invite me in?" Muldoon asked. The grocer had disappeared, leaving only the two of them on the step.

"Uh . . . aye, certainly," Kavanagh said. "If you want . . . though I don't know what it could be for. I thought I answered all your questions."

"So, you haven't heard, then?" Muldoon asked as he swung the nightstick rhythmically into his hand. Thwack, thwack, thwack.

"Heard what?" Kavanagh glanced over his shoulder as if afraid of what might be out there. He motioned toward the door. "Well, come on, then." Muldoon's gaze followed where Kavanagh's had gone, hoping to catch sight of . . . what? Crimson cat-eyes reflecting the dim glow of the streetlamp?

He followed Kavanagh to his room and entered its darkness. Muldoon wanted to see the man's expression. Kavanagh fumbled about for a moment, then struck a match. It sputtered, a bright pool flashed for just an instant before flickering out. Muldoon remembered the cheap matches. He'd used them himself. Now, he bought only the good ones, phosphorous that hadn't been mixed with a touch of dirt. Maybe the man was exactly what he portrayed? A white-collar office worker down on his luck. Kavanagh lit a second match and set it carefully to the stub of candle on the table. The faint light barely reached into the corners.

"Sorry," Kavanagh said. "I can only afford the one candle."

Muldoon used whale oil lamps in his own place. At first, he'd hesitated at the extra expense. But as he grew confident in his ability to earn money from wrestling in addition to his regular policeman's pay, he gave in. He wasn't paid particularly well, and certainly wouldn't have been able to afford to live in the style he was beginning to enjoy, except for his skill in wrestling. He earned more from grappling than he received from the city. Was Kavanagh, like him, a man on his way up . . . or down?

"Now, what can I help you with?" Kavanagh asked with an air of innocence. He pulled his spectacles from his shirt pocket and swiped a cloth across the lenses.

"Where were you last night?"

Kavanagh stared at him sullenly, a veil of distrust clouding his expression.

"I know you weren't here. So, don't even try to say you were. Your landlord's already told me so."

"I . . . I . . . " Kavanagh looked wildly about, as if searching for a way to escape. Finally, he dropped his gaze to the floor and shoved the spectacles back into his pocket. "I was gambling," he said.

"I thought you weren't a gambling man. The way the grocer has it, you're an upright man, just a bit hard on your luck right now. Is there something else you need to tell me?"

"Well . . . um, I have a bit of a problem. With the dice, I mean. I can't seem to stop myself. That's where I was last night. I spent the day looking for work . . . and then," he looked down at his shoes as a splash of red spread across his face. "And then I spent the evening gambling."

"You didn't come home?"

"No. I . . . I stayed the night in a saloon. This place would've been all locked up. So, I didn't even try. I just stayed out."

"So, you don't know about the murder."

"Murder?" Kavanagh asked. "I've already told you, I was asleep when that man was killed."

"No," Muldoon said. "The one last night was a woman."

Kavanagh snapped straight, as if a soldier to attention. "Another murder? Here?"

"In the same place as the last."

Kavanagh moved to the window and peered out into the gloom. The candle's paltry light reflected in the black glass.

"If I'd been home, maybe I would have seen something this time. Maybe she wouldn't be dead."

"She was dead already. Dumped, just like the last one."

"Strangled again?"

"Aye." He damned the press for printing so much information. How could he tell what a man knew, or what he'd learned from reading it in the paper?

Muldoon searched the man's face, but he couldn't see any hint to his thoughts. Kavanagh wasn't nearly big enough, he reflected. He might have killed the girl . . . but Schneider? He didn't know why he wasted his time. This was obviously a dead end.

"By the way," Muldoon asked, as he opened the door to leave. "Where, exactly, were you last night?"

"Billy McGlory's," Kavanagh said. "All night."

Muldoon nodded and stepped out into the darkened store, and then outside. He walked toward home. He'd found out all he could this night. He needed to see Kelly, but the Captain had barred him from going to the Tombs. Perhaps Benson could go for him tomorrow. And he'd go see the sisters. He hadn't had a chance yet. Still, something bothered him. What am I missing? He adjusted his collar against the cold, then looked up at Kavanagh's window as he passed. Two glittering red eyes glared out at him. And then they were gone. His heart lurched, and then he almost laughed at the trick his imagination played on him. Beyond the wavy glass, Kavanagh's single candle flickered. Muldoon took a step back and the flame seemed to split into two through the undulating glass.

CHAPTER 17

April 19

MULDOON couldn't sleep. He rolled over and looked again at the twin sticks on the low table next to his bed. No candles were lit, but light filtered in through the space between the curtains that covered the big front windows. He'd left them open several inches to take advantage of the weak light, plus, he didn't really want to be alone with his thoughts. Keeping them open seemed to connect him to the mass of New Yorkers slumbering through the night. He remembered Meg McAllister's prophecy. Was the girl the lamb she'd spoken about? Five, maybe six deaths? And what was the darkness within? He shivered, then shook his head angrily. He didn't believe in fortune telling. Meg was ill, maybe crazy. He couldn't believe in some kind of demon stalking the night. His quarry was a man.

His gaze kept returning to the sticks. He picked them up and felt them. He had retrieved the first, the one from Schneider's place, taking it from the vault at headquarters. Nobody cared. The booze, too, had disappeared he'd noticed. The case had been solved as far as the department was concerned.

He slid up into a seated position, his back against the headboard. He picked up the sticks and felt their smoothness. Someone had spent a lot of time carving them, carefully shaping them so each fit the recesses between a man's fingers. Their surfaces were wavy, not flat. Each was long and thin, like a writing instrument, or the handle of a letter opener, or maybe a bit wider? More like a very fine walking stick? The bare wood was pale, lightly aged, not too many years old, nor yet recently formed. He placed them end to end and fitted the broken edges together. The jagged ends fit perfectly, two pieces of a whole. Their six inches became twelve. The softly ridged wood formed a pattern, a spiral, winding slowly down the length. And along the spiral those two initials, A.R. repeated themselves. But what bothered him was the other broken edge. The first stake, the one from Schneider's was broken at both ends. That meant there was at least one more piece out there. One more piece to find. A thought nagged at him, like the missing section. Did it mean that the killer's work wasn't complete? A wrestler . . . and a pampered young woman. He had to find the connection! If he didn't, it seemed likely someone else had an appointment with death. Not the least of whom was Kelly McAllister.

Thump.

Muldoon glanced up at the shadowed ceiling above. He was certain it was a footstep, stealthy, not the normal groans and creaks of an old building settling for the night. He held his breath a moment and listened, but the sound didn't repeat. But . . . yes, there it was again, further down the room. Casper Biggs kept the room up there. What could he be doing in the dead of night? He slipped from his bed, thanking God he was below, not above, where Biggs couldn't hear the sounds of his movements. He moved quickly to the wall and placed his hand against the partition. He felt it shudder lightly as Biggs's door silently opened and then closed.

A pair of brown canvas pants and a dark shirt, civilian attire, hung on a peg by his door. He yanked them on, pulled the suspenders over his shoulders, slipped on his boots, and grabbed his flat Irish cap. He shrugged on a heavy workingman's coat. As the front door clicked shut, he stood behind his heavy drapes, thankful he hadn't yet replaced them with transparent Irish lace. Casper Biggs stopped just outside the door and glanced back at Muldoon's window, then moved quickly off the porch and stepped into the darkness of the street.

Muldoon slipped out of the building behind Biggs. He was confused. Where could the man go in the middle of the night? Why hadn't he noticed before? Then, he realized he hadn't had rooms directly beneath the man before. He remembered Mrs. Dunn had lost her keys a couple of months back. Biggs must have taken them, and got a matching key made. He fumbled in his pocket, feeling for his own key. Then quietly, furtively, he followed Biggs. He stuck to darkly shadowed areas, hurried through pools of light under streetlamps, and evaded Biggs's occasional backward glance.

Avoiding the Points, Biggs led Muldoon toward the docks. The small man's hand returned again and again to his side, and Muldoon knew it was for the comforting touch of a gun in his belt. Biggs knew his route well. He paused to avoid a policeman's path, and stayed in the darkest parts of the street. It made Muldoon's job easier. He, too, remained hidden in the dark.

What could the man be doing? Muldoon wondered. As they neared the shore, he watched from the shadows. Biggs clambered down into a small boat. Several other men were already aboard. Quietly, a big man pushed the craft away from the dock, toward Jersey.

He was baffled. He didn't like the man, but he still couldn't figure why Casper Biggs would be out in the middle of the night. The man had a secure job, and he was a cantor in his church. Maybe not a pillar of society, but still, he was relatively respected in the community.

As the boat slid out of sight, Muldoon ran across the dark pier toward three other boats tied there. He pulled up short, surprised to see them occupied. He'd expected to commandeer one, "borrow" it for his short expedition across the harbor. But each had a man at the oars.

Quickly, he regained his composure and climbed into the nearest. The grizzled seaman eyed him suspiciously, as he took in his working man appearance.

"Take me across," said Muldoon as he fished in his pocket for cash.

But the man just sat there.

He handed across a wad of paper bills. He didn't particularly like the greenbacks, but they were quiet in a cop's pocket. Nothing worse than coins jangling at the wrong time. The man took the bills and smiled appreciatively. Muldoon knew he'd overpaid, but he needed to get across and this man knew he wasn't one of his regular fares.

As they moved out into the light fog rising from the sea, Muldoon leaned forward in his seat. "There'll be double that if you wait for me on the other side."

The man smiled wickedly, the blackened ruins of his teeth bared. "All right, mister," he spoke in a nasal, low-class twang. "You ain't one of them. Maybe youse a copper? Or a niggah lover? I don't know, and I don't care. But I'll get you across. And if you get out of there, I'll even be waiting for you. But I need some more of that green afore you leave. As security like, in case you don't make it back. Make it worth my while to ditch out on my regular fares."

Muldoon nodded, and then counted out a couple more bills. The man grabbed quickly, his gnarled fingers closed around the cash and stuffed it into his pocket. He wouldn't hang around on the Jersey side waiting for his return, that was certain. No, he'd quickly go back to the far shore and ferry more men across. But the promise of additional cash might bring him back for one last, secret pickup.

"Who are they?"

"Don't know, and don't care," the seaman spat a long stream of tobacco juice across the bow. "Since you ask . . . " He leaned closer toward Muldoon. "I think they're the devil worshippers. The one's that have the papers buzzin'. Long as they don't harm me, and come carryin' lots a green, I don't care."

As they neared shore, the boat turned aside and made its way to a little-used, dilapidated pier. They ducked in on the far side and skimmed as close to shore as possible. "Be back nigh onto four. That's when I'll be leaving. Can't wait no later, else I get caught." He hitched his pate toward the near-silent movement of a distant boat. "And them'll be over to the other side by then."

Muldoon nodded, grabbed hold of the ramshackle ladder, and pulled himself onto the wreck of an abandoned pier. He hoped the ruin would bear his weight. Without a look back, he made his way to shore. He knew the man would leave as soon as he was out of sight. Quickly, he turned left and slipped into the shadows. Somewhere up ahead Casper Biggs must have climbed onto another pier, one of a thin stream of men crossing from New York City.

As Muldoon drew near the men, he paused behind a stack of crates. Just ahead, several men clambered onto the pier. Biggs wasn't among them. He was sure the man had already come ashore, but these men would lead him along as easily as Casper Biggs. Sticking to the shadows, he followed as the docks were left far behind. And, soon enough, most of town, too.

A low iron fence lined the street, and beyond it glowing white pillars were just visible, the cemetery's headstones that reflected what little light gathered in the gloom. This side of the harbor drew in the fog like a living thing, it curled among the stones. Ahead of him, the queue of men turned in at the gate. Muldoon glanced behind him and then stepped over the fence. Moving through the graveyard, he paralleled the men on the path. They continued on to enter the stone church. Light spilled out into the gloom from the open door. Quickly, Muldoon slipped behind the wide arms of an oak tree.

"Welcome, Brothers," a hushed voice floated across the graves.

The light extinguished as the big door shut behind the men. Muldoon waited in the shadows as the trail of men grew thin, the door opened and shut again rhythmically. In the distance, a clock boomed twice. Two o'clock. He waited to be sure there were no more stragglers. After fifteen minutes, he peered at the face of his pocket watch, holding it up to catch what little light filtered out from the dark-shuttered windows. No one else had arrived. Carefully, he eased from behind the tree and moved cautiously toward the building.

"Friends Meeting House" a placard above the door announced . . . Quakers. But he knew Biggs was no Quaker. He was Church of England stock, Episcopalian through and through. What was Biggs doing in a Quaker meeting house? Muldoon moved closer toward the brick building. It was federal style, a sturdy, two story rectangle, twin chimneys atop its peaked roof. Though shuttered, the windows stared at him, daring him to invade their sanctity.

"I wouldn't go no further if I was you."

Muldoon spun about. Peering in the gloom, he searched for the man who'd spoken.

"You don't want to be going in there. Them's real bad news." A dark figure separated itself from the shadows behind a tree, just opposite Muldoon's own sanctuary. The man glanced furtively about and then moved closer. "Follow me," he said, and ducked back amongst the stones.

Friend or foe? Muldoon didn't know. He took a deep breath, and then followed the shadow deeper into the blackness. As he came up behind the building, the man stopped and Muldoon moved close. A strong hand grabbed his forearm hard and leveraged him toward the ground.

"Shhhh," he whispered as Muldoon pulled his arm free. The man turned toward him. It was George Army, the African wrestler. "We stay low a ways from here."

Muldoon felt a momentary relief. But . . . did he trust this man? He's big enough, he reminded himself. Army could easily have killed the girl, and he was one of the few who could take on Schneider. But right now, he was after other game. He decided to trust Army. At least for now.

"What is it?" Muldoon asked as he nodded toward the building.

"It's bad news, is what," Army replied.

"Quakers?"

"Nope. They just use the building. It was Quakers . . . once. But they're all gone now. Killed during the war, or just moved on. And then this place, it was taken over, like. By them inside. And they're real bad . . . real bad news."

"Who are they, now?" Muldoon asked.

"I don't know. But I been watching them. Past few months anyway."

"I've got to get inside." Muldoon edged toward the building and searched its broad expanse with his gaze.

"Wait," said Army as he laid a big hand on Muldoon's arm. "Used to be a station. You know, on the railroad. There's a secret way in. To the attic. We can see everything from there."

They wound their way a short distance between the gravestones. A dilapidated shack solidified before them, the mist curling away as they neared. Army glanced furtively about, slipped in, and then pulled the broken door roughly closed behind them. The darkness nearly blinded Muldoon as he adjusted to the deeper gloom inside. The hovel's interior was empty, save a rusted, battered barrel wood stove near the back wall. Its stove pipe was broken in two, one part rose several feet above the stove, the rest hung crazily from the ceiling. Dead brambles filled the room, waiting to spring to life with the new season. Army grinned conspiratorially, grabbed a rusted bucket by the door, and poured its contents into the pipe. Muldoon watched in confusion, but took the bucket from Army as he held it toward him.

"Go fill that with dirt and leaves," Army said. "And put it back by the door."

He quickly filled the bucket, then watched as Army slid his fingers under the stove's belly, lifted it up and tilted it backward. To Muldoon's surprise, a portion of the floor lifted with it, revealing darkness below. He stepped forward and peered down into the gloom.

"Come on," said Army as he lowered himself into the yawning hole. A cold shiver slid down Muldoon's spine as he climbed down into the same graveyard dirt that held the dead. And he still didn't quite trust George Army.

It was dead dark below once Army pulled the secret entrance closed behind them. "This here's the best part," whispered Army as he reached blindly in the dark for Muldoon's hand and guided it to a wood and skin contraption that hung just below the trap door. "Give that a mighty squeeze."

Muldoon felt the device, two wooden paddles connected by loose skin . . . a bellows! He pulled the two sides open wide and felt the air fill the bag. *Whooooosh*, he forced them together again. Just above, he heard the patter of dirt, twigs, and leaves as they rained down on the floor. The surface would be lightly covered with a new layer of dirt. Of course, he realized. All signs of their recent passing would be hidden. Tracks might remain, but they would look weeks, maybe months old. And the bare floor beneath the stove, where they had lifted it, would be covered again . . . just where the dirt had slid away when the door was raised. It was ingenious.

Even if he couldn't see it, Muldoon knew Army was grinning. "Come on," said the African. "It's a bit of a ways in the dark."

They walked quietly, Muldoon's hands brushing along both sides of the dirt tunnel. It smelled of damp soil, the deep, musky scent of crumbled earth. But the tunnel was straight, and led back toward the meeting house.

"This where we go up," whispered Army. "Don't make no extra noise. But they get loud, so they might not hear anyways."

Silently, Muldoon followed George Army up the ladder. It seemed the very pressure of the air changed, from the closeness of the tunnel to an even more suffocating stillness between walls. He could feel a brick wall on all four sides, as though he were climbing up a chimney. The inner wall was warm, and he realized he was, truthfully, inside a secret tunnel attached to the chimney. To the casual observer, the extra compartment, tacked onto the back of the flue, would be invisible.

"We're over the kitchen," whispered Army as Muldoon climbed up into the attic. "This side has a double floor. Can't hear nothing down there. So we're okay to move around. But over there . . . " He pointed to the open rafters across the attic. "Gotta stay away from over there."

Muldoon glanced about curiously. A little light filtered up through cracks in the rough ceiling that separated them from the big gathering room below the rafters. He imagined groups of escaped slaves living in this attic, perhaps hiding for days on end and waiting to be ferried across the harbor to the anonymity of New York City. Many had stayed in the city. Others moved on to Canada. Either way, this had been just one more stop on their way to freedom. Had Army hidden in this same attic, a refugee from the South?

It wasn't particularly safe in the open attic, he thought. The trap door they had entered was hidden in the warped floorboards. Its back edge, where it backed up against the chimney, was straight. The floorboards jutted out in different lengths to camouflage it. There was no obvious, square door, with a handle. There was no rug thrown over it. It had to be cleverly hidden to fool anyone who came looking for the people who hid in the tunnel. He imagined that the Quakers had crates and old furnishings, and attic bric-a-brac piled on this sturdier side, and people hid among the stacks, darting into the dank tunnel when the authorities came to call. Men with the power over life or death . . . freedom or slavery. Men like him.

Muldoon lay on his belly next to George Army. They peered through the cracks between the ceiling boards and into the room below. He pressed his face close and scanned the figures in the room. Chairs filled the open space, bodies crammed into the room. From his hidden perch, he had a view mostly of the backs of heads. Somewhere below him, Casper Biggs sat lost in the sea of men.

Near the wood stove across the room, three men stood facing the crowd. Each wore a white mask over his eyes and a long cape over his shoulders. Are these the Satanists? A cold-bladed shiver ran down Muldoon's spine.

The tall man in the center spoke loudly, shouting over the tumult. At first, Muldoon couldn't understand the words the men shouted, some angrily, others excited, but all seemed to have something to say. Not all of them wore masks, but many did—the masquerade type, covering just the eyes. He caught site of Biggs, masked, but he recognized the man's clothing and manner.

"Quiet . . . quiet, now!" the man at the front of the room called. "Let's hear what Brother Angelo has to say."

As the crowd settled, Brother Angelo stepped forward. "Thank you, Brother Vincentio," he began in a singsong preacher's tone. Not their real names, Muldoon realized. "I understand you, Brothers, we all feel the same."

The crowd roared wildly again. As the room quieted, the pale man began again. "This country is not safe for us. The African has been freed, but does he show his gratitude? No! He comes into our cities and takes our jobs. Why didn't he stay on the plantations where he belonged? Some say it was the Freedman's Bureau. It put high-and-mighty thoughts into his head, told him he deserves what the white man has."

"Boo!" the room filled with howls of anger. Men leaped from their chairs, fists in the air. Muldoon shifted uncomfortably next to George Army. Not Satanists, he thought. Unless they combine devil-worship with racial hatred.

The man who called himself Brother Angelo held his hands out to calm the crowd. "We don't wish the African any harm . . . " He spoke calmly, placatingly. "But we don't want him in our homes, either. He was given a new opportunity . . . send him and his kind back to Africa . . . to Liberia. But does he go? No! And what about a home in the west? Kansas? Oklahoma? Should we allow him to take prime land away from the white man?"

Again, the crowd went wild. "No!" they screamed.

"I say NO!" cried Brother Angelo over the roar. "I say the free African is more of a threat to our world than ever he was when enslaved. He threatens to overwhelm us, take our jobs, move into our homes . . . " he paused and continued in a hushed voice, "and next he'll want our women."

Again, the crowd screamed, a wicked sound, filled with hatred.

What is this? Muldoon might expect to hear this kind of diatribe somewhere in the South, but here? And these men? His gaze moved across the crowd below. He recognized many of them. They were well respected men, some were businessmen, and others were men of the cloth. But they were also Nativists . . . white Anglo-Saxon Protestants. Men of English derivation. Muldoon shook his head. Was this somehow related to his case? Schneider was German, he was an immigrant, and so the target of Nativist animosity. But the girl was probably one of theirs. Perhaps the sister, or daughter, of someone in this crowd. Whoever they were, this group needed to be watched.

As the crowd settled down, Brother Angelo stepped forward. Eyes flashing, the man began again. "Friends!" he shouted. "My friends, we have yet another threat to the sanctity of our lives. It is a new threat. One that fills our gutters with the waste of human society. I'm talking of the Irish ape, the Papists swilling whiskey in the streets. They flood in by the hundreds . . . nay, brothers, by the thousands. They cling to our shores, filthy hands out-thrust, begging outside our very doors. They are the vermin-waste of the Old World, filth-encrusted, pestilential beasts taking our jobs . . . I say, OUR JOBS. Have you seen them working in our stores, taking positions at lower wages, forcing young Native men from their liveli-hood? We must turn to our friends, like Brother Escalus here." He patted the shoulder of the stooped, graying man at his side, the third man of the trio. "He comes to us from Tennessee, yes, Tennessee, brothers. Together, we must re-forge the bonds of brotherhood. Reach out to our neighbors in the South, those who seek answers to the encroaching evil, from within and without."

Muldoon had heard enough. He began to scoot back from the edge when a familiar figure sitting near the back of the crowd, a big, blocky shape, caught his attention. He recognized him, but he couldn't believe Sergeant Hugh Collins, a fellow police officer, would be down below.

He nudged Army. Quietly, the two departed the way they had come.

Muldoon didn't fully understand what was happening in the meeting house, but he was sure it wasn't something the Quakers would have appreciated. Whatever it was, it was dark . . . of that, he was sure. Northern gentlemen and industrialists (he'd even recognized several prominent abolitionists and temperance men) secretly meeting with Southern extremists? He was sure the men speaking were Confederate officers, gentlemen of the South . . . men outlawed by Lincoln, but par-doned by his successor, Andrew Johnson, with his Amnesty Proclamation.

These men were organizing under a single banner . . . a banner based on racism and ethnic pride. He'd understood that much. And he had also understood the targets of their poisonous diatribe, their "other" of blacks, Irish, Catholics, and immigrants. He wondered if there were a connection between this new organization and the two murders. He knew he'd have to take a closer look at Casper Biggs.

CHAPTER 18

MULDOON paused on the step before the first house on Sisters' Row and waited impatiently for a response to his knock. He'd spent the morning combing through various newspapers across from Detective Benson in the crowded little office. Discarded papers were heaped in the corner atop old files. There would be fewer papers tomorrow. Some of the city's papers were dailies, but most were weekly. It seemed the city had hundreds of separate papers, one for each district, and several overlapping territories. And any of these might carry a small advertisement seeking information about a missing young woman. It was the one part of police work he disliked the most, spending so much time looking for written clues in old papers, files, and documents. Hours of sitting left him aching for physical activity. Still, he knew he couldn't have arrived at the sisters' before early afternoon. The girls kept late hours.

He and Benson had lunch at a little café not far from Headquarters. Then, Muldoon had set off at an ambling pace, timing his arrival for one o'clock. Now, he stood before the seven adjoining houses on West Twenty-Fifth Street that had come to be known as Sisters' Row. They were tall, thin row-homes, looking as if they'd been squeezed together, with not even an alley between. Each was gaily painted, though not gaudy, giving no hint of their immoral inhabitants. If not for their proximity to saloons and bawdy houses of a baser nature, an unknowing passerby would have no cause to suspect the activities inside.

He rapped again on the door and waited silently on the small porch. A faint drizzle pattered on the slight overhang above his head. The air was chill with a light spring wind. Within the building, he could hear the sound of steps drawing near. The door opened a crack, revealing a diminutive dark-skinned girl dressed in a maid's black and white outfit.

"Yes, Sir?" she asked, eyes large at the sight of a policeman on her stoop.

"I'd like to see your mistress."

"You'll have to wait here while I ask her."

Shortly, the maid returned and pulled the door wide. "Come in," she said. "Miz' Ada be right with you."

She showed Muldoon to a bright, well decorated sitting room where he again waited. Standing in the center of the room, he surveyed the artwork on the walls. They were portraits of women in compromising positions, yet somehow tasteful. Not like the ones so common in bawdy houses. These had expensive gilt frames, and subdued colors that contrasted with the yellow floral-print paper on the walls. A deep green settee angled in one corner with several plush chairs grouped nearby. A small fire burned in the hearth in an attempt to draw the damp from the room. Muldoon appreciated its warmth.

Lace curtains hung in the bay window, and a graceful table was centered in front of the opening. Soft light filtered onto it through the rain-streaked glass. A vase stood on a deep green doily, a bouquet of flowers artfully arranged. One lone stem lay across the crochet fabric, its single bud graced the table. Muldoon noted the carefully posed scene cynically. Below his feet, an expensive but subdued Chinese rug decorated the floor. The entire room was purposely arranged to provide a semblance of domesticity and wealth. It contrasted sharply with his thoughts of the murdered girl for whom he'd come.

Standing before the fireplace to take advantage of its warmth, he picked up an egg-shaped curio from a small grouping of Russian enameled trinket dishes. He rolled it lightly between his fingers then returned it to its place as the tap of shoes came from beyond the door. A petite woman entered the room. She was stunning, in a pale yellow house dress of China crepe trimmed in deep green, which just brushed the floor. The bodice plunged deep, drawing his gaze, green trim emphasizing the curve of her breasts. Though her dress was long-sleeved, they were of the thinnest gauze, and he admired the pale length of her delicate arms visible through the material. Her deep red hair was crimped, in a long chignon that fell to her shoulders. Several jewels were clipped above tight curls that adorned her forehead.

She moved forward gracefully, hand extended.

"William, my dear," she said in her carefully trained voice. The hint of a New England accent was just perceptible.

"Hello, Ada," he said.

"You haven't visited in the longest while," she purred, and held her hand toward him, a kerchief gripped in her long fingers. Ada Everleigh had introduced him to the pleasures of a woman's flesh several years before, as she was just establishing her business in the city. He'd been a shy country boy on his way to war. "Can't waste that," she'd said, all those years ago, running a gloved hand across his chest. And, though she entertained only the wealthiest gentlemen, she welcomed him into her home, pleasuring herself as much as him.

He took her slim hand and raised it to his lips.

"What brings you here?" The hint of a smile bowed her lips, but he could see a hardness in her eyes. Angry he hadn't come earlier?

"I'm here on a case."

She pouted prettily. "A case? Only a crime can bring you to my home? And we, who are so close?"

He knew he was welcome in her home, and had come several times since returning from the war. They came together in sharp, passionate need, and then she'd return to her duties and he to his. She was the Madame and ruled over the seven adjoining houses and their occupants, but rarely did she entertain, and never for pay. Her girls were to be bought, even her sisters, but Ada gave herself only to those she chose.

She turned smoothly and moved gracefully toward the settee, her gown swaying softly. "Come, William," she purred as she indicated the closest chair. "Sit, and tell me what you need to know."

She was cultured, so refined, he, and the rest of New York, often wondered where she'd come from. Perhaps she was the daughter of some country gentleman in an obscure New England village, the accent slightly evident in her words. She was well brought up, but something had drawn her into sin. He, too, had come from a small town. His own father had a degree of wealth. But that had been lost when he died, his estate gone to pay debts Muldoon hadn't known existed. So, he went to the city, to Five Points and the Bowery, where he could barely afford to live. He imagined it was the same for her. But she didn't have his strength and skill to support her. She had just one thing . . . her beauty. Rumor said she'd spent her inheritance to purchase the seven row-homes, one for each of the sisters. And that became their fame, drawing gentlemen from near and far, to taste the delights of their homes.

"I'm looking for a young woman," he said.

"Oh, William," she giggled. "Every man is looking for that!"

"Aye, there's always that. But that's not my meaning. A woman was murdered, perhaps seventeen or eighteen, by the look of her. I'm trying to find who she is. A name, a home, a family. She was found in the Points, at Paradise Park. But she isn't from there, I'd wager. Either she's from a high-class place like yours, or she's the daughter of a wealthy man."

Ada studied Muldoon through her lashes. Her eyes softened, her former irritation with him easing. She looked at him seductively. "All of our girls are accounted for. But there are several more establishments you may want to check. You can try Josephine Wood's over on Eighth

Street." She listed several more high-class bordellos. He knew most of them, but waited for her to finish.

"Thank you," he said at last, and wrote the addresses in his small notebook.

"What did she look like?" Ada asked. "In case someone comes looking for her here?"

"I can't say, really," answered Muldoon. "She was young, and quite beautiful, I think. But beyond that . . . " He shrugged. "Her hair was gone."

Ada pulled back suddenly as if struck, a hand straying to her own lush locks. Then, a thoughtful look crossed her face. "Did you try the wigmakers? If her hair were long, it would have been quite valuable."

Muldoon looked at her questioningly.

"For hairpieces, silly," she exclaimed and shook her lovely head, the hair waving to and fro. "Did you think all of this was mine?"

Several hours later, Muldoon emerged from the house. The thing about Ada was, every time he saw her they couldn't help themselves. She drew him up to her boudoir, where they spent hours in each other's arms. He couldn't get to Billy McGlory's Armory Hall too soon anyway, so he had time to spare. He'd have to work late again, to check up on Kavanagh's story.

CHAPTER 19

McGLORY's was a nasty dive on Hester Street. Muldoon secured his equipment on his belt so nothing could be easily taken, but he kept his nightstick handy. Just in case.

As he neared the saloon, he noted several leaner, meaner types loitering in the street. The rain still hadn't let up, so they leaned against buildings, trying to stay under the overhang to keep dry. Muldoon passed them . . . pretended he hadn't noticed. He knew what they were there for. Some unsuspecting drunkard would be accosted from behind and left in the gutter, his money and belongings gone. These were the first of McGlory's boys.

After these men had seen to the drunkard and his possessions, the "lush" workers would go after him. They would search his pockets all over again, seeking hidden valuables missed by the bouncers. And often they'd relieve the man of his clothing as well, leaving him lying naked in the street. If this was where Kavanagh spent his night, he was lucky, indeed.

Muldoon turned to the saloon and pushed open one of the big double doors. Inside, he passed down a long, narrow hallway. The walls were painted strangely black, giving an eerie, funereal aura. Fifty feet on, the dark hall ended with a door opening into the bar-room. Beyond that was the dance-hall, theater-like, with balcony seats arranged around an open space filled with tables and chairs. It was a huge room, capable of being occupied by perhaps seven hundred men.

Waitresses strolled to and fro, carrying an endless supply of drinks. To the side of the stage, three men played piano, violin, and cornet, providing music for the dancing girls. The women paraded around the stage in skimpy costumes, swishing skirts high to bare their legs and undergarments.

Muldoon strolled through the place, watching the action. A group of men looked up at him, disturbed at his sudden appearance, momentarily halting the throw of dice. Others turned quickly away as he approached. What they did in here, many wanted to keep here. A hand reached around from behind him to lie flat on his broad stomach. It slowly lowered, a seductive movement. Reacting suddenly, he grabbed the wrist and yanked the whore around him, forcing the offender into a deep knee bend.

"Ow! Ow!" the boy-girl exclaimed in a curiously low voice, masculine melding with feminine. "Don't you want some sugar?"

"Not from the likes of you," Muldoon said, staring frostily at the man. He was dressed as a woman, all frills and lace, a stunning hairpiece on his head. Except for his voice, he was hardly discernible from any number of prostitutes in the city. Muldoon knew this particular establishment catered to men of that taste. Even the beauties on the stage, he knew, were unnatural women.

"Well!" exclaimed the whore before flouncing off to find some other, more willing, partner.

Muldoon circulated through the big room. So many of the clientele were dressed expensively, with full mutton chop sideburns. They were wealthy men "elephant hunting," slumming on a Friday evening. At some point, he knew, McGlory would have to come over to him, to dissuade him from disturbing the clientele. And disturbed they would be, he knew . . . New York's upper crust playing with boys while an officer of the law strolled by.

As he predicted, McGlory soon appeared at his side.

"Sergeant Muldoon!" the weaselly man exclaimed. He rubbed his hands constantly together, as though desperately trying to wash away a multitude of sins from his past.

Muldoon looked at him with disgust, eyeing the man's long greasy hair, tucked tightly back behind his ears. He wore plaid pants under a more sedate black vest and coat, his watch chain hanging loosely. A man with his wealth, Muldoon knew, could easily afford better, and certainly could be clean. But after all, the man was born in Five Points and had never known better. He aped what he saw as best he could, and didn't realize his own appearance was so cheap an imitation.

"My guests," he tried again. "They . . . um . . . they're rather . . . uncomfortable." He said it almost as a question, bending over strangely even while he looked up at Muldoon, his neck cocked back to hold his head at an odd angle.

"They should be accustomed to policemen," Muldoon said curtly.

"Aye, I'm certain many of them are . . . but what of the 'quality?' Couldn't you move back into the bar? On their account?"

"I suppose I could, if you're up to giving a little information."

"You know I can't do that. I've got a reputation."

"Aye, and so have I. You know me from the past, McGlory. You know it's not just the police I represent, but the Bowery B'hoys, too."

"That's a hard thing to be reminding me of, Muldoon. You made your choice when you went to the law."

"Aye, but the law came to me first, over at Harry Hill's, as you know. A politician needs his men, and a neighborhood needs its politician. Someone who'll watch over them, and give them a hand when they need it. Tammany Hall gives us that, so we need to give an arm to the Boss now and again. And that arm's me. But I serve both masters. Once a B'hoy, always a B'hoy, and we take care of our own."

McGlory nodded unhappily. His gang was the Chichesters of Five Points, but he'd made his own choice when he moved out of the

Points and into the Bowery. The immediate vicinity might be filled with McGlory's own, but Muldoon recognized several faces at the gambling tables. He nodded to them as they passed. If need be, they'd support the B'hoy.

"Come with me to my office," wheezed McGlory as he lit up a smoke.

Muldoon shook his head. "No, I don't think so. I prefer to talk in the open." There was no way he'd enter a private room with this man. Then he'd be totally alone. As it was, he'd have to make it out of Hester Street and its environs. He wasn't going to play into the little weasel's hands in here. Keep him outside where he had plenty of witnesses.

"You're a hard man," McGlory said.

Muldoon nodded, a curt gesture, toward an empty table by the wall. The two walked over, and he slid into the seat against the wall where he could protect his back.

"Two murders," Muldoon said. "I need some information."

"Aaaah . . . the two at Paradise Park. I heard about that. A man and a woman. Strangled." Muldoon almost laughed. McGlory didn't realize he'd confirmed one of his most closely held secrets, that he couldn't read. He could only listen to the boys on the street corners selling their news. They called out exciting headlines, often making up a more exciting, even more outlandish tale than the one already in print.

"Aye," Muldoon said. "That'd be them."

"And what do you think I can tell you about them? I don't know anything aside from what I've heard."

Muldoon pulled out three small pictures—two photos, one a sketch. He held them like playing cards, carefully fanned. Selecting one, he slid it across the table, flipping it over just in front of McGlory.

"Do you know this man?" he asked. It was the photo of a man in a Union Sergeant's uniform. Karl Schneider, in the picture he'd picked up in the man's apartment.

"Looks familiar, but I can't say as I know who it is."

"Try again," said Muldoon as he lifted it from the table and angled it to catch the weak tavern light.

"No, can't say," McGlory said again.

"How about this one?" Muldoon asked, holding out a well-drawn sketch. Danny Ryan, the coroner's clerk had drawn it for him. The boy had a fair hand with a pencil. He had objected to going in amongst the dead. Muldoon had laughed at him, joking about his choice of jobs. But he knew it could mean the difference between survival and starvation. So, he'd offered the boy a dollar and a new book. Danny reluctantly agreed to make the sketch, and the deal done, he'd carefully made a detailed likeness of the pale woman from Paradise Park.

"What about the hair?" Danny had asked, and Muldoon had told him to sketch something in, but not too dark, since they didn't know what color it should be.

"Can't say I know her, neither," squeaked McGlory in his grating little voice. "But she's a sweet piece o' meat."

"A piece of meat is right," Muldoon said. "She's lying cold in the morgue."

"Aaaah, so she's the one."

"Aye."

Muldoon slid the third picture toward McGlory. "And how about this one?"

"Again, I have to say, I don't know. I don't know any of them."

Muldoon's lips tightened in anger. "Aye, you do. And I say, if you'd lie about one, you would lie about them all."

McGlory started as if surprised, straightening in his chair. "I tell you, I don't know a one of them!"

Once again, Muldoon showed him the picture of Karl Schneider. And again, McGlory shook his head. Muldoon reached forward suddenly and grabbed the little man by the back of his slimy head, and pushed his face down toward the table top where the picture lay. He shoved the single candle that lighted the table toward the man. "Take a long look, McGlory . . . and tell me what you see."

"A'right, a'right," McGlory said, a touch of fear in his voice. "It's Karl Schneider."

"Aye. Very good. And of course, we both know he was one of your boys."

McGlory nodded, caught out in his lie. It was hard to believe this same man had once been Captain of the Chichesters, one of the most notorious gangs in the Points.

Muldoon let go of the man and allowed him to sit straight once again. McGlory rubbed the back of his head where Muldoon had held it forcefully. Again, Muldoon slid the drawing in front of the gangster.

"I swear to you, Muldoon, I don't know this one. I ain't never seen her. If I'd seen her, I wouldn't have allowed her to get killed. She'd have made me a bundle, she would. Least, until she was a bit older, anyhow. Then, maybe I wouldn't have cared what became of her. Maybe passed her on to another establishment."

Muldoon narrowed his eyes. He didn't care for this man and his wicked thoughts. The girl wasn't an object to be used and then tossed aside. But he believed him. He hadn't seen the girl before. He slid the final picture across the table. Kavanagh's. Muldoon had pinched it from the man's flat. McGlory studied it for a moment.

"He's a regular," McGlory admitted.

"Was he here last night?"

"Aye, he was."

"All night?"

"I don't watch the crowd that close," McGlory said. "He was here for awhile . . . " He paused, as if in thought. "And then I think he left. But he came back, and yes, he was here all night. I remember, he made a big show of losing."

Muldoon nodded. It didn't mean much. Kavanagh wasn't a big enough man to have killed Schneider. Even he would've had a hard time with it. But he couldn't help being a bit curious. After all, two bodies had been dumped just outside the man's window . . . and he claimed to have no knowledge about either. Muldoon stood up to leave, then turned back.

"Does he have any certain folk he meets here?"

"I don't know, I don't look that close at my guests," McGlory said. "For God's sake, Muldoon, I got room for seven-hundred in there."

"Aye, that you do," Muldoon said. "That you do."

He exited through the same dark entrance he'd come through some time ago and opened the outer door cautiously. It was full night now. The streetlamps threw their weak glow in contained balls of light, dotting the street like stars. The rain had let up for a bit, and tendrils of mist rose from the damp road. Muldoon knew the loiterers were out there, hidden in the darkness. He glanced uneasily behind him, knowing a signal from McGlory would send a dozen men into the night after him. Some of the other cops had started carrying guns, but he hadn't gotten one. They weren't supplied by the department, so he'd balked at the extra expense. He hadn't carried one since the war. Times like these made him debate whether he should. The "equalizer," he'd heard some say.

Pulling his nightstick out of its sheath, he held it ready on his left, right hand loose beside him. He had to walk several blocks to Mulberry, then only a few more to Police Headquarters. The street was far from deserted, but he knew few would be of help to a cop. Most folk distrusted them. When existence depends upon the ability to steal, the law and all that represent it are on the wrong side.

He stepped onto the street and turned toward Mulberry. He walked with self-assurance, straight and tall. His pace was measured, not too slow, but certainly not fast, either. In this district, you couldn't show any sign of fear or weakness, or the rats would descend upon you in an instant. A cop moving quickly would be seen as either being in chase, or being chased. In this instance, it would clearly be chased. He'd quickly lose the respect of the population, and no longer be able to perform his job effectively. He'd be no good to Boss Tweed. And more important than that, he'd lose the respect of the wrestling community. He'd be laughed out of the very thing he loved the most.

Muldoon continued down the street unmolested. Prostitutes stood in small bunches on corners, calling out to him and other passersby. They made themselves as desirable as possible in their way, not caring who would take up their proposition. What mattered to them was the pittance they could take home to their families. Or in these parts, to McGlory, or some other whoremonger.

He passed under the light at Mulberry and turned the corner. Quickly, he moved from the dim glow into blackness against the wall of a dilapidated building. He pushed tight against it, knowing he couldn't be seen. The light couldn't penetrate beyond the wall. He waited, sure someone had followed him. The silence was overwhelming. Around the corner, he knew, were men sent by McGlory to take him out of action. He, a cop and a B'hoy, had violated the sanctity of the man's own establishment. He didn't know which was worse, that he was a policeman . . . or a B'hoy. Either was sworn enemy to the man, one competing with him in criminal intent, the other, at least pledged to protect the law. Of course, he wasn't naïve. He knew the City Police weren't angels. They really weren't much more than yet another gang. So many of them took bribes . . . and gave them, pimped and whored, gambled and protected criminals. They were part and parcel of the vice in New York City. But then, there were some like him, men who sought clean and lawful streets. Detective Benson, too, wanted to protect the law. But Muldoon knew alcohol drew that man down. For himself, he had to work within the boundaries of both law and environment. He had to protect the law even while he lived among the people. So, he walked an uneasy tightrope—working with, and using, both law and criminal. He was a cop . . . but he was also a B'hoy.

Hiding in the dark, pushed tight against the side of a building, Muldoon tried not to think of these things. He knew them. They were a part of his psyche. If someone came around that corner, he'd do what he had to. In this part of New York, it was survival of the fittest.

And around the corner they came. Three men, thugs, wearing loose, ill-fitting clothes, though of good cut. Muldoon knew they'd been taken from drunkards, left lying naked and beaten in the street, to find their way home in the morning.

He let the small group pass him in the blackness. He thanked God the night was pitch-black, clouds filling the sky. The rain had begun again, leaving everything a thick swill of mud.

"Where'd he go?" muttered one of the men.

"Don't know," answered a second. "Got to be around here somewheres."

Muldoon nearly held his breath. Not because he was afraid, but to see if any others rounded the corner behind them. His heart thudded loudly in his ears. In the distance, he could see several women loitering under a streetlamp. A cab passed in the street at a swift pace, the horse's hooves sloshing through the mud. Its driver sped up, no doubt, at the sight of the rough-looking threesome. Muldoon shifted the nightstick a bit in his grasp.

The biggest thug stepped backward a little and rolled onto his toes, as if he could see better if only he were taller. Then, he turned and headed back the way they'd come.

"Well, we better get back." He spoke jauntily, as if he were in command of the situation. But Muldoon knew this was the far edge of his territory. It wasn't particularly safe for the men to move beyond the little patch of light at the corner.

As they moved back toward the streetlamp, the small man in the back of the group paused and turned his head. Something had caught his attention . . . a glint in the shadows, perhaps. And suddenly, Muldoon knew. Some tiny movement of his, and the dim light had reflected off his copper badge, or one of his brass buttons, all so prominently displayed on his chest. He had hoped to avoid this fight. It wasn't his way to hurt, if hurting didn't need to be done. Not since the war, and all the killing he'd done.

With a swift motion, he leaped forward, swung the baton and caught the small man on the wrist, forcing his gun from his hand. The man cried out in pain, and Muldoon felt the bone break beneath the weight of his stick. He began to feel the rush of combat, the excitement that he'd come to love and to hate. The taste of blood quickened his heartbeat. He stepped forward and kicked the pistol into the shadows where he'd stood only moments before. With a quick movement, his right fist flew forward, crunching into the man's face. Blood spurted from his nose, and the small man dropped to the ground, unconscious.

He spun about. The smallest was out of action, but he was also the easiest, once parted from his gun. The two remaining men rushed him in unison. He could almost smell their fear, but they charged nonetheless, and he respected them for that. Still, it was him or them. He had to act first. He dropped his nightstick and grabbed their loose jackets as they came. Using their own speed, he slung the two men together, jarring them for just a moment. He stepped in and slid his left foot forward, tripping the closest to the ground. The bigger man fell over the sudden pile at his feet, and lurched forward toward Muldoon. He grabbed the man's arm and pulled him into a tight half-nelson, until he heard, and felt, a slight pop. The man dropped to his knees with a muffled shriek. His arm now hung uselessly at his side, the shoulder dislocated.

The one he had tripped now faced him alone. His eyes bugged out with fear as Muldoon made a lunging motion toward him, and the man turned and ran as if the very devil were behind him. Muldoon laughed, but it wasn't with mirth. These streets were mean, and it took a meaner man to make it through.

His uniform was ripped. He hadn't felt it happen. If it was too badly torn he'd have to buy a new jacket. He turned to the shadows, and kicked around a bit with his feet until he felt a hard object. It slid further back, hitting the wooden building with a metallic twang. He leaned forward and carefully picked up the pistol. He raised it toward the streetlamp, so he could see it better. It was a Colt Model 1862 "Police" Percussion Revolver. It had been taken from some cop, he figured, so now it had been returned to the boys in blue. He slipped the heavy pistol into his waistband and retrieved his nightstick from where it had fallen.

He grunted with satisfaction at the silent figure on the ground and the other moaning as he hugged his arm to his side. He turned, and alarm bells jangled his senses—a frisson of fear slid down his back. At the far end of the street red eyes glared at him. He felt riveted to the ground, and before he could react the dark figure disappeared.

CHAPTER 20

April 20

MULDOON tested his muscles, stretching one arm, then the other. He grimaced at the stiffness in his right shoulder, but pushed past the pain. McGlory's thugs hadn't left any real injuries, none that could have much effect on his evening's bout. Harry Hill had paired him with an out of town challenger. The kid was still a bit inexperienced, but a match was a match. He'd soon have some green in his pocket. He stood in front of his bureau mirror and studied his bare reflection. New bruises splashed across his flesh. He poured water into the basin and cleaned the raw wounds, bandaging them tightly. Harry Hill, Boss Tweed, his fans, they all had confidence in him. They thought he couldn't lose. He was becoming their hero. Some of the local kids acted like he was Achilles. He remembered reading about the Greek hero when he was a kid. His father had beaten him for it. It wasn't a Christian book. But he'd loved reading about Odysseus' and Achilles' exploits and hid a copy of Homer's Iliad in the hay loft. He wanted to be like them. Looking in the mirror, he wondered if he was. When Achilles failed, he'd died. If he failed, Kelly would die.

He checked out his torn and bloodied uniform, then discarded it for the clean one hanging from a peg. He hoped he could get it mended. Tossing it over the back of a chair he dressed quickly, then slipped out of the dark house. Only the maid, Betsy, was about so early. He held his finger to his lips. He didn't want to disturb Ma McAllister. Betsy nodded mutely, a tiny, forlorn smile on her face. For a moment, he wondered why she always looked so sad, but shrugged it off. Everyone looked sad. War does that. Leaves a lot of sorrowful, empty smiles behind.

His thoughts turned back to the crimson-eyed figure he'd seen again the previous night. He clenched his jaw. Was it real? Or a phantasm of his imagination? He ignored the soldiers that assailed him from all sides. Three trailed him. One stopped before him, and he crossed the street, continuing up that side as he headed to work.

Benson was already in his office when Muldoon got to headquarters. The detective's clothes were more rumpled than usual and Muldoon noticed a space had been cleared on the floor near the desk. Benson's overcoat lay on the floor.

"You slept here?" Muldoon asked.

Benson peered at him with bloodshot eyes. "I was too drunk to get home."

"You need to give up that stuff."

Benson's skin had a slight, sickly tinge of green. A pale glow filtered from the shadowy hall and through the partially-opened door, barely lighting the room. Muldoon turned the key on the wall, and the flame rose in the gas-lamp.

Benson shielded his bloodshot eyes. "Do you need that?"

"Aye,' Muldoon said. "And so do you."

He seated himself in front of the desk, Benson on the far side.

"At least, you might want to pick up your coat," Muldoon said. "Just in case the Captain comes in. I don't think he'd like the thought of your staying all night, just because you were drunk."

"Probably not." Benson reached down to snag the coat and flung it over a pile of files.

"Of course, he probably doesn't like those, either," Muldoon said, indicating the stacks of files.

"No, but like you . . . I've got the threat of Tammany Hall over him." Benson grinned.

Muldoon wondered about that. He was a strong arm for Tweed, but Benson wasn't near big enough. And the man was distinctly old native blood, not Irish. He couldn't imagine what connected him to William Marcy Tweed. And he knew better than to ask. A man's story was his own.

The Captain had to be crazy over it, he thought. He didn't like either of them particularly well, and what made it worse, he couldn't fire them. He was stuck with them, because of their connection to Tweed, the most powerful man in New York City. Muldoon wouldn't be surprised if he were told Tweed's ring spread across the entire state, if not further. He might even be big enough to influence national politics. He certainly could, as far as the New York City vote. He hired men to force people to vote and then scare them into casting their ballot for the 'right' candidate . . . the Tammany Hall Democrat. He hired men like Muldoon.

Captain Hayle, like the rest of the old English stock, couldn't stand Tweed and his party of Irishmen. The Nativist English thought the Irish were poor because they wanted to be. Up to a point, Muldoon agreed. But there weren't jobs, and what could be had didn't pay well. The easiest way to get out was to move west. Horace Greeley wrote "Go west, young man" in the Times. As if the poor could head west. They couldn't even get out of the city. Those who did get out had to have made a small grubstake somehow. Make enough to buy their way west. He planned on being one of those men. He was Irish, like most of the others in his district. But he had skill on the mat, and he had the size and strength to back it up.

"Did you find out anything of value yesterday?" The scrape of a heavy desk chair yanked Muldoon from his reverie as Benson pulled his chair out from under the desk. He sat down heavily, running his fingers through his untidy hair.

"Aye, a bit." Muldoon pulled out the revolver and laid it on the desk between them. "Got this off one of McGlory's thugs."

"I never thought I'd see you with a gun, Muldoon." Benson picked up the pistol. "There's no telling who it might have belonged to." He turned it over and inspected its smooth blue finish. It was a five-shot .36 caliber weapon with a 4 ½ inch barrel. He hefted it, and Muldoon knew he'd find it nicely balanced, the walnut grip smooth in his hand.

"Not since the war," Muldoon said. "I'll only carry when I need to. Seems to me it's easier to get shot bringing your own gun."

"Three months and the men are still laughing at Sergeant Miller. Shot by his own pistol." Benson laughed, then put a hand to his temple. "Damn throbbing won't go away."

Muldoon raised an eyebrow, but didn't say anything. Benson had to stop. But he couldn't. He slipped the gun into his waistband. "Think how easy it is. I got this gun off its owner during a fight, same as happened to Miller."

They didn't say anything, each lost in his own thoughts. Then suddenly Muldoon pushed back in his seat. "So, did you see Kelly McAllister?"

"Yes, I did." Benson's expression darkened. "He's not doing too well. You said he was injured in that match last week, but how badly?"

"He was fair hurt," Muldoon said. "Couple broken ribs, and I had to pop his shoulder back into place. But nothing else I could find. Course, I'm not a doctor. I know he was hurting mighty bad."

"He doesn't seem to be much better. He should be, after a week."

Muldoon frowned. It hadn't seemed Kelly was that bad. Within a week, his own body would have been well on its way to recovery, even with the ribs and shoulder. He might not be able to wrestle for a while, but he'd be up and around by now.

"He's taken to his bed, Muldoon," Benson said, a serious tone in his voice. "And he doesn't seem to be eating. At least, that's what the guards say."

"Well, who'd be eating that filth?" Muldoon asked, and rose to pace the small room. "I've got to get him out of there. This case just doesn't seem to be going anywhere."

"No, but it's only been a week. We've made a bit of progress. You've got a good lead with Kavanagh."

Muldoon shook his head. "He spent the night at McGlory's, just like he said." His thoughts turned dark as he wondered at the quick speed of trial and sentencing of his friend. "And we only have days before Kelly swings."

CHAPTER 21

Surely someone saw the bodies get dumped. There had to be a witness. If Muldoon couldn't find someone Kelly McAllister didn't have a chance. He spent the rest of the morning walking Cross Street, questioning and re-questioning folks. Nothing. Shortly after noon, he returned to Police Headquarters. Detective Benson had already left, so he headed wearily home. The spring in his step was gone. He felt so tired. Muldoon knew he was lucky. Because of his connection with Boss Tweed, he only worked half day on Saturday. He should stay out there, but he had to rest before the match. The late nights, the worry, the dreams. He was so weary. He wanted to ditch the fight and sleep for a week. But he couldn't. His pocket book was getting thin, and he needed to bring home the purse.

"Kelly," he mumbled. "You damn, sorry kid. I can't lose another friend . . . another brother." Not like Patrick Ryan. After the battle at Fort Pickens Paddy had just . . . disappeared. He wasn't among the dead or injured. The New York 6th Infantry's reputation had preceded them south. Even among the Yanks they were called hooligans and gangsters. The Rebs threatened to destroy them, and said that they'd never take one alive. If the Rebs captured him, then he was probably dead.

Now he might lose another friend. Muldoon had seen Kelly grow from a thirteen-year-old kid to a strong young man, just beginning a wrestling career. He taught Kelly to fight, and he'd taught him to read.

The boy had learned his letters from his Ma, but he didn't put much use to it. Then when Muldoon got the fever, Kelly and Ma McAllister took turns at his bedside. They read out of the bible, and off scraps of newspaper Kelly found. Then Muldoon sent the boy out to search for cheap books. He brought back a book of poetry by Keats, and stumbled over the words. Muldoon never asked where the books came from, or where they went. Probably stolen. But he listened while Kelly read stories of war, or love, or adventure. And he quietly corrected the boy's reading of Shakespeare and Homer, Nathaniel Hawthorne and Edgar Allen Poe.

He pushed away the memories as he entered the boarding house. The door to the front parlor stood partially open. So much for getting into his room unnoticed. He sighed quietly as Mrs. Dunn called out to him before he could pass.

"Come, sit with us for a while." She gestured toward an empty seat near the door. He slid into the chair and leaned back heavily. He knew he appeared vulgar, but he was too tired to care.

Heavy blue curtains had been pulled open to let in the subdued light of an overcast day. A momentary shaft of light broke through and he idly watched as dust motes traveled down to the worn Chinese rug. The furniture, too, was worn, but of once-good quality. Mrs. Dunn had patched the torn fabric, and then hung oblong doilies over the chair backs. A matching cover draped over the fireplace mantle, a collection of vases carefully arranged there, and a gaudy blue and gray floral painting hanging above them. Muldoon studied the small fire laid in the hearth. It barely cut the chill in his bones. Some days, he felt much older than he was. In the flames, he could see buildings burning. When the Rebs evacuated Pensacola, they'd torched the city. They hadn't wanted to leave it for the Yanks, and much of the town was destroyed. When he gazed into the flames . . . Pensacola was on fire again. An oil factory, storehouses, some small boats. All burning. And then the house. Women and children screamed out. Southern voices. No one helped them. Not even me.

Was it that he couldn't . . . or that he wouldn't? He didn't know anymore. The thoughts haunted him. His blood began to freeze, his jaw
muscles ached with tension, and his fingers tightened on the chair arms.

". . . Sergeant Muldoon?"

He pulled his gaze from the fire, turned to Don Hardin, who sat
near Mrs. Dunn.

"Sorry?"

"I was asking about the elections coming up," Hardin said. "Are
you interested in them at all?"

"Oh . . . aye." Muldoon sat a bit straighter in the chair. He
flashed a glance toward the door. He wanted to get out of uniform. The
first chance a cop got, he wanted to get out of it and into civilian clothes.
He turned back to Hardin. "I'll be working at the polls."

"You will?" Mrs. Dunn asked, her eyebrows rising. "I didn't
know you were political."

"Aye, well," Muldoon began. "They need as many folk as they
can get . . . you know . . . to keep things in order." He couldn't quite
bring himself to admit his role as strong-arm. He'd be there, not to keep
order exactly, but to make sure registered Democrats voted for
Democrats. Boss Tweed got his job for him, so he owed his loyalty to the
political machine. If Tammany Hall lost its position of power, then he'd
lose his job to some Republican.

Meg McAllister leaned forward, momentarily forgetting her tat-
ting, the light blue threads trailing across her lap. "Have you heard anything about the convention?" she asked. "Have you heard what they're
going to talk about?"

"I haven't heard" Muldoon said. He was glad Meg seemed to fit
in. There had been none of the raised eyebrows he expected. The two
had concocted a bit of a story, not a long stretch, but one the others
could believe. So, with a new, second-hand wardrobe, she became a distant relative of his, come to stay for a while.

"I heard something about giving the black man the vote." Casper Biggs addressed the room with a superior air.

The room erupted in violent discussion as they debated the likelihood of allowing black men to vote. It quickly became apparent which side each was on. Personally, Muldoon didn't care. He really wasn't political. But he did think reform was a good thing. Finding his eyes drooping, he excused himself from their company, went to his rooms and closed the door firmly behind him. He yanked off his uniform, hung it over the back of a chair, and lay down on the bed to rest. He had a wrestling match coming up. He'd already asked Betsy to get him up by four.

Still, he couldn't help but think of Casper Biggs. The man had sat close beside Meg. At the age of sixty, he was the only person in the boarding house who didn't call her Ma, aside from Mrs. Dunn, who considered hers a business relationship. Did he consider himself a prospect? Muldoon didn't like the man. He'd been at the Quaker meeting house. Worse, he publicly proclaimed his hatred of the Irish. The man was an enemy. What he was playing, where Meg McAllister was concerned? Muldoon didn't know. And he didn't like it. Not one bit.

CHAPTER 22

Harry Hill's was the most sought-after entertainment hall in the city. A two-story frame building on West Houston Street, it sported bright paint to attract passersby. A blue and red lantern lit a huge sign on the side of the building:

Punches and juleps, cobblers and smashes,
To make the tongue waggle with wit's merry flashes.

A line of men filed in the large door. Beside them, brightly clad women smiled and waved, disappearing through a small door just for them. A brawny man stood at the entrance, collecting twenty cents from each man who entered. The women got in free. They were part of the entertainment.

Muldoon bypassed them, and entered the back way. In the storeroom, he stripped down to his tights, and then made his way to the bar. The early bouts soon ended, but the final event was delayed as a skinny man from Trenton, New Jersey shouted obscenities in support of the visiting grappler. A burly bouncer forced his way between him and several local boys. One, a freckled redhead, reached around the bouncer and poked the Jersey man hard in the shoulder. "Officer Muldoon will make mincemeat of your boy," he said, as the bouncer pulled them onto the stage and let them at each other. Harry Hill never allowed a brawl to get out of hand. His was an orderly establishment, by the standards of the city. If you wanted to fight, you did it on the stage.

The unexpected entertainment excited a flurry of new wagers. Muldoon didn't join the betting, but remained focused, preparing for his match. He wasn't a betting man. He did like a good boxing match, but these two went at it slap-happy. Neither had the discipline, or the skill, to be real boxers.

Harry Hill crossed the room toward Muldoon. He was a short, stocky fifty-year-old with the build of a boxer and a face to match.

"Heard about your match with the African," Hill growled as he approached, his voice low and raspy as a bulldog's.

Muldoon shrugged noncommittally.

"If it was anyplace but the Black and Tan, I might be worried about your loyalties." He rubbed his crooked nose. "Gave 'em a show, did you?"

Muldoon nodded. "Aye, but it was for Kelly McAllister. Had to get him safely out of there. That George Army would have killed him for sure."

"I might not be too happy with you," Hill said. "But it seems to have whetted their appetite." He nodded toward the mass of men who'd come for tonight's bout. "They're interested to see how you do tonight. I've heard some saying you're done for. That you've lost it. They say it shows from the fight with Army. You were slow to take him down. Even lost a fall. That was mighty good of you."

"He's a natural talent, but no real training. And, it kept the crowd going. That first fall had to go to Army. If not, neither one of us might have gotten out alive."

"I suppose. If he'd lost quickly the crowd might have got mad. Nice of you to let him save face . . . but you showed he was near equal to my champ. I don't appreciate that."

Down the bar, two women yelled at one another over some alleged offense. "Hey! Hey, girls," Hill called out. "None of that in here."

He tapped Muldoon on the arm. "Excuse me, but that's not happening here unless it's up there."

The battle on the stage played itself out. Both men, bloodied and bruised, were carried from the stage and dumped unceremoniously on the sidewalk outside. They were replaced by the cat fight, and then it was Muldoon's turn. He strode toward the stage, the crowd parting easily before him.

"Go, Muldoon!" someone called.

"Peter Boyle, he's a great fellow!" Someone in the back cheered the Jersey man.

And then, they were both on stage. Muldoon raised his hands high, playing to the crowd. The fans went wild. He loved this part of it, the anticipation of the crowd, their shouting adoration. At Harry Hill's, five-hundred spectators squeezed into the room. It was a big crowd, but someday, he planned to wrestle in the Gardens, with a gathering of thousands. Someday, he swore, it would come true. And then he'd be out of the slum he had to sleep, work, and play in.

He wore white knee breeches and flesh-tone hose, lightweight shoes on his feet. His chest was bare, bulging muscles sliding loosely beneath tight skin. He turned to the kid from across the bay. Peter Boyle dressed similarly, in a single-piece leotard, blue from his toes to the suspenders over his thick chest. A rhythmic tick jumped over his eye, betraying his nervousness. The New York crowd booed and hissed as Boyle raised his arms to them. Muldoon decided to get this one over quickly. He'd toy with him for a bit, and then end the match.

The crowd might be disappointed, but he didn't care. He was tired, and would rather make an early night of it. He needed to be thinking about Kelly McAllister, and Karl Schneider, and the dead girl. He turned to Boyle and took his stance. Squaring off, they waited until the referee dropped his hat, and then grasped each other tight. Boyle wasn't unaccomplished, he'd give him that, but he was no match for Muldoon.

Quickly, Muldoon maneuvered behind him and got him in a headlock, his left hand gripping the kid's bicep. Just a quick movement, he thought. Then Boyle would be dead. Neck snapped. Kelly couldn't have done it. He knew it with absolute certainty. It would take a man who didn't care. Or one who liked to kill. Army? Maybe. Who else? Nobody else he knew of. Within a minute, he had the kid down. Boyle bridged, resisting the pressure exerted on him, but within a minute and a half, his shoulders were pressed to the mat. The first fall was over.

The second fall didn't last much longer.

"That's a foul," Boyle complained. "Plain as can be. He came at me before the hat fell."

"Boo!" the crowd roared at Boyle and a scuffle broke out in the rear between factions.

"Boyle cries foul," yelled Hill over the din.

"Don't you believe it," the crowd yelled, then, "Muldoon, Muldoon, Muldoon," drowned out the calls of, "Boyle, Boyle, he's a great fellow."

The Police Gazette had supplied the official, and the man raised his hands in the air, calling for quiet. "The fall doesn't count," he yelled, and the crowd roared in anger and disbelief.

The two started once more. And again, Muldoon had Boyle down without much effort. The third fall, too, was quickly dispatched. Harry Hill glowered.

The crowd went wild. Hill stepped toward Muldoon and raised his hand high. Muldoon flexed his muscles, just for the crowd, and they cheered to see his biceps, sweat gleaming across the broad muscle.

"You could have given me a show, too," Hill growled.

"I'm tired tonight," Muldoon said. "And the boy had nothing there. I can't make a show out of nothing. Find me a real opponent, and you'll get your show. Besides, now they know I haven't lost it."

He waved as he left the stage and fans reached out to him, patted him on the back, felt his well-developed muscles. With the money he earned tonight, he'd be able to pay for three months' rent, even with the price of four rooms. The kid's backers had put up a good sum for this match, plus his share of the take, he'd be rolling in dough. He'd be able to get a new uniform to replace his ripped and bloodied one. And then he'd buy a new suit, finely-made boots, trousers, vest, and jacket. And maybe a top hat and cane, if he could find them second hand. The rest he'd put in the bank to add to his growing savings.

Across the room, a flash caught his eye, just for an instant. He turned toward it and searched the crowd. In the distance, a top hat came down on a man's head. The man turned toward the stage, a worried expression on his face. He was tall, with a fair complexion. Muldoon didn't know him, but something about him seemed familiar. He frowned.

"Muldoon!"

Recognizing the voice, he spun about. Kavanagh . . . a bundle of bills clasped tightly in his fist. The man beamed, waving his winnings high in the air, a mug in his other hand. Muldoon nodded, then turned back toward the door. The man in the top hat was gone.

CHAPTER 23

April 21

MULDOON could find nothing on Kavanagh. It just didn't seem like he was the right man. He'd have to turn his sights elsewhere, but he had no other leads. He and Benson had gone before Hayle, and they were grilled for more than an hour. The Captain had been furious.

"This should have been an easy one for you two oafs." Captain Hayle's face grew red. "The woman was a whore. All you need to do is arrest someone. It doesn't matter who."

Muldoon didn't understand the Captain's rage. If she was a prostitute, then why did he care? Was somebody else behind the scene? Somebody who wanted to find an answer to the death of the girl . . . or cover it up? Or was he afraid the two might connect her to the Schneider murder?

"What's so important about this case?" Muldoon asked. "If you're right, and she's just a whore, then it shouldn't matter. Whores are killed almost every day down here."

"Yes, but this one is unsolved."

"Most of them are."

"Don't challenge me, Muldoon. It's of interest to the City."

He wasn't satisfied, but he didn't dispute the Captain further. Hayle didn't know any more than he or Benson did. But, curiously, he hadn't handed the case over to Graham. Normally, it would have been, as soon as it became important . . . like Schneider's case. That one had made a big splash in the papers, so it had to be solved quickly. And Hayle's favorite closer was definitely Graham, not Benson and Muldoon.

CHAPTER 24

A low fog rolled in during the night, and the relentless drizzle ceased, at least for the time being. Muldoon dressed in civilian clothes. He wasn't on police business today. It was Election Day, and he chafed at Boss Tweed's bit. But he didn't have any choice. Tammany Hall had called him into action. He joined the rest of the household for breakfast. Casper Biggs had the New York Times spread out on the table before him. He looked up as Muldoon entered.

"Are you going to the polls?" he asked.

"Aye, I'm assigned to the sailor boarding house on Cherry Street."

"That's a bad district."

"And that's why I'm going there," Muldoon agreed. "To bang some heads if I have to."

"Sergeant Muldoon!" Mrs. Dunn confronted him, hands planted firmly on her broad hips. "I'll not have that sort of talk at my table."

He apologized quickly. Meg McAllister stifled a giggle behind her hand, and turned it into a cough instead. "So, who are you supporting, William?" she asked. "You haven't talked much about it."

"I'm for a straight ticket," he said.

"Of course," she said. "But then, I don't know much about politics. Only what I've heard."

Mrs. Dunn harrumphed loudly. "And what you've seen in the papers, I'm sure. I've seen you looking."

Margaret Flannigan leaned forward, coming to Meg's defense. "It's not like she doesn't have a right to know what's in the news, Mrs. Dunn. I've taken a peek myself, now and then."

"Well! I don't know why you'd even want to know about it. It's not as if you can vote."

"But that's exactly what this convention is about, Mrs. Dunn," Muldoon said. "To decide who can, and who can't vote. Aren't you interested in that?"

"No. My father brought me up right. And my husband did the voting."

"You no longer have a husband, though. Don't you think you should have a say in political affairs, as the head of your household?"

"No, I don't, Sergeant Muldoon. And I believe that's enough of this talk. Don't you have to go now? I'd expect you should be there before the voting actually takes place. Whatever it is that you do."

Muldoon nodded. "Aye, I suppose I should get going." He bent over and kissed Meg on the top of her graying head. She blushed at his display of affection, but grasped his fingers and squeezed them lightly. She might not speak of it, but he knew she wanted him to know she appreciated what he was doing for her, and for her son. His fingers tightened on hers, a silent apology for not being able to help Kelly today.

He straightened, and hurried out the door, his light overcoat flapping open as he walked. He'd put on his best suit. It was an important day in the city, and he wanted to look well turned out. He might be threatening to break heads, but boss Tweed expected him to look good while doing it. He walked quickly toward Cherry Street. It was a rough area, but then, so was any neighborhood in the fourth ward. He knew many of the people who lived in the ward, knew where they lived and worked. They would fear him, if only for that. Having to enforce party voting was the part of his relationship with the Boss he liked least.

By the time he arrived, the sun was beginning to break through the clouds for the first time in over a week. He took off his coat and handed it to the man behind the Democratic Party table. Looking around, he watched as various factions set up in the open room. Their table, piled high with literature, stood to left of the entrance. Several large boxes held new ballots, printed with the names of the Democratic candidates. Muldoon glanced at one, reading the names: Sam'l L. Garvin, A. R. Lawrence, John E. Burrill, and Charles P. Daly. He didn't know a single one of them. But he was the Democrat's strong-arm at this polling station. Boss Tweed and the Party had chosen these candidates to represent this district at the Constitutional Convention, and Muldoon was here to make sure they got elected.

Directly across the room, the Republicans got ready for the day. Mirroring the Democrats, a pile of literature and boxes of ballots sat on their table. These, he knew, listed only Republicans. The Radical Republicans set up a third table, straight in from the door.

This last group was an offshoot of the regular Republicans. They agitated endlessly in the streets, standing on soapboxes and holding rallies. Personally, he thought all Republicans were the same . . . wrong. But only because they weren't interested in immigrants. They met boats at the docks with signs and speeches calling for the abolition of alcohol. Muldoon smirked at the thought of fat politicians meeting a boat full of Germans, or Irishmen fresh from Erin, and asking them to join the Republican Party . . . but by the way, no more Irish Whiskey or German Beer Gardens.

The Radical Republicans, he knew, railed against the blanket conciliations President Andrew Johnson had given the southern states. They wanted his impeachment. Articles came out in the press periodically, debating the pros and cons, or presenting one view or the other. And they wanted suffrage for the black man. This last was the biggest debate, he thought. The one issue that had people up in arms, especially connected as it was to the question of woman suffrage. In today's election, black men could vote . . . provided they had the two hundred and fifty dollars required by law. But that was only for them. Any white man could vote.

If he had to make a choice between the two, the Radicals, with their ideas of reform, were the group he'd be drawn toward. But there was still the issue of Nativism bothering him. In New York City, that meant Irish immigration. Men and women from old, established family lines, and even recent English immigrants, held prejudices toward the Catholics and to a lesser degree, to the German Lutherans who flooded into the country in mass numbers. Signs like "Irish Need Not Apply" popped up in business establishments across the city. And Irish were barred from living in certain neighborhoods. "Black Irish" became a common term. Both Republican parties were Nativist. Let the black man have the vote, the Radicals said, but the Irishman can go home.

Muldoon leaned against the wall and waited for the poll to open. Across the room, a burly, red haired man set down a box of ballots, balancing it carefully on the edge of the table, one hand holding its side. He asked a question and was directed behind the table. He picked the carton up again and shifted it under one thick arm, carried it around the table, and set it on the floor next to an empty chair. Muldoon watched idly, then scowled as the man turned around, revealing the wide facial features of Sergeant Hugh Collins. He stood on short, heavy legs, like two tree trunks merging into one barrel-shaped body. Big arms stuck out from his sides, instead of hanging down easily. He was like a grotesque caricature of masculine strength. If Muldoon didn't have to tolerate him, he wouldn't. Collins was one man he'd gladly smash in the face at the slightest provocation. But he wouldn't hit a fellow police officer. Not unless it was a mighty big provocation.

Collins raised his beefy hand in the air, a not-quite smile on his face. "Muldoon," he said in his deep, gravelly voice. "I didn't expect to see you round here."

Muldoon wasn't fooled. He knew there wasn't much respect between them. He nodded in greeting, a small, sharp movement.

"So, we're across the aisle from each other," the stocky man laughed snidely. "Aren't we always? But then, Detective Graham does have a way of solving your cases. Wasn't there a recent one? Something about a wrestler."

Muldoon raised one side of his mouth in a half smile, but no mirth reached his eyes. The remark was meant to hurt. Sergeant Collins often worked with Graham, just as he did with Benson. He eyed the man's tatty suit, once of the best style, but now years out of date. He might have bought it at some second-hand store, but more likely, he'd taken it off the back of a drunk booted out of some bar.

The man thinks he looks sharp, strutting like a peacock around a handful of hens, Muldoon thought. But the show was lost on a roomful of men. And there wouldn't be any women coming through. Even so, he doubted they'd look much at him, except maybe in disgust and fear. He didn't think the man knew how revolting he was. But then, he wasn't a woman, and you could never tell about their taste in men.

"So, you're here for Tammany, eh?" Collins asked.

"Of course," Muldoon bared his teeth in a replica of a smile. "It's why I have my job."

"Oh, that's right," Collins exposed his own teeth. "You're a copper because you know Tweed. Not because you earned it."

"That's right," Muldoon said. "And I'm here to protect my interests."

"Well, I'm here to protect mine. And that means . . . well . . . that you get fired!" Collins tilted his head back and laughed.

Muldoon tightened his lips in another imitation of a smile. "If it's up to this district, that isn't likely to happen. It's primarily Democratic, you know. And the last time I heard, so is most of the city, thanks to those huge numbers of immigrants you love so much."

Collins glared impotently.

"Oh, and thanks to you Republican's inability to sway new voters," he added.

But then again, a lot of dead men voted, too. He kept this last thought to himself.

They walked outside the building, each carrying a handful of flyers. A man from the Radical Republicans came out with his own pile of flyers, though he wasn't a party strongman like Collins and Muldoon. The Radicals hoped to gain votes on their merits, not on coercion. Muldoon rather liked that approach. But as long as Collins stood on the other side of the door, he would stand on his, making sure his voters weren't bullied into voting for the Republicans.

A line of men stood waiting to vote, ragged men and well-kept alike, one behind the other. As each man reached the door, he turned to Collins or Muldoon and took a flyer. Stepping inside, the column separated into three distinct lines. Once a man reached the table of his choice, he took a ballot. Then, when he reached the ballot box he'd drop his selection into the container.

Muldoon had to make sure the registered Democrats voted a straight party ticket. The ballot they picked up at each table had only the names of that party listed on it, but that didn't mean they couldn't scratch one off and write in a different name.

"Hey!" Collins growled suddenly. "I see that, Clark."

Muldoon turned to see what was happening. A skinny, bespectacled man had tried to write in different names, but got caught. Muldoon recognized him. He was a clerk for a local coal distributor, but he wasn't a Democrat, so he wasn't Muldoon's problem. Still, he thought, Collins was maybe going overboard a bit. The clerk shook visibly as the sergeant threatened him, then grabbed hold of his collar and dragged him to the Republican table for a fresh ballot. As he took the new ballot, Collins snatched the pencil from the man's trembling fingers, bit it in two and spat the pieces into an empty box. Then, he pulled the man to the front of the line, guided his hand to the ballot box, and forced his shaking fingers to drop the unchanged ticket in the slot.

"There! That wasn't so bad, now, was it?" Collins snarled, an ugly grimace on his face. "And now, you can go shave off that mustache and vote again."

Muldoon wondered what he looked like when he stopped someone from changing a ballot, as he knew he'd be doing not once, but many times this day. He hoped he didn't look like that. Suddenly, his attention shifted. He turned his head sharply, looking for the source of a snatch of conversation he'd just overheard. His gaze flicked over the faces in the line, settling at last on two men several steps away. The breeze happened to have blown his direction, sending their words toward him. As they drew closer, he could hear what they said.

" . . . didn't come home."

"That's unusual. She seemed such a considerate child. But what of the companion? She didn't return home, either?"

"No. The Colonel is beside himself. Or so my Bess told me."

"I won't believe it was foul play. Young Margaret was so sweet when she came into the shop that time. And she bought slippers . . . not one pair, but two. I remember, the first was pale blue, and the other was violet. She wanted those colors particular so as to match ribbons she'd brought with her."

Muldoon stepped between them. "When was she due home?"

The two men stepped back at the intrusion. "Oh," said the first man suddenly. "It's Sergeant Muldoon! With the police."

"Aye," Muldoon said. "That'd be me."

"So, your wanting to know . . . would it be official business?"

"Aye, it would. I need to know when this young Miss Margaret was due home, and how she was getting there."

"She was coming in on the Atlantic and Great Western, as my wife Bess heard it. Coming from Dayton, on the main line. A carriage was waiting for her at the station on 27th Street, but she never got off. Waited 'til the train was empty, so they say. But she wasn't on it."

Muldoon leaned back on his heels. This "Miss Margaret" might not be his murder victim, but this was certainly the best lead to come his way.

"When did she go missing?" he asked.

"Yesterday evening, about seven o'clock, I suppose. That's when the coachman returned home without her. Like to get his head cut off, so Bess told me."

Muldoon studied the man for a moment. He was a short fellow, in a cheap but well-made brown suit. Probably off the shelf. He looked respectable enough, a guy you could trust.

"Your wife is a maid in this 'Colonel's' house?"

"Aye. That she is. My Bess is a right good worker. She used to be a seamstress, but her fingers get tied up a bit if she works too hard on it. So, the Colonel's wife, she comes to the shop where Bess was working and she says to her, she does, 'Why don't you come and work for me?' I guess she noticed how Bess's fingers was hurting when she was putting them pins in. So, Bess, she says she would. And that's how she come to work for the Colonel."

Muldoon turned to the other man. "And you're a cobbler? You make shoes?"

"I certainly do, and I'm good at it. Better than those new shoes you can get ready-made. I been making shoes my entire life. I learned it up, from apprentice to master. I'm a master now." The second man looked challengingly at Muldoon. His shoes were a product Muldoon knew he couldn't afford. Used were the best he could get, though he had great respect for the man and his dying craft.

"What's his name? The Colonel, I mean?" asked Muldoon, turning again to the first man.

"Why, he's Colonel Hamm. Lives up on 5th Avenue. He's got one of them fine big houses."

Muldoon had heard of the man. Colonel Hamm was head of National New York Bank and Trust. Muldoon had been on 5th Avenue just once. It was a fabulous thoroughfare of mansions and money. He'd have to visit the Colonel with Detective Benson, it was more his kind of area. The men had moved beyond him, and he continued to direct others toward the Democratic table where they could pick up their ballots. He scanned the crowd for pencils and shifting eyes. Really, he decided, this was a good job for a copper.

CHAPTER 25

April 22

THE New York Times sat in its usual place on the table. He knew Biggs would be irked, but he didn't have time to wait for the man to read the paper. It wasn't his, anyway. Mrs. Dunn continued to have it delivered even after her husband had died, though she didn't read it herself. Or at least she said she didn't. He wouldn't be surprised if she took it to her own room at the end of the day and scanned it for interesting stories. Casper Biggs thought it was his right to read the paper first, since he was the oldest man in residence. Right now, Muldoon wanted to see the election results before heading uptown. He scanned the front page, and then flipped through until he found the article on page five. As he expected, Lawrence, Garvin, Daly, and Burrill each had an asterisk next to their names, indicating they'd won the election. All of them had over 9,000 votes, but Muldoon snorted to see the various numbers, ranging from 9,194 for Burrill to 9,344 for Lawrence. So much for biting pencils, he thought, recalling Collins' antics the previous day. Each of the Republicans, he noticed, had only a little over 2,000 votes. It was a landslide for the Democrats. He folded the paper as neatly as he could and replaced it before heading for Police Headquarters. He really didn't care about Biggs, but he'd keep the peace for Mrs. Dunn's sake.

A short time later, he hurried up the steps and crossed the large entry to the back hall and Detective Benson's office. It would be best if the two went uptown together, he thought. He was out of his element when it came to Mrs. Astor's "400" as they were called, the crème de la crème of New York City. But the detective wasn't in any condition to accompany Muldoon. He lay on his floor fast asleep, the ravages of alcohol apparent on his face, deep rings around his eyes, a slight green tinge to his cheeks. Muldoon shook his head with irritation. He'd have to do it himself. There wasn't much time left. If the Captain got wind of the missing girl, Margaret Hamm, the case would be handed over to his 'pet,' Detective Graham. Right now, Colonel Hamm's reluctance to go to the police worked to his advantage. He suspected the Colonel's motivations had more to do with having his dirty laundry aired in the press.

He quickly scratched out a note to Benson, informing him of the new development. "The case just might take me out of the City," he warned. "If it does, cover for me if you can. I'll dispatch another note if necessary."

He stopped at the desk on his way out. Sergeant Foley was doing his report, figuring last-minute changes in the daily assignments.

"Hello, Tim," said Muldoon, running his hand through his hair.

"Muldoon," said Foley without glancing up. "You off on something for Benson?"

"Aye," Muldoon said. "He's got a new lead he needs me to look into. It might take me a couple of days. So, don't expect me in tomorrow. Maybe not even the next day. But if it takes longer, I'll wire Benson and let him know. Then he'll fill you in."

"Where you going?"

"I don't rightly know yet."

Foley scribbled something next to Muldoon's name. "Got you covered, boy-oh. Now take off, before the Cap'n comes down and sees you. Then you'll never get out of here."

"I'm going," Muldoon said. The enmity between him and Hayle was well known by now. With a sardonic salute, he turned and strode out the door. He grabbed a streetcar at the closest stop and headed toward 5th Avenue. He rode silently, anticipating the coming meeting with Colonel Hamm. He expected the man would be at home rather than at the bank. If he had a missing kid, he thought, he'd be at home with his wife and family. Or out on the streets looking for her. But then again, Muldoon wasn't a bank executive.

The horse-drawn streetcar left Bowery and plodded along the iron tracks that led up 4th Avenue. He leapt off at 32nd and walked the long block over to 5th Avenue. As he neared, he caught site of the mansion. The big box-shaped house looked more like a government building than a private home. Its many windows stared down at the street from three stories and an attic. It was red brick, with Greek columns next to the door, and a triangular roof over the porch. It looked like a monstrosity to him, a kind of combination of Greek and Federal style architecture.

He felt awkward in his policeman's uniform as he walked up to the front door. But he was there to see the master of the house, not the kitchen staff. Dredging up confidence, he rapped on the door. He heard the tapping of heeled shoes as somebody neared the door. A second later, a pert little face peered up at him. She wore the traditional black and white maid's dress and apron.

"Yes, sir?" the woman asked. She took in his uniform. "Oh, are you here about Miss Margaret?" Her perfect English was studied, carefully practiced. She was clearly Irish, but worked hard at her acquired Native accent.

"Aye, that I am," Muldoon said.

The maid stepped aside so he could come in. He doffed his hat respectfully.

"If you'll follow me, you can wait in the drawing room."

"Thank you, Miss," he said, following her across the large entry and through a door on the right. She left him there and he turned to look at the room, hoping to get a gauge on the man who lived here. The place was immaculate, the type of room he'd only seen in pictures. Muted coral paper with thin stripes and tiny heart-shaped flowers adorned the walls. The white cornice contrasted with the pale coral ceiling. Deep red, intricately designed Oriental carpets covered the floor. A marble fireplace dominated one wall, a small fire burning on the grate. He marveled at the wealth that would allow someone to keep a fire burning in an empty room of this size.

Two sets of French doors led out to a garden patio. They were closed this time of year. But around them, velvet curtains, red to match the rugs, were open to let in the feeble morning light. The ever-present rain had started again and spattered against the window. Between the doors, an ornate grandfather clock stood sentinel. Two wing-back chairs skirted the fireplace, providing a warm, cozy place to read. He imagined sitting in the bigger of the two, the red chair, and putting his feet up on the little footstool. The other chair was a pale coral, smaller, feminine. Seats for the Mister and Missus. But the fabric was little worn, so the set-up was mostly for show, he gathered.

Before the grouping by the fireplace, a second set of furniture was carefully arranged. Here, there was a delicate settee and two fine chairs arranged around a smaller Oriental rug, this one in coral tones to match the fabric of the chairs. A small round table stood beside the settee, draped with a floral tablecloth and topped with an expensive vase filled with huge blooming flowers. Needlepoint pillows decorated each of the seats in the room. The daintiness of the furnishings spoke of a woman's touch. A slight stain on one showed this was the setting most used.

Muldoon didn't sit, afraid to break the delicate chair legs with his weight. So, he stood and waited. He moved to the fireplace and gazed into the flame. But when he saw burning houses, he turned away. It was his demon . . . those burning houses of Pensacola. He paced the room, returning periodically to the fire's warmth.

Nearly forty-five minutes passed before the Colonel entered the room. He was a tall, aristocratic man, nearly six feet in height and razor-thin, a pointed goatee dignifying his chin. He stopped abruptly at the sight of Muldoon in front of his fire, but seemed to regain his composure almost as quickly as he'd lost it. Muldoon narrowed his eyes. Why had the man seemed surprised to see him? Hadn't the maid gone to get him? Or was he hiding something?

"What can I do for you?" The Colonel asked a bit gruffly.

"I'm from the Metropolitan Police," Muldoon began, his eyes narrowed thoughtfully. He recognized this man. He had been at Harry Hill's. He was the man with the top hat. And he'd been at the Quaker Meeting House, Muldoon was nearly positive. Had he been sitting just to the left of the speakers? He'd been in profile, an earnest expression on his face as the men spoke their revolting words.

"So I can see," the Colonel said, looking pointedly at Muldoon's uniform. "But what are you doing here? I certainly didn't make any reports."

"No," Muldoon said. "But I've had a report nonetheless. It's about your daughter."

"My daughter?" The Colonel strode toward Muldoon and paused just inches away. Challenging. Authoritarian. Military.

Muldoon stood his ground. The man had inadvertently put him at his ease. He knew how to handle a military man. And even though only a sergeant, he was suddenly on equal footing with the Colonel. He was the one with the information Colonel Hamm needed.

"It's come to my attention your daughter is missing, that she was expected two days ago off the New York & Atlantic, but she wasn't on the train."

"How did you come by that information?" the Colonel asked.

Muldoon raised an eyebrow and shrugged.

"Yes, that's true," the Colonel affirmed, turning slightly away. "But she sent a message. It was delivered by the porter."

"And that message was . . . "

"That she'd decided to stay for a time."

"The message was written in her own hand?"

"Yes, of course. I mean . . . I don't know. You'd have to ask her sister, or her step-mother."

Muldoon was taken aback. This man had raised a daughter and didn't even recognize her handwriting? Colonel Hamm turned to the fire and traced a finger across the big mirror above the mantle. Muldoon shook his head slightly. Some servant would have to come back in here and wipe away all sign of the smudge the man left behind. But, in the small action, he could see the Colonel's worry.

"This isn't usual for her?" Muldoon asked.

"No. In fact, this was her first time out of the city alone. Well, not alone. She was with her companion."

"And the companion didn't return, either?"

"No, of course not! She certainly couldn't return without Margaret. After all, that's what I pay her for." He spun about, angrily, to glare at Muldoon.

"Aye, sir."

"So, what is it you want from me?" the Colonel demanded.

"I wish to offer my services," Muldoon said. "As an officer of the Metropolitans. I'd like to set your mind at ease. You're a busy man. I propose to go and make certain your daughter is well."

"I've sent a letter by post. This very morning."

"Aye, but this is quicker. I suppose you could send a telegram, but then it might look like you're worried. And you don't want to give that impression, I'm sure."

"No . . . no, you're right. I'd like to know that she's all right." The Colonel reflected for a moment. "Yes, I'll take you up on your offer. Margaret is at my sister's and her husband's home in Dayton. Let me give you an address and a letter of introduction." He penned the two items on crisp white paper, folded the letter, and slipped it into a matching envelope, tucking in the flap. Muldoon accepted them and slid them into an inner pocket of his uniform jacket.

"I suppose they don't pay you much, do they?" the Colonel asked suddenly.

"Enough," Muldoon said.

"That is to say . . . " the Colonel began, and cleared his throat. "I expect you won't be paid for this trip? You'll need some money?" He reached into his desk and pulled out several bank notes.

"For expenses only." Muldoon accepted them, rather discomfited. One day, he promised himself, he'd have the money and the house. He picked up a small picture from among a grouping of frames on the Colonel's desk. She was younger than the dead girl. He couldn't be sure it was the same girl. He tried to picture her without hair. "Is this Margaret?"

"Yes."

"Can I borrow it?"

"Whatever for? She'll be at her uncle's home." Colonel Hamm turned his back on Muldoon in an obvious, and curt, dismissal. His hands, gripped tightly behind him belied his poise. The man was worried.

Once outside the front door, Muldoon donned his hat and turned up his collar against the rain. As he began down the steps, a small, shy voice stopped him.

"Excuse me, sir."

He paused and then turned back. The little maid stood in the door, looking uncertain.

"Aye?"

"Are you . . . are you gonna bring back the little miss?" Her Irish accent threatened to appear. "We're all oh-so frightened! It's just not the same here."

Muldoon took a step back toward her, his head tipping a bit to the side. "Who's in the house?" he asked.

She glanced behind her, as if afraid. "Well, the Colonel, of course. And his wife . . . and her daughter, Miss Melanie. And then there's the baby, of course."

Muldoon nodded thoughtfully. "I'll do my best to bring her home."

He cocked his head. Why did she seem so concerned when the Colonel wasn't? He'd been surprised to see Muldoon, and even more so in connection with his daughter. But this maid had made that same connection herself. "Is there something I need to know?" he asked. "Are you afraid of somebody?"

"No . . . nothing." A shadow dropped over her features as she smoothed them, and her apron, into blank uniformity.

Loath to share his own fears, he turned away and descended the stairs, then headed back toward the streetcar line over on 4th. It would take him close to home, where he could pack enough things for a short trip. But it would be civilian clothes, not his blues. He'd be out of his area of authority, and his uniform would look out of place so far out of the city. Before leaving, he needed to scribble out a short note to Benson, to explain where he was going . . . and another note addressed to Harry Hill to put his next match on hold. Hill wouldn't appreciate that. The saloonkeeper and Dick Fox, editor of the Police Gazette, had made arrangements with a grappler who was traveling from Buffalo. He hated missing the bout. Each contest brought him closer to a match with the renowned national champion Clarence Whistler, not to mention the larger amount of cash he earned each time.

He said he'd try to bring Margaret home. But he was afraid it wouldn't be the way they wanted.

CHAPTER 26

THE connecting door creaked slowly open and then stood quiet. Muldoon set down his bag and pushed it further open. The room beyond was shadowed and silent, the curtains tightly drawn. Orange glowed from the charred embers on the grate.

"Come in," Meg said from the darkness. "Sit a moment before you go."

He sat. He didn't remember this table. It wasn't here when he'd occupied the room. He sat across from her, tête-à-tête. She reached across the table and took his hands into hers. As she pulled them toward her, she turned them palm-upward as if to read his fortune.

"William," she began. "I was the daughter of a rich man. You know that, of course. But my mother was a Traveler. Do you know what that is?"

Muldoon shook his head.

"Gypsy is what they're called here. Grandda didn't approve of the match, so Da took us away. We lived far from the family, off in Kildare. But when I was six, my mother died and we returned to my father's home. Da shouldn't have taken me there. See, when I was just a tiny *leanbh*, just a babe, my family already knew I had the gift. I always knew when things were out of place."

A chill slid down his spine. Her flesh was icy where his hands touched hers.

"That first night, I had terrible nightmares. I slept little and Da had to stay with me. Each time I closed my eyes, a man came to me. He was a gnarled, crooked man and he shook his cane at me. I screamed, and he ran after me. He was swifter than he looked. Just as he reached me with the crook of that evil cane, I would wake. And Da would be there."

The embers shifted in the grate, popped and hissed, and sparks rose up the chimney. But they did little to warm the room.

"I had that nightmare every night, until finally Da asked Grandda where the cane was. He knew it was my gift speaking through the dream. The cane was old, and had been passed down through the generations. It was kept in a chest in the empty room next to mine. When I laid eyes on it, I knew it was an evil thing, more a *shillelagh* than a cane. She came to me for the first time then . . . the bringer of my gift. I don't know her name, she just 'is.' She told me that cane would bring pain and tragedy. Grandda destroyed it, or so he said. But I know he didn't. Because everybody is gone, and now I'm far from my beloved Erin, and my only son is soon to die for a sin he didn't commit."

"I won't let him die," Muldoon said, tightening his hands around hers. He looked down so she wouldn't see the doubt in his eyes. He loved her, but he couldn't believe in her gypsy magic.

"Look at me." Something in her voice brought his gaze back up to her eyes. "You must watch for the man with the cane."

He thought of the broken stakes he'd found with the letters A.R. carved onto them. They could be part of a broken cane. Two pieces of a whole.

Chapter 27

THE loud, smoke-belching engine blasted steam as Muldoon grabbed the rail and climbed aboard the train. With a lurch, it left the station, threatening to toss him off balance as he looked for an empty seat. He had bought second-class. The round-trip ticket ate up more than half the Colonel's bankroll. The carefully folded bills in his wallet hid safely inside his inner breast pocket. He'd had an extra flap stitched over the pocket and secured with a button to deter thieves. He'd been a B'hoy and a cop long enough to appreciate their abilities.

The ride was long and dirty. Smoke from the stack blew back against the cars as they moved swiftly along behind the steam engine. He slid into a seat across from a black-garbed elderly woman. She looked him over, then promptly closed her eyes and went to sleep. He opened the Police Gazette he'd brought along for the ride. He enjoyed reading its exaggerated crime stories and sports coverage. Not as reliable as The Times, so far as news stories go, but it had one thing the better paper didn't. Cards. He scanned the advertisements to see who challenged whom, and for what event and venue.

The train stopped at Salamanca. The old woman debarked to walk to and fro along the platform. Other passengers purchased food from local vendors. Muldoon finished the meal Mrs. Dunn had packed for him, a piece of salt pork between two thick slices of bread and wrapped in old newspaper tied with a string. He got up to take a turn himself and stretch his legs.

"Good evening, sir," the conductor said as he stepped off the train. "It's nice weather for a stroll."

"That it is."

"Are you going on to Dayton?"

"Aye, I am." Muldoon paused, then on impulse, pulled a picture out of his pocket and showed it to the conductor. "Have you ever seen this woman?"

The conductor angled it toward the weak light that filtered down from the pole lamp behind him on the platform. "I can't really say . . . maybe. But then, so many folk pass through on the train."

"She would have been traveling not much more than a week ago. And she might have been up there . . . in first class. Going back to the city."

The conductor looked again. "There's another train on this route. You might check with the conductor on that one."

Muldoon nodded thoughtfully and then held out the photo of Kavanagh. "How about him? You ever seen him?"

He shook his head, and then looked down at his watch. He called out, "All aboard!"

The train started with a jolt as Muldoon settled into his seat. The old woman was gone. She had changed seats, perhaps for companionship. A young couple sat across from him now. They jabbered on and on about their marriage and their new life together, until finally he closed his eyes, feigning sleep as the old woman had.

THE train slid up to a long rectangular building with a wide roof that covered the platform. Stacks of barrels and crates stood under the lamp post at the far end. Wagons, and buggies, and their drivers cheerfully welcomed home long-absent relatives as people exited the train. Other passengers walked to and fro on the platform as they had at the previous stop. Muldoon pushed through the throng and entered the building to find the Dayton station master.

The man stood just inside the door watching the travelers debark. He held a large watch, its chain hanging loose from his fingers. He'd marked the train 'on time' on a large chalkboard on the wall beside the door. Muldoon stopped in front of him.

The station master slid the watch into a pocket. "Can I help you?"

"I'm up from the city," Muldoon said. "Got business in town, and I'll be needing a place for the night. Where can a man like me find a decent place to stay?" Where can a Mick get a hotel room, he thought.

"There's a good hotel just on the edge of town, name of Beasley's. They've got clean rooms and a fair price."

Muldoon nodded his thanks, and stopped on the platform to retrieve his bag. He headed the direction the station master had indicated. There weren't any streetlamps this side of town, but the evening was bright and the moon lit the road as he walked. It was a short walk, by city standards. The town was still small, though obviously growing rapidly because of its railway connection. Freshly painted new buildings glowed in the moonlight. Beasley's stood back from the road with a large front lawn, and flowers in wide beds. Beyond it, he could see little, the night broken only by the occasional light from a window. The place was on the edge of farmland. He turned, strode up the path, and mounted the steps to the broad porch. He raised his hand to knock, but noticed a small sign pasted discreetly by the knob. "Enter and ring the bell," it read.

He turned the knob and stepped into the hushed interior of the rambling country-style farmhouse-cum-hotel. The building was long, two stories high. The path had brought him to a door at the left of the structure, what had once been an attached carriage house, and at some point, turned into living quarters for the proprietor. Inside, a lamp burned low. He crossed to the counter, which ran the full length of the room from the door to the back wall. At the center, a book lay open, and a pen and glass ink bottle sat to its right. A bell stood on the other side. Muldoon lifted it and rang, and its clear metallic tinkle broke the quiet.

Within moments, a man came out from the back room, spectacles on his nose with a loose chain drooping from them to the clip connecting them to his vest. He was in his shirtsleeves, his vest unbuttoned. His gaze traveled over Muldoon, taking in his large frame, and noting the distinct Irish caste of his features.

"How many nights?" he asked. He was gruff, but soft-spoken.

"Just tonight," Muldoon said. "I'll be leaving tomorrow, if my business goes well."

The man pushed the book toward him. Muldoon dipped the pen into ink and scribbled his name: William Muldoon.

"Luggage?"

"Only what I carry."

"Room eight, top of the stairs."

He nodded his thanks, and turned to find his room.

"Oh," added the proprietor with a sudden smile. "Breakfast's at seven in the dining room, if you care to join us. Most do. My wife bakes the best sweet bread in town."

Hiding a yawn, Muldoon muttered his thanks and took his leave. He was tired, and had a hard day tomorrow. Maybe not physically, but certainly mentally. He wasn't sure what he'd find . . . a living girl, safe with her aunt and uncle . . . or a dead one back on a slab in the morgue.

CHAPTER 28

April 23

HALF past seven. His forehead ached. Visions of a crooked man with a living walking stick running around Pensacola had haunted his dreams.

There isn't a crooked man. He didn't believe in Meg's visions, he believed in science. Newton had proved gravity with his apple. Galileo had proved the sun, not the earth, was at the center of the solar system. Myth and superstition died, and science took their place. The greatest evil was man himself, and Muldoon was certain a man was at the center of this crime. First, he had to go to the home of Mrs. Hannah Wannamaker. He hoped he'd find Margaret Hamm there, alive and well. But he had the cold feeling he got when he expected the worst. He dressed with care and went downstairs. The matron was cleaning up the dining room.

"Good morning," she said as Muldoon stepped into the room. "You've missed breakfast, but there's a little bread left if you wish."

She took the covers off a plate of sweet raisin bread and a dish of butter and poured him a glass of fresh milk. Between mouthfuls, he asked her where the Wannamaker home was.

"Oh, just head on up the road," she said as she wiped crumbs off the far end of the table with a damp rag. "Take the first left, about half a mile on. You can't miss it."

"Thank you kindly, Ma'am." He shut the door behind him and headed out. The air was chill and scattered patches of icy snow still lined the road. Few clouds marred the blue expanse of sky, but back toward New York City lay a bank of ominous black clouds.

Muldoon approached the house slowly. The long, tree-shaded drive led to a large house, a modern Queen Anne-style building three stories tall, with gingerbread and towers. It was painted muted shades of plum, pale green and forest. He wasn't sure he liked the style, it was almost garish, yet something about it was attractive. A large, wrap-around porch with an inviting swing beckoned. A dog barked. He saw it tear around the building, leaping from the steps and scattering gravel as it ran toward him. It stopped short and instead of baring its teeth aggressively, it wagged its tail, tongue lolling from its mouth. He offered the back of his hand, and then rubbed the fluffy yellow animal on the head.

As he reached the house, the front door opened and a maid holding a feather duster in her hand stepped onto the porch and began to shake out its dust.

"Oh! I didn't know . . . I mean . . . can I help you, sir?" she stammered as she hid the duster behind her back.

"I'm here to see Mrs. Wannamaker."

"Is she expecting you?"

"No, but I've come from New York. From her brother, Colonel Hamm."

She stood still a moment, face turned slightly, and studied him. "Well, if the Colonel sent you, then it must be all right. Come in, come in." She opened the door wide and stepped aside so he could enter.

"If you'll wait in the morning room, sir, I'll let the Missus know you're here."

She showed him into an open room, East-facing windows dominated one wall and filled the chamber with sunlight. A gilt-painted cornice bordered the high white walls near the ceiling. A white marble fireplace across from the windows was trimmed in matching gold, and two gilt wall sconces bordered a giant mirror above the hearth. A collection of clocks lined the mantle, their backs reflected in the glass. A white settee and two chairs sat at an angle to the fireplace and a curio cabinet stood in the far corner of the room. Muldoon walked over to it and gazed in at the various statuettes inside. They were all delicate white porcelain women . . . like the unknown girl in the morgue.

"My brother sent you to me?" A woman's voice floated across the room. "I hope he's well."

Muldoon turned as Mrs. Wannamaker entered the room. She was a gaunt woman, her housedress barely able to conceal her angular bones. "He seems so," Muldoon replied.

"And Mrs. Hamm? You know, of course, she gave birth several weeks ago. Is she well, and the child also?"

"All seems to be well with them. Mr. Hamm sent me to inquire after his daughter."

"Oh, she was quite well. But tell me about the child." She seemed to steer him away from the topic. "He was so robust when last I saw him. He was born here, but then of course, you already know that. Elizabeth . . . that is to say, Mrs. Hamm, retired to the country to have the child."

Muldoon hadn't known, but the woman seemed talkative. It might be the easier way to get the information he was looking for. "She was accompanied by her daughter?"

"Yes, of course. A woman doesn't travel alone. She had a maid, as well. A mulatto girl . . . Lydia, I think I her name was." She waved a fine-boned hand, as though dismissing the servant.

"And Miss Margaret, she enjoyed her stay in the country?"

"Certainly. As well as any child of her age, I suppose. She prefers New York, I'm sure, with its parties and socials, the opera, and symphony . . . " Her voice dropped, became dreamlike, as she reminisced. Muldoon sensed she thought more of her own past than about Margaret Hamm's.

"So, tell me, Mr. Muldoon," she said suddenly, a curious expression in her eyes. "What exactly are you here for? Are you on business for my brother?"

"Of a sort," he replied. "I'd like to speak to Miss Margaret, if I may. He sent me with a message for her." He hadn't a message, of course, but if he were to see Miss Hamm, he'd mumble an excuse, feign some inconsequential message from the girl's father, and beat a hasty retreat.

Mrs. Wannamaker had a habit of patting her coiffure, to make certain it was in order. She froze, one hand on its way, yet again, to her hair. "But . . . " she began. "Isn't she at home?"

His heart sank. "Madam, may I speak with your husband?"

The woman walked stiffly to the bell pull and summoned a servant. Within moments, the maid who had answered the door appeared. "Susan, would you please send Johnson in to the Master? I require his presence."

He assumed Johnson must be the butler. No doubt, Mr. Wannamaker was in his office, a room many men kept off-limits to women, including the staff. The butler would be responsible for keeping that room in order.

Mrs. Hamm moved slowly, trancelike, toward the settee. She sat stiffly erect and motioned Muldoon toward a chair across from her. He knew politeness required him to sit, so he perched stiffly at the edge of the chair, afraid to sit back in case the delicate-looking thing broke under his weight.

Shortly, a tall man of about fifty entered the room. Like his wife, he seemed all angles, reminding Muldoon vaguely of President Lincoln. The man's eyes were drawn to Muldoon as he rose from his seat.

"My dear . . . " Mr. Wannamaker began, as he turned to his wife. "You requested my presence? You know, of course, I'm working on a legal matter." He turned to Muldoon. "I'm an attorney," he explained.

"This is Mr. Muldoon. He has just come from the city," said his wife, her words barely more than a whisper.

Mr. Wannamaker turned again to Muldoon. He didn't proffer his hand. His gaze slid over Muldoon's not-quite-so-fine suit. "Please, Mr. Muldoon, have you business in this household?"

"Aye, I'm afraid I do." He pulled the letter of introduction from his pocket and handed it to the man. "I hoped to inquire, and finding everything satisfactory, take my leave without alarming anyone. But I fear that's no longer possible. It appears young Miss Hamm has gone missing."

Mrs. Wannamaker breathed in, a sudden shocked sound, and raised one hand to touch the center of her breastbone.

"I'm sorry to bring the news in this way. I hoped it wouldn't be necessary," Muldoon said, concerned for the woman.

"No, no, it couldn't be helped," Mr. Wannamaker said. He strode swiftly toward the pull and rang the bell hard. Within moments, the maid returned. "Get Mrs. Wannamaker a tisane tea, Susan. She's had a shock."

"So, you're a police officer," Mr. Wannamaker continued as he turned back to Muldoon.

"Aye. I'm investigating the disappearance, it would seem. I'm sorry, but I must ask some questions."

"Of course," Mr. Wannamaker said, and took a seat beside his wife. He took her limp hand in his protectively.

"When did you last see Miss Margaret?" Muldoon began.

"It was almost two weeks ago."

"Yes, on a Tuesday," Mrs. Wannamaker added. "She was leaving for the train. She was so excited." The woman's face paled even more and she slumped back against the sofa cushions.

"She left suddenly?" Muldoon asked.

"Yes." The lawyer's hand tightened about his wife's. "She was retrieved . . . or so we thought."

"Retrieved? That's an odd expression. As though she were banished here."

"In a manner of speaking, she was. Her mother had left with the child, but she was to remain here . . . until sent for."

"And somebody came for her. Who was that, exactly?"

"It was the footman, I don't know his name. He arrived on Monday with the news that she was expected the following day. Her train fare had already been purchased. Then, the three of them left. My man drove them to the train."

"The three of them?" Muldoon asked.

"Yes. Margaret, the footman, and her maid."

"Lydia, you said?" Muldoon turned to Mrs. Wannamaker.

"Yes, I believe that was her name. But it's hard to know . . . with somebody else's servants."

The maid returned with a tray. She set it on the small table before the settee. Mrs. Wannamaker mumbled a quiet thanks and waved her away.

"Just a moment," Muldoon said. The girl stopped and turned to him with a surprised, hesitant expression. "Miss Margaret's maid . . . was her name Lydia?"

"Yes, sir," said the girl, bobbing a curtsy. Her eyes flicked to Mr. Wannamaker. He nodded to her, and she apparently took it to mean she could speak with the strange visitor.

"Can you tell me what she looked like?" Muldoon asked.

"She was kind of brown-skinned, but light, like. With freckles. And her hair was a reddish-brown. She was very pretty, sir." She glanced quickly again toward Mr. Wannamaker. "If I do say so myself. Oh, and she was real tall."

Muldoon nodded at her.

"Thank you, that will be all," Mr. Wannamaker said, curtly dismissing the servant. She turned and fairly ran from the room.

"Do you have more questions, Mister . . . or should I say Sergeant . . . Muldoon?"

"Just a few, if you don't mind. Her father, Colonel Hamm, seemed to think she was due on the train this past Sunday. Why would that be?"

"I can't imagine," Mr. Wannamaker said drily.

"Oh!" his wife exclaimed. "She had a letter after she left." The woman stood, rather wobbly on her feet, for just a moment. "I hadn't sent it on to her yet, it's on the tray." Stiffly, she went into the hall and retrieved a letter from a table just outside the door. She handed it to Muldoon, and then sat back down beside her husband.

"May I?" Muldoon asked, and slit the envelope with his index finger. Inside was a folded sheet, the same stationary on which Colonel Hamm had written his note to the Wannamakers. It was a cursory letter from her father, train tickets enclosed. There was little emotion to the letter, perhaps even a hint of coldness. It was certainly something to look into.

"This came in the post?" he asked, and handed the contents to Mr. Wannamaker. His wife read over his shoulder, raising a trembling hand to her lips.

"Yes," Mrs. Wannamaker answered. "But I didn't have any idea what it was, or I would have opened it."

"You can't be blamed," her husband said, and patted her arm comfortingly. "How were we to know? After all, it was her family's own footman that took her!" He glared at Muldoon.

With a sigh, Muldoon pulled the blue bible out of his pocket. He opened it and slid a folded piece of paper from between two photos.

Unfolding it carefully, he held it out to Mr. Wannamaker. "Is this your niece?" he asked.

With a little shriek, the woman fainted.

"You have your answer," Mr. Wannamaker said. "May I ask why you carry a sketch of Margaret? Especially when you had no knowledge that she was actually missing? Certainly, her father would have given you a photo."

The man knew. Muldoon could see it in his eyes. He spoke quietly, respectfully. "I'm investigating a murder. Two, actually. This drawing is a likeness of the most recent victim."

Mr. Wannamaker nodded slowly, holding his wife close in his arms. Muldoon rose, crossed to the pull, and rang the bell. The lady would need to be cared for, the doctor called.

As soon as she'd been helped away, leaning heavily on her maid, Mr. Wannamaker turned his full attention to Muldoon. "So, she hasn't been officially identified as yet."

"No."

"Then, I shall come with you. I would save my brother-in-law this one thing. He'll have sorrow enough."

Muldoon thanked him, told him which train he'd be on, and then took his leave. He suddenly had more inquiring to do in this town. He hoped he could find out all he needed with a stop at the police station.

Immediately upon returning to town, he went to the station. It was a small building, nothing at all like the behemoth he worked out of in the city. A pleasant young man sat at the desk, and Muldoon doffed his hat respectfully, and then introduced himself.

"What can we do for you, Sergeant?" the officer asked.

"I'm investigating two murders, and the disappearance of several people."

The young officer sat upright in his seat. "Here?" he said. "We've only had the one, and that was a Negro."

"A woman?" asked Muldoon, already certain of the answer.

"Well, yes. Perhaps you'd like to speak to the Chief?"

"Aye, perhaps I should."

The Chief was a big, burly man, but soft-spoken. "She was a Negro," agreed the Chief. "But she's been buried already. In the African burial grounds, out of town."

"Can you tell me what she looked like?" Muldoon asked.

The description matched that of the missing maid. He was sure it was the same woman. As he expected, she'd been strangled. He showed the two photos to the Chief, but the man didn't recognize either person. To his knowledge, neither Mr. Kavanagh nor Mr. Schneider had ever been in town. No, she didn't have any mysterious bruising on her abdomen. And the police hadn't seen any stakes with initials carved into them.

"One more thing," began Muldoon before leaving. "Mr. Wannamaker . . . he has a busy court schedule?"

"Busier than most," the Chief said. "He's the best in town."

"And he's been in town the last couple of weeks? You wouldn't happen to know if he had to go out of town or anything?"

"No, he's been in court every day, up until a couple of days ago. He had a major case, a legal dispute between the bank and the railroad. But he got it settled."

"That's good," Muldoon said as he took his leave. So, he could scratch Mr. Wannamaker off his list of suspects. Now, he needed to find the footman, but there wasn't a trace of him in Dayton. His trail, Muldoon suspected, would take him to New York City.

The return trip had been uneventful. Mr. Wannamaker rode in first class, Muldoon in second, so he had been spared the uncomfortable silence that would have enshrouded them. Upon their arrival in the city, Wannamaker took a hotel room, saying he was loath to visit his brother-in-law until after he had identified the body. He wanted to be certain before disrupting that family's peace.

Muldoon was glad for the break. He returned immediately to his own rooms, where he was met by Meg McAllister, who demanded a full recital of his travels. He told her about the trip in a vague way, describing people and places. And no, he told her, there was no sign of the man with the cane. What he didn't tell her was that this had ballooned quickly from a single murder to a triple homicide.

CHAPTER 29

April 24

MULDOON watched silently from behind his heavy curtains as Casper Biggs slipped out the door. The man snuck across the front porch and inched his way forward in the darkness, carefully avoiding the squeaky spots.

Hurriedly pulling on a pair of pants and a clean undershirt, Muldoon stepped into the dark hall. He was sure Biggs headed for another assembly in the Quaker meeting house. He didn't need to follow him this time. Instead, he made his way up the stairs. He wanted to take a look around the man's room.

At the top of the steps, he turned left, and then followed the landing toward the front of the house. When he reached Biggs' door he paused, and listened intently to the small noises of the house. Quietly, he pulled a small tool kit from his pocket, inserted a pin into the lock, and twisted it about until the mechanism released with a snap.

Again, he held still and listened intently. The house was silent. He pushed the door open and slipped into the dark chamber. The upstairs rooms weren't connected to the gas main, so, unlike his own rooms, there wasn't a lamp on the wall with the constant low glow of flame. A sliver of light filtered in from between the heavy curtains, and he strode toward them. He peered out onto the street. Biggs was gone, and he couldn't see any movement out there. He pulled the curtains wide so the dim glow from the streetlamp could brighten the room a bit.

The place was extremely tidy, but he knew that was due more to Mrs. Dunn than to Casper Biggs. The bedcovers were turned down and slightly rumpled, as if waiting for its occupant to return. The table beside it held a stubby candle on a dish, a box of matches at its side. Several books lay atop the table, stacked neatly. Muldoon flipped through them, just in case something was tucked inside. But they were clean.

He turned to the small bureau and methodically rifled through the drawers, careful to leave no trace of his search. At the bottom of the second drawer, he found a stack of envelopes, each slit open at the top. He pulled them from the drawer and carried them toward the window. In the dim light, he could just make out the writing. All were addressed to Biggs. He slid the first letter from its packet and held it up to the dim light.

"Dearest Brother Casper," it began. Muldoon raised an eyebrow. The man didn't have a brother . . . did he? He turned again to the letter.

"I have received your letter of February the 3rd. We are very interested in your activities in New York. As brothers in this endeavor, we would certainly like to see our little enterprise spread its roots in your Northern region. Perhaps even beyond, to Massachusetts, and to Maine! It takes this kind of effort to form any party, and we hope our brotherhood can become an organization to challenge that of the Democrats and the Republicans. Of course, we are most concerned with the new Radical Republicans, and would gladly see a demise in its membership. Still, that is for another day!

As for the brotherhood, if you can arrange the use of the meeting hall you spoke of, we can guarantee a slate of speakers. You must, as always, work quietly. Though this is the noblest of causes, it is one which stirs angry sentiments among those unenlightened few who praise the Negro and the Irish . . . "

Something outside moved!

Muldoon dropped to one knee and peered from behind the curtains. He was sure he'd seen a slight movement out on the street. There . . . it came again. He could just make out the shape of a man in the shadows beyond the streetlamp. The figure turned furtively about, and then ran toward the boarding house.

Quickly, Muldoon replaced the letters in the bureau drawer and smashed the one he'd read, along with the envelope, into his pocket. He paused at the door, then opened it a crack. Over the landing, he could see a slowly growing patch of light as the front door opened and the top of Biggs's head came into view. Damn, Muldoon thought. How the hell do I get out of this one? Biggs must have forgotten something, he reasoned. Perhaps the very letters he'd held, and now come back to get. The man would come up the stairs and find him in the room . . . and he had no excuse. He might have his suspicions, he knew Biggs was involved with some strange brotherhood, but he had no real knowledge of their plans. As long as they took no action, they could say anything they wanted. At this moment, it was he, Muldoon, who was in the wrong . . . won't the Captain enjoy this one, he thought.

Muldoon shut the door with a tiny click. Quickly, he moved toward the window, pried it open and slid it up in the frame. He pushed the table to the side so he could get close. Carefully, he pulled himself through and balanced on the sill. He looked down at the shingled porch roof, praying that it would hold his weight. He stepped out onto the roof . . . it held. Spinning quickly about, he reached up and pulled the window closed behind him . . . just as the inner door opened.

He dropped to his hands and knees, then crawled to the side of the porch and dropped off the edge, landing heavily on the ground. He pressed against the wall, hiding in the shadow. Quickly, he inched between the two buildings. It was a tight squeeze. New Yorkers liked to fill every spare inch with structures. His own window was shut tight. He continued to push his way between the buildings, toward the back, hoping to break out into the open space before Casper Biggs caught him.

Up above, he heard Biggs open the window through which he'd just made his escape. He imagined the man's features twisted with rage, wondering who had invaded the sanctity of his space. The man climbed out onto the porch roof. Muldoon heard feet scraping on the wooden shingles.

Suddenly, he reached an unlatched window. It was open wide, not his own, but Meg McAllister's. He thrust his upper body back, and balanced across the windowsill. He walked his feet up the next building and pushed himself through the window, rolling as he hit the ground. A table nearly fell over when he hit it, but he grabbed it, steadied it. Glass tinkled as it broke . . . some trinket, or perhaps a cup and saucer. Quickly, he regained his feet, yanked the window down, and pulled the curtains closed. Just in time, he breathed . . .

CHAPTER 30

Muldoon arrived at the morgue a few moments before Mr. Wannamaker. Hesitantly, the man walked the length of the chill hallway to the marble room of the dead. He held a handkerchief tightly against his nose to minimize the smell. Muldoon felt sorry for him. He knew the man would feel guilty for a long time to come.

When Bob Gamble pulled the sheet away from the girl's face, the man blanched. Then, he nodded and stumbled from the room. Muldoon followed. Outside, Wannamaker breathed deep, gasping breaths of not-quite-fresh city air.

"Who . . . what monster," he amended, "could have done that to that beautiful girl?"

Muldoon knew he referred not just to her death, but also to her shaved head. Stubbles of hair had appeared on her scalp, an odd remnant of life. Gamble hadn't pulled the sheet any lower, didn't share with him the awful bruising on her abdomen. The bald head was shock enough.

"Catch him, Sergeant. Catch her killer."

"I intend to," Muldoon said. Not just for the young woman laid out on the slab, but also for Kelly McAllister, whose hanging was just days away now. If he couldn't connect the two cases, and bring them to a quick conclusion, the boy would hang.

Muldoon accompanied Wannamaker to the Hamm mansion on

5th Avenue. This ride was different from the last time he'd traveled there. A cab carried them through the streets.

"I . . . I'll tell them," the attorney said. "It's my responsibility."

Muldoon nodded. It was preferable that way. He'd rather not bear bad news of that sort. It would be hard enough just being the attendant policeman. He prepared himself for the episode as best he could.

The two were ushered into the house quickly, the tall, gaunt man in expensively tailored attire followed closely by Muldoon. They waited together in the drawing room. The lawyer seemed to draw comfort from him. Within moments, Colonel Hamm entered the room, trailed by his wife. He stopped abruptly at the sight of them. His gaze shifted from one to the other, knowing the news was bad.

"Elizabeth, leave the room," the Colonel said.

"No! She's my daughter, too."

It was the first time Muldoon had seen her. She was a petite woman with palest blonde hair, strikingly pretty, with even features, full lips trembling. She was much younger than the Colonel, perhaps in her later thirties.

She was the stepmother, he knew. But perhaps she had loved the girl. Somewhere in the house, there was another daughter, the product of this marriage, and an infant son.

"Richard," Wannamaker began. "I . . . " He glanced at Muldoon, as if for support. "We've brought terrible news. It appears . . . I mean . . . I've been to the . . . "

The man was floundering. Muldoon rescued him. "I'm sorry, sir. Madam. Your daughter, Margaret Hamm, is dead. She's been murdered." He didn't really like to say it that way, but he knew it was best said quickly.

Mrs. Hamm slumped against her husband. The Colonel wrapped his arms around her and held her tight.

"You're certain?" the Colonel asked as he helped his wife to the settee, settled her there, and turned to the bell pull to order her a tisane. It was a curious re-enactment of the scene just a day before.

"I've been there . . . to the . . . " Mr. Wannamaker glanced pointedly at Elizabeth Hamm. "Yes, it's Margaret. I've identified her this morning."

The Colonel nodded, and then turned to Muldoon. "Then, Sergeant, I expect you to do your best to apprehend the beast."

Muldoon nodded. "And, I'm sorry, but I have some questions I must ask."

"Of course," the Colonel said, and took a seat next to his wife. Mr. Wannamaker perched at the end of a chair across from the other two. He accepted a cup from his sister-in-law after the maid brought in a refreshment tray and set it in front of Mrs. Hamm. She looked uncertainly at Muldoon. He shook his head, just the smallest movement. She gave him a grateful smile and poured her own with shaking hands.

"The most pressing question I must ask," Muldoon began, "is the whereabouts of your manservant. The footman who went to Dayton not two weeks ago."

The Colonel looked at Muldoon, confusion in his eyes. "I didn't send a footman."

Mrs. Hamm placed her hand on the Colonel's arm, and closed her eyes as if in pain. "That would be Martin."

"Martin?" Muldoon asked.

"Yes," the Colonel said. "He left my employ two weeks ago."

"Left?"

"He was let go. His work . . . left something to be desired."

"So, he may have held a grudge against the family."

"Against me, you mean. I would say that's likely. He didn't leave under the best of circumstances. And I didn't give him a recommendation." Muldoon knew what that meant to a man in Martin's circumstances. He wouldn't work again. He had been turned out on the streets. He almost asked about the offense, but he noticed Mrs. Hamm's hand, the one on the Colonel's arm, as her fingers tightened in alarm. He glanced up at her eyes and saw the concern. There was definitely something there. He'd have to get at it a different way.

"I'll need to speak to the servants," Muldoon said. "And I'd like a list of your daughter's friends."

"Her friends?" Mrs. Hamm asked, that fear again in her eyes.

"No," the Colonel said. "I cannot allow that. The servants, of course. You can speak to them. I'll arrange it with the butler. If you come back later, you can see Burnes. He'll help you with the staff. As for her friends, I'm afraid I can't allow that. Their fathers wouldn't allow it, either."

"Colonel," Muldoon said. "We're talking about your daughter. I need to speak to any possible witnesses."

"Those girls cannot have been witness to such a horrible deed!" The Colonel slammed his hand down on his knee. The slap echoed through the room. Mrs. Hamm jerked back, then quickly concealed her sudden fear. Muldoon raised an eyebrow. The woman had been hit. Had the children? Had the Colonel created the bruises across his daughter's abdomen? But, certainly not those on Schneider. He appraised the man's build. Not so gaunt as his brother-in-law, yet nowhere near the bulk of Muldoon.

"The girls may have some knowledge, however slight, that may help shed light on the case. Something even they don't realize is important," Muldoon said.

"No." The answer was emphatic.

A tiny movement at the door caught Muldoon's eye. At first, he ignored it, not wanting to see his specter, but his eyes flicked toward it. The door slid silently shut. Perhaps a servant listening in, he thought. Not one of his silent soldiers.

"I'll send a man later to question the servants," Muldoon said, giving in to the Colonel's steadfast position. "May I speak to your other daughter?"

"No," Mrs. Hamm said. "I won't have her disturbed. She's only ten . . . and this will be hard enough on the child."

Muldoon nodded. He hadn't expected that interview, considering the Colonel's attitude about the friends.

"And now, Sergeant. I believe we've answered enough questions. Send your man. If he calls at the back door, the staff will be expecting him."

Muldoon put away his little notebook and stubby pencil. He wasn't sure where the new information was taking him. He'd have to study it a bit further. "Thank you, Sirs, Madam," Muldoon said, bowed slightly, and took his leave, shutting the parlor door behind him.

As he retreated through the house, a slight sound from the staircase drew his attention.

"Sir . . . " There it was again, the tiniest little whisper. He turned aside from his direct route to the door and paused near the banister. A little girl, perhaps ten years old, stood a few steps above him. Tears marked her face. He smiled at her reassuringly.

"You must be Miss Melanie," he said. "Your aunt told me you're Miss Margaret's sister?"

"Yes, I am," the girl said. She was a pretty little thing. Though only half-sibling, she was a shadow of her elder sister. Muldoon could see the likeness. That would be hard for the Colonel and his wife in the years to come, he thought. Her appearance would bring memories of the promising young life they'd lost.

"Her friend is Alva," the girl said.

"Alva?"

"Yes . . . oh! Smith, Alva Smith. It's unfair Papa wouldn't tell you. She was Margaret's best friend. If she can tell you something . . . I mean, if she can help . . . then you should know."

"Thank you. I'm certain she can help. But I don't think her father will let me speak with her."

"You can find her at the track. She goes on Saturdays. I know her papa doesn't like it, but she does what she wants. They say she's a woman of her own mind . . . well, anyway, Margaret always said so."

"And how will I know when I see her?" Muldoon asked.

"Oh, ask any of the boys," she waved her hand in the air. "They all know her."

Muldoon smiled at the child's naiveté. The little girl's voice talked about adult things, but didn't fully realize that Miss Smith was, perhaps, a bit scandalous.

"Thank you," Muldoon said.

"Oh, but don't go in that!" she exclaimed, then covered her mouth. She glanced about quickly, as if hoping no one had heard. She continued quietly, "You need to wear your very best clothes. You'll be quite dashing. And then she'll talk to you. I don't think she would if you only wear your policeman's clothes."

"Thank you for the hint," he said, and squeezed her hand lightly as he noted the tears welling up again in her eyes. She squeezed back, then turned and ran lightly up the stairs.

Outside on the step, he wrote again in his little notebook. Who was Alva Smith, he wondered?

CHAPTER 31

BENSON was in his office when Muldoon got to Police Headquarters. Notebooks, sketches, and descriptions of missing property, and lists of possible suspects lay before him on his desk.

"It looks like you're making some progress," Muldoon said as he sat down.

"Yes. It's coming together quite well." Benson leaned back in his chair and pushed aside his work for the moment. "How is it going for you? Did you find anything in Dayton?"

"Aye," Muldoon said, a cheerless tone in his voice. "It was her. Margaret Hamm."

"Then we've got to go to the Captain. Don't be surprised if he pulls us off this one . . . "

They climbed the stairs to the Captain's office. Half an hour passed before he called them in. Muldoon was sure he kept them waiting out of spite. Detective Graham lounged in his chair in front the big desk. Benson slid onto the other chair, and Muldoon stood just inside the door, hat in hand.

"So?" Captain Hayle leaned forward in his chair and glowered at them as if at intruders. "Have you solved the burglaries? Or is it the dead woman. Or one of the other unsolved cases piling up in your office?"

"I . . . I'm making good progress, Captain. But it's about the woman. I've learned her identity," Benson said.

Muldoon clenched his jaw. He couldn't appreciate the way Benson got credit for his discoveries. But he liked the guy, and working with the detective got him off the beat.

"So?" the Captain asked.

"She's Margaret Hamm," Benson said. "The daughter of Colonel Hamm. Of Fifth Avenue."

"You're certain of this?" Captain Hayle straightened sharply.

Benson looked up at Muldoon. He took the cue.

"Aye, Sir. The body's been identified by the Colonel's brother-in-law, one Mr. Wannamaker . . . of Dayton, New York."

A slow smile curved across the Captain's face. "And you've interviewed these men?"

"I have."

"Good," Captain Hayle said. "Carry on."

"This is a case I would be interested in!" Graham leaned forward in his chair and tapped the desktop with his index finger. "I have a much better reputation for closing cases."

"Perhaps. But I would prefer these two continue their investigation." Captain Hayle leaned back in his chair, elbows bent, with fingertips together to form a steeple. The oddly benevolent smile didn't reach his hard eyes. "You're dismissed."

They stepped into the hall. Muldoon pulled the door behind him with a click. "What was that all about?"

"He expects us to fail." Benson glared back at the closed door.

"Why? With such a prominent family . . . why would he want us to fail?"

"Exactly for that reason," Benson said. "Because then he would have reason to fire us . . . Boss Tweed be damned."

"I'm not gonna let him do that," Muldoon said. "I'm sending Sergeant O'Malley to question the staff. And we need to find that footman. He brought the girl back to New York, so he's got to be somewhere in town."

CHAPTER 32

ULDOON pushed his way through the throngs of people at the racetrack. He'd changed into his new suit, the one he'd bought with his wrestling money. Ready-made was his first choice. It was cheaper to get clothes off the shelf, but it was hard to find his size. He'd paid well to get a tailor-made suit, and lucked out when the second shop he'd walked into had a suit already made. The original buyer had changed his mind, and all it had needed was taking in around the middle. The suit was a soft gray-black with a top hat to match. He chose a polished maple walking stick with a gold knob at the top. It was relatively simple, he didn't go in for ostentation. But he knew he looked as fashionable as any other gentleman who strolled through the stands.

He didn't stop at the windows, but moved on past. He wasn't a betting man, and didn't feel the pull of excitement at the thought of winning a wager. The thrill of gambling paled next to the exhilaration of actually participating in an event. Let others lay bets, but he would take part in the action. He tore his gaze away from a soldier leaning in at the window. He couldn't be Paddy Ryan, but a specter haunting him even here. His heart beat rapidly, and he could hear the rush of blood in his ears. Panic rose, and he felt the urge to run, as he did so many nights. Run from the sight of bloodied, half-gone men, arms or legs dangling . . . or missing altogether. And his friend, missing among them, yet haunting him still.

He paused where he stood, in the center of the wide hall, and drew in a deep breath. He held it as gambling men shoved past him on their way to or from the windows. And then he started again, his emotions under the taut veneer of control that filled his waking hours.

Somewhere, Alva Smith, a woman he didn't know and couldn't picture, sat hidden in the crowd. His gaze slid past living folk, and occasional others. He turned his mind to the girl. It would help if he had an idea of what she looked like. If he followed the society pages he would probably have recognized her. But he didn't, so he wandered aimlessly through the multitudes, looking for a brash young woman surrounded by men. The problem was that at the track, most women fit that description.

And then he saw her, or at least he thought he did. She wasn't particularly beautiful, but she had an air about her, one that attracted the men . . . almost a devil-may-care kind of attitude. She lounged gracefully in a private box, delicate opera glasses pinned to her blouse. She was a sight, really, in a pale blue grosgrain walking dress and a royal velvet casaque. Her dark hair was pulled back into an elegant coiffure, royal blue ribbons woven throughout. She wore a tiny cap, tilted forward at a saucy angle. Above her head, she twirled a parasol, oblivious of frowns from behind her. He judged her to be eighteen or so.

He made his way down the steps toward her. As he came closer, he realized her features were more striking than he had at first given credit. Her eyebrows were finely arched over flashing eyes. Her nose was perhaps a bit too small, and her lower lip rather pouty. But it was her zealousness that shone like a star, and attracted the various men and youths gathered about her. She drank it in like sustenance. At one and the same time, Muldoon was drawn, and repelled.

"Miss Smith?" he asked as he neared.

She glanced up at him, then turned in her seat, sudden interest reflected in her eyes. "Do I know you?" she asked.

"No, Miss."

"Good! Then it shall be all the more delicious finding out who you are."

He was a bit put off by her forward remarks. He wasn't used to a woman quite like this. At least, not one who called herself a lady.

She stood up and moved away from her companions as if they no longer existed for her. One young man made a move to follow her, but Muldoon stopped him with a look. Cowed, the man sat again, grumbling loudly. The others jostled him good naturedly, but they all watched enviously as she mounted the steps to Muldoon's side. He turned to walk with her.

"Tell me," she said. "What is your name?" She tilted her head and gazed up at him through the corners of her eyes.

"William Muldoon."

"Muldoon . . . " she said, tasting the name in her mouth. "I rather fancy that. It's not a name I've heard before. Is it Irish?"

"Aye, Miss Smith," he said.

She laughed, a low tinkling sound, and glanced sidelong at him through lowered lashes.

"You're not concerned about your race, then?" Muldoon asked, and looked back toward the track where high-bred thoroughbreds paraded the field.

"No," she said. "It's just a passing fancy. I come here, because my father says I shouldn't."

He could hear a slight southern twang in her voice, but there was something else too, as though she had spent years in another country. It added an element of excitement to her that he hadn't ever felt before. His pulse quickened, and he struggled to control it. This was definitely a woman he could not have.

"Why have you sought me?" she asked suddenly and turned to face him. She placed a gloved hand against his chest.

He took her hand away, afraid she would feel the rapid beating of his heart. He tucked her arm into the crook of his own. Drawing her beside him again, he continued walking.

"I need some information, and I believe you may be able to provide that to me."

"I see," she began. "You're an investigator. This must be about poor Margaret." She raised a finger and barely touched the corner of her eye to wipe away the tiniest tear. At first, he thought it was for show, but the rapid changes in her expression told him that she fought hard to hold back the flood that threatened. Muldoon didn't speak again, but waited for her.

"And what is it that you need from me," she whispered at last.

"Is there any reason that you can think of," he began, hating to be blunt. "Any reason somebody may have wanted to kill her?"

"None I can think of," she replied quietly. "Really, Mr. Muldoon, she was so good. Not like me. There must be so many boys who want me dead. Any one of that lot back there." She gestured vaguely toward the men who'd surrounded her moments before.

Muldoon couldn't believe that. Though right at this moment, those men might feel that way about him.

"Was she a popular girl? Sought out by the boys?"

"Certainly, in her way. She was very beautiful, but perhaps a bit too shy. Still, she had those with whom she danced regularly. But no. No suitors, if that's what you mean."

Muldoon nodded. He could understand that lack, with Miss Smith as her best friend. Margaret Hamm, pretty as she was, would be outshone by this belle. They'd reached the end of the promenade, and turned back the way they'd come. Muldoon walked quietly, there wasn't much more he could ask her. There were more questions he had, but he couldn't answer them without getting inside the Hamm's house. But he knew that wouldn't happen, not for an Irish cop from the Bowery.

"What is it you're thinking?" Alva asked. "Whatever it is, I want to help." Her voice quavered a bit, and she dashed her kerchief angrily across her eyes, trying to maintain her composure. For the second time, she rounded on Muldoon. Her eyes sought his, demanded all his attention. His gaze was drawn to hers, as if her searching eyes could see into his soul.

"I want to help," she said suddenly and stamped her foot. "What is it you need?

He caught her hand as it slid from the crook of his arm, and skimmed down his forearm. "I need to know what was happening in that house. There's something there that I don't understand. It's like she was banished, sent to her uncle's for some reason, and kept there, until allowed to return home."

"I'll go visiting then, and learn what I can. Where can I find you again?"

Muldoon colored slightly. "I'm . . . I mean . . . I didn't mean to deceive you." He let go of her hand, and turned toward the track. The race was over. He hadn't even heard them call it. And shouldn't someone have blown a horn?

He turned back to the girl. "I'm a policeman. A sergeant. I work out of Police Headquarters on Mulberry. But you can't go there, it would be unseemly."

"Then tell me your address, and I'll send a note."

Muldoon nodded. It was a good plan. He scribbled the address on a sheet torn from his little notebook and handed it to her. She smiled as she took it, pleasure gleamed in her eyes. "Be careful," he said as she took the slip of paper. "It could be dangerous."

She smiled wickedly.

PART TWO

CHAPTER 33

April 25

ALVA sat in her room and brushed her long hair, then pulled the front back and tied it up with a ribbon in a young girl's style. She knew her father liked to see her this way, looking young and innocent. He had no idea how innocent she really still was. She simply liked to play the part of a coquette to shock Mrs. Astor's '400.' Of course, her father thought she was partly to blame that they hadn't been fully accepted into society. But, she knew it was because of their Southern heritage. For goodness sake, her family spoke with a twang! She'd been born in Mobile, Alabama just eighteen years previous. It was where her father, Murray Smith had made his fortune . . . in cotton, of course. Then, just before the war, they'd moved to New York City. But, their accent made integration into society impossible. Southerners were definitely not welcome in the North during the war. Most people looked at them suspiciously, as if all Southerners were rebels. So, for the duration of the war they went abroad, to Paris. And then they returned here.

As she lay the brush on the table, she thought of the previous day's events. It had definitely been a memorable afternoon. She'd left the racetrack almost immediately after Muldoon. He'd escorted her back to her box, where she sat beside her companions for a moment, but she'd lost all interest in the races. Feigning a headache, she asked her escort to take her home, which he quickly agreed to. She was sure the man blamed Muldoon. She smiled wickedly at the thought. He was a very handsome man. She couldn't believe how big he was. She had contrived to place her hand on his chest, and was surprised at the firmness. She had expected a layer of softness, like her father, or like the men who courted her. She'd never known a man with that amount of muscle. And when they walked arm in arm, she'd felt the fluid strength of his muscles. A delicious shiver of . . . was it fear? . . . slid down her spine and lodged somewhat lower. He was definitely a dangerous man. Perhaps more dangerous because of the reaction to him that she felt. She'd had a shock, almost of recognition, when he spoke her name. She'd turned to see the largest man she had ever known, gazing down upon her.

Like a fool, she'd scrambled out of her seat and abandoned her escort and her entourage. Poor Joseph Vanderkook, she'd made him whip his horses to a fast trot and he'd cut through traffic at a breakneck speed just to get her home because of her 'sudden' headache. She smiled at the thought of that brash young man . . . he must be so worried that his courtship was about to be overthrown.

Until now, she'd never met a more exciting man. Suddenly New York glowed! But then he was only a policeman, and she had so many plans for her future. She simply had to marry well . . . someone like Joseph. Still, this William Muldoon . . . he was thrilling! She'd spent the rest of the day anticipating her glorious adventure. She would go to the Hamm's to express her condolences. It was expected anyway, though perhaps not quite so soon. And then she'd see Mr. Muldoon again.

She dressed in her most sedate outfit. Luckily, she liked blue. She found a deep shade, nearly navy, with epaulets, and military trim. She pretended to be unaware of the disapproving frowns it provoked when she donned war-inspired garb. It was the height of style, and just because she was originally from the south didn't mean she shouldn't wear the newest fashions. At ten o'clock she called for the carriage, and accompanied by her mother, drove to the Hamm residence. They were let in immediately, and shown into the morning room where Mrs. Hamm held court.

At the moment, they were the only guests. The room had been draped in black crepe, to match that worn by Mrs. Hamm. She'd prepared the scene perfectly, to demonstrate the depth of her loss, as guests arrived to offer condolences. Mrs. Hamm was ensconced on her settee, a pot of tea on the table before her, little cucumber sandwiches displayed proudly. Cucumbers were nearly impossible to find this time of year. They were clearly a show of ostentation. The woman didn't greet them pleasantly, though she was cordial for the sake of her step-daughter's friendship with Alva. After this day, she probably didn't plan to readily accept the Smith's into her home again.

"Good morning, Phoebe, Alva," she said, a small smile frozen on her lips.

"Good morning," Mrs. Smith replied warmly, and the two seated themselves on chairs opposite their hostess. They each accepted a cup of tea and a sandwich. Alva nibbled on hers, she didn't really like cucumber, but after all, one must be polite. She hid a sigh. She liked stilted, polite conversation even less.

"We are so sorry to hear of your loss," Mrs. Smith began. "My dear Alva is beside herself with pain. Margaret, of course, was her dearest friend."

Mrs. Hamm nodded her head politely. "Yes, they were dear friends." The woman spoke as if Alva wasn't there. She desperately wanted to argue, to make Mrs. Hamm acknowledge her, but she needed to keep quiet. It wasn't her way, but she had to listen to the conversation, to catch any untoward nuance. But little of note was said, only the simple inanities of polite conversation.

After a few moments, she decided she'd had enough. This wasn't at all what she'd expected. She had looked with excitement on investigating the murder. And she truly did want to help find her friend's killer, but this was ridiculous. Nothing was said that could even hint at scandal.

"I need a breath of air," she said to the ladies. She needed to escape the somber atmosphere.

"Oh . . . well," her mother said. "If you aren't feeling well I suppose I must accompany you home."

"No, Mama, it isn't that," she began again. "I am simply overcome with sadness for my friend. I feel the need to walk in the garden. If I may?" She glanced at Mrs. Hamm. She tried to put the right amount of sadness into her expression, but hadn't realized how easy it would be. She really did miss her friend.

"Of course, my dear." Mrs. Hamm tilted her head imperiously. "Please, take a walk and refresh yourself."

Alva gratefully exited the stifling room, shut the door and leaned heavily back against it. Well, she thought, she had certainly ruined that. It had been her one chance to find out something of note. She walked into the room across the hall, nearly identical to the one she had just left except for the color of its furnishings, and exited through the French doors. Slowly she strolled through the garden, knowing she had let down Sergeant Muldoon.

"Hello." A tiny voice broke through her reverie.

As she spun about, Alva noticed the small figure of Melanie Hamm curled up on a stone bench. The girl dropped a book into her lap.

"I was trying to read . . . but I can't. I, I can't stop thinking about my sister." She wiped tears from her eyes. "I'm glad you're here. I was afraid you'd stay away. Since you two were best friends. And, you know, since Mama and Papa are so . . . well you know. You are from Alabama." The child scooted over and patted the bench next to her.

"Do you want to sit here?"

Nodding, Alva perched lightly at the edge of the seat, mindful of her dress. She took the girl's hand in hers. Suddenly Melanie threw herself into Alva's arms, big wrenching sobs wracked her small body. Alva hugged her close, holding her own tears at bay, knowing this moment was for the child.

As her tears finally subsided, Melanie pulled back, and Alva handed her a silk kerchief. The girl wiped away her tears, and turned to look at her sister's friend.

"They never talk to me." Melanie shook her curls angrily. "It's like Margaret never was."

She twisted Alva's kerchief, pulling desperately at the lace trim. "Did you . . . did you see the policeman?" she asked between gulping breaths.

"Ah, so you sent him?" Alva smiled.

"Yes, he was so very nice. Don't you think so?"

"I most certainly do."

"He thought you might know something about the . . . about Margaret."

Suddenly Alva had a thought. Perhaps the girl knew something that she didn't realize was important. Excited, she carefully began to lead the conversation.

"It must be terrible for you, that Margaret was so far away when this tragedy happened."

"Oh yes, Mother came home alone. I was never so surprised. I expected to see Margaret, too, but Mother said she wasn't well. She said she would come home in a few weeks."

That was the first time Alva had heard of that. She knew Margaret had accompanied her mother to Dayton to have the child. And she, too, had been surprised when Margaret hadn't returned. But she didn't know about her illness. And her friend hadn't even written to her the entire time she was away.

"Did your mother say what was wrong?"

"No. Just that she was very ill."

"Was your mother angry with her? That she had gotten ill?"

"No, but Father was. He said she could stay there until he was ready!"

"Does your father get angry a lot?" Alva patted the child's hand.

"Oh no!" Melanie exclaimed. "He's the most wonderful father in the world. He never gets angry with anyone. Well, except for Mama sometimes. And the footman."

"He was angry at the footman?" Alva felt a growing excitement.

"Yes, he said terrible things, things I ought not to repeat. Mother says it's bad language, and the Lord won't forgive me if I say those things. But a man is different. He's allowed to say what he wants."

Alva nodded. "That's what they say." She didn't particularly agree, but it wasn't her place to argue with the child. "So, why was he mad at the footman?"

"I don't know. But he wasn't given a reference. The man was very upset. He kept saying he didn't do it, and that it wasn't him. But I don't know what they were talking about."

"When was this?" Alva wondered what could possibly have happened to make Colonel Hamm so angry.

"Just a couple of weeks ago." Melanie screwed up her face as she tried to remember. "Just after Mother came home. Father was in his office, and I followed Mother there. I had a question . . . but I don't remember anymore. She went in, and she didn't shut the door all the way, so I . . . well, I listened." The girl hung her head, shamefaced. "But that's when he got mad. Mother had just told him about Margaret, that's all!"

"What did she say?" Alva held her breath, her heart knocking heavily against her ribs.

"She said that . . . Margaret said . . . that it was somebody Father knew. Somebody really close. Whatever it was, I guess he thought that meant the footman."

"Was the footman really close?" Alva asked. She couldn't see how.

"Well, I guess so," answered the girl. "He was going to be Father's valet. His old one died, you know."

"No, I didn't know."

"Alva!" The call broke through the silence of the garden around them.

"Well," Alva said. "I suppose I've been out here much longer than I meant. It was very nice of you to keep me company."

The young girl gave her another swift hug.

"I suppose you won't be coming so much anymore," she whispered. "Now that Margaret's gone."

"I don't suppose your parents will let me." Alva smiled sadly.

She rose from the bench and pulled a little pin from her hair, with a tiny crystal dragonfly adorning the end. Reaching forward, she slipped the pin into the girl's hair, then leaned toward the small blonde head and kissed her where she had placed the jewel. Then she turned and walked away, tears fresh in her eyes.

When Alva finally stopped crying, the carriage had just pulled up in front of their grand house. Her mother tried to console her, but she really did miss Margaret. She put on a brave show most of the time, and now she had lost Melanie, too. Suddenly she wanted to see Sergeant Muldoon. She had planned on sending him a note. But right now, she needed someone to lean on, somebody who wanted nothing from her, and to whom she owed nothing.

"I'm going to take a little ride, Mother," she said. "I just can't go in yet."

"Then you will wait for Mary." Mrs. Smith looked at her disapprovingly.

"I'm not getting out, Mama. I'll stay in the carriage, I promise." Alva didn't want a fight, but she wasn't about to have the maid listening in on her conversation. What she had to say was private, between her and the policeman.

Phoebe looked at her a long time. Finally, she agreed. "You do seem particularly distraught, my dear," She leaned forward and cupped her daughter's cheek in her hand, then gently wiped away a tear. "Fine, but I will speak to the coachman. He'll make certain you don't get into trouble."

Alva waited in the carriage until her mother was safely inside, then she was whisked away, on up 5th Avenue, as if for a drive through the park. When she was a safe distance, she tapped on the window between her and the driver. Simmons, the coachman, slid the little door open and turned his head a bit so he could hear over the clatter of the street.

"Yes, Miss?"

"I would like to go to Elizabeth Street," she said, and gave him the address.

"No, Miss, I can't. I promised Mrs. Smith you wouldn't be stopping anywhere."

No matter how much she pleaded with the man, she couldn't get him to agree. He'd made a promise, and while she was in his care, she was definitely not getting out of the carriage. At this moment, the man's loyalty to her parents irked her.

"Well," she said suddenly. "Then the footman can carry a message to the door for me. I won't get out at all."

The driver thought about it, and then finally gave in. She smiled smugly as she leaned back against the seat. He'd only promised her mother that she wouldn't get out, not that she couldn't deliver a message. The carriage turned about, picking up the pace now that they had a particular destination. As they headed into the Bowery, Alva looked anxiously out the window. The coachman might have thought he'd made a mistake after all. But, despite any misgivings he might have, he continued on his way. She relaxed back into her seat, but pulled the curtain back a little from the window. If the neighborhood got too rough, he could simply turn around and take her home. The neighborhood was poor, but well kept, so they continued slowly down the street. She read addresses as they passed by, until they finally stopped in front of Mrs. Dunn's boarding house.

She watched as the Footman leaped down, strode up the walk to the front door, and rang the bell. A maid opened the door, stiffened in surprise, her lips forming an "O," then she spun about and slammed the door behind her.

CHAPTER 34

ULDOON opened the door and looked at Betsy inquiringly. She struggled to speak, her lips moving silently, her eyes huge. She just looked from him to the front door—and back again.

"Ooohh, Sergeant Muldoon, sir," she finally blurted out. "I've never been so surprised in my entire life. A man, dressed ever-so-fine, he's out on the step. A . . . a grand carriage waiting behind him. He says he has a message for you, sir."

Suddenly, she crumpled down in a heap of black and white skirts. "Oh Lord, oh Lord, I ran off to your room and I forgot to invite him in. I'll lose my job for sure."

He reached down, took the maid by the hand, and pulled her upright. He stepped into the hall and looked curiously in the direction she kept staring. He was surprised to see the footman waiting patiently outside the open door.

"May I help you?" he asked as he looked beyond the man at the carriage and four.

"If you are a Mr. Muldoon," the footman replied.

"I am."

"My mistress would like a word with you, sir. In the carriage. If you would care to get your hat and coat, I will escort you back."

Muldoon raised an eyebrow, but returned within a moment, coat on and hat in hand. He wasn't dressed for it, he knew. He wore rough woven brown pants and a plain shirt. He couldn't match his new jacket over these pants, so he took his regular one, a coarse working man's coat. And his hat was a flat, newsboy style cap, buttoned down to the short front brim, giving him a very working-class Irish appearance. He followed the man out to the carriage.

The footman opened the door, and stood to the side. Muldoon waited for the occupant to lean out and speak to him.

"Well, get in!" An impatient voice floated out of the darkness.

Muldoon climbed up with a smile on his face, though he was rather embarrassed by his appearance. "Hello, Miss Smith," he said, as he seated himself opposite her.

"Mr. Muldoon." She nodded.

The driver grumbled almost inaudibly. "Never said she could pick up a man,"
but he whipped the horses on. The footman closed the door behind him and climbed aboard, tapping for the coachman to get moving.

He'd never ridden in a carriage before, and Muldoon glanced around at the beautiful appointments, trying not to look gauche. It was early Sunday afternoon and when they reentered a more fashionable district, they slowed to promenade pace along with the other carriages. Alva kept the curtains shut, and Muldoon knew she was embarrassed by him. She wouldn't have hidden one of the beaux she had been with at the track, he knew. But then, if he was in his new suit, she might have opened the curtains.

He looked at her, eyebrows raised. "I'm certain you didn't just want a ride with me, agreeable though it may be. Did you have some news for me?"

"I went to the Hamm residence this morning," she said. "After Church. I know it was a bit awkward, visiting on a Sunday, but I needed to. She was my friend after all. I . . . I loved her!" She sat erect, her gloved fingers stiff in her lap, an angry, challenging expression on her face.

Muldoon nodded genially. He knew the rich weren't like the poor. In his neighborhood, all the visiting was done on a Sunday. During the week, folks were too busy working to waste time. Of course, it helped when everybody went to the same church. For him, it was the Catholic one several blocks away from his rooming house, though he rarely darkened that door.

"You don't need to justify it," he said gently.

SHE didn't know why she needed to defend herself, especially to him . . . a stranger. For some reason, she was angry with him. She didn't understand it, just knew that she was. He was too damnably amenable. She was embarrassed even to think the word, blushed a bit as it passed through her mind.

He looked at her with a quizzical expression, as if he wondered what she had thought about. And that made her even madder, that he could somehow read her emotions so easily! Still, she couldn't help but admire him. He had shrugged out of his jacket, and placed it and his hat on the seat by his side. He sat across from her, leaning back nonchalantly with his legs rather farther apart than a man of her class would do, one foot braced against the base of her seat. She fancied she could see his muscles through the light fabric of his shirt, her eyes drawn to his chest on more than one occasion. And each time she blushed. And then he would smile that crooked not-quite-smile, one side of his mustache rising higher than the other. It was a wicked grin, as if he knew something that she didn't.

"I . . . I think she was expecting," Alva suddenly burst out. She couldn't believe she had said it! She really should have written it down, then she wouldn't have had to endure the humor in his eyes. Just saying it brought her mind around again to . . . well . . . IT. The act of passion between a man and a woman. And she knew he had to be thinking of it as well, though maybe not in connection with her, as she definitely was thinking about him. She had to get control of herself. She had never been like this about a man before.

SITTING across from her, Muldoon couldn't help but grin each time her gaze dropped to his chest . . . or lower. He rather fancied that this was a bit like what a woman felt when a man kept staring at her bosom. But of course, he wasn't angry, or embarrassed. He wondered if women were truly either one of those, or if they flushed for the same reason he felt the blood surging through his own veins. Still, it was a bit fun, to be on the receiving end of that look for once.

"Why do you think she was expecting?" He asked, raising one eyebrow. She seemed to deflate with his business-like tone. Had she wanted him to think of her in that way?

"Well, because she went to the country with her mother. And then she didn't come back . . . "

"Is there something unusual about that?"

"No, not really." Her eyes flashed with irritation.

"Then, tell me what makes you think it." He cocked his head to watch the fleeting expressions that chased across her face. Was it really just a hunch? Woman's intuition? Or did she know something that she couldn't, or was too embarrassed to tell him?

"Well, I do think maybe it's a little odd." She tilted her head in an echo of his movement just seconds before. "And she never wrote to me. Not once."

"Maybe she didn't like to write letters?"

"Oh, she did. She wrote many letters each week." Alva leaned toward him and spread her hands as if holding a stack of mail. "She must have written a letter each day, to cousins, and to friends. And then we would sit together, and read the answers. It was so much fun." Her voice began to quaver, and she seemed angry with herself again, as if she shouldn't have feelings. "I wrote to her so many times while she was away . . . and never once received an answer."

She was feeling sorry for herself, he could tell. But, he believed in women's intuition. That's one of the things about having an Irish mother. They almost always know what you're up to. Sometimes, it seems, they know before you do yourself.

Alva cleared her throat. "And then Melanie, that's her little sister, said that Margaret was sick. That's why she didn't come home. But, her mother came home with the baby right after it was born. It seems to me that the person having the baby should be the sick one."

Muldoon found himself agreeing with her. It was beginning to sound a bit suspicious.

"Have you any ideas who the father might be?" he asked. "If she really is the mother, I mean?"

"Well, I think it might be the missing footman. I think his name is Martin."

"Why do you think that?" It made sense, he thought.

"Because, Mrs. Hamm told the Colonel that it was somebody close to him, and then the footman was fired. Now what could she have meant by that? 'That it was somebody close to him,' unless they were talking about the baby's father?"

"You might be right, but that'll be nearly impossible to prove."

They had come around again to his rooming house. "I'll look into it and send you a note," he promised. Then he alighted, and her carriage was gone. Carrying his hat and jacket in hand, he turned and went into the building. Judging by the slight movements of curtains, he would have some explaining to do at dinner tonight.

CHAPTER 35

April 26

MULDOON hurried to the morgue. Margaret Hamm's body hadn't been released yet, but he suspected the family's mortuary would be collecting her this morning. And he needed to get some questions answered before she was lost to him. The door was still locked when he got there, and he waited impatiently, finally catching sight of the doctor as he strolled up the path.

"You're here early." Gamble greeted him. He pulled out his keys and fumbled with the lock, until the door finally clicked open. "I don't have any new ones . . . so, let me guess, you must be here about the girl."

"Aye," Muldoon said, and pulled the doctor quickly inside.

"Hurry up!" he called to Danny Ryan who had just appeared from around the corner, ever-present book in hand. The boy looked up in surprise, and then sprinted the final distance.

"What's the matter?" he asked as he slid to a stop.

"We've gotta get in, quick."

Muldoon glanced up and down the sidewalk, and then pulled the door shut behind him. He latched it and moved further into the room.

"Keep it down," Muldoon said quietly, preventing Danny from pulling up the shade. "I need to know something, and I need to know it before the family comes to get her."

"It's that important, is it?" The coroner smiled. "Okay, then. Danny, nobody gets in here until we say so."

Danny winked conspiratorially, and then nodded his head. He was enjoying the game. He set his book on top of his desk, and walked back to a small closet just down the hall. Pulling out a broom, he began to sweep.

"I've been so busy sweeping, just in case the mortician fella peeks in, that I couldn't hear anyone knocking. How's that?"

"Thanks, boy-oh," said Muldoon with appreciation. He turned to follow Gamble to the back room.

"I need to know if Margaret Hamm had a baby," Muldoon said as he closed the door behind them.

"I thought it was much more than that," Gamble laughed. "That's an easy request, it doesn't even take any cutting. I didn't consider that in my report, because we were just dealing with an obvious murder. But let's take a look here."

He pulled the body out of its niche and uncovered its lower half. "A large number of women, those who have given birth that is, have perineal tears. And if the birth was recent, we should still see some evidence of swelling, even without the tear."

Within moments, the doctor stood, shaking his head. "I'm sorry Muldoon. I didn't think it was necessary. You're right. She's had a child, within just a few weeks of her death."

Muldoon stroked his mustache. The whole scenario had just changed. This meant the child that Colonel and Mrs. Hamm claimed as their own was really their grandson. And it meant that he'd found an awfully good motive for murder. Now he had to find the footman. Clearly, that's who the Colonel suspected as the father . . . or did he know it? But then again, Muldoon wasn't ready to set aside the Colonel, himself. He was certain the man hit his wife. And the man was a clear bigot, a member of a secret society based on prejudice. Could his biases turn to murderous anger over a daughter gone bad? Especially if Martin turned out to be Irish?

"What Should I do?" Bob Gamble pushed the gurney back into place, and turned to Muldoon.

"About what?" Muldoon looked back at him, confused.

"I've already turned in my report. Cause of death: strangulation. I didn't mention this . . . I didn't even know. God, man! I should have looked. My report was incomplete, like I was an amateur."

"Just write an addendum. You know I'm not going to say anything." Muldoon knew he was thinking of his job, afraid he would lose it. "You can date it back to when you looked at her first, if you like. And I'll witness it. But then file it away, lose it somewhere. She's a part of the Knickerbocker crowd, and you're bringing out something ugly . . . something they don't want to see. And, the Hamm's have already claimed that child as their own."

"I know," said Gamble, his voice dropping low. "I don't want to have that kind of wrath come down on me."

"Just put it away. It doesn't matter, yet. We may need the report, when it comes to a trial . . . but if we don't need it, I'll never say a thing."

Gamble thanked him, then turned to pull out another corpse. Muldoon walked back up the cold hallway, passing Danny along the way. He winked as he opened the door, and came face to face with an irate little man standing out on the step. A black wagon waited on the street "Tilden's Mortuary" stenciled on the side.

"Sorry," Muldoon said. "I must have locked it on the way in."

He ambled nonchalantly away, the balding mortician cursing indignantly. Then, as he noticed the looks he attracted, the man obliterated the anger from his face, and plastered on an undertaker's vacant, slightly concerned expression. He entered the morgue to collect Margaret Hamm's body. But not without one last, piercing glare. Muldoon laughed.

CHAPTER 36

Suddenly, Muldoon was making headway in the case. All he needed to do, he thought, was find the footman and he would probably have his murderer.

"O'Malley here?" he asked the desk Sergeant as he entered police headquarters.

"Nope." Tim Foley looked up from his paperwork. "He's out on the beat. Captain wouldn't let him out of it. Not even to help on your case."

"You mean, especially not to help me." Muldoon scowled.

"Aye, more likely that." Foley threw a sympathetic look at him. "But Benson's here. He's in a right jubilant mood, he is. He solved his case."

For a moment, Muldoon's heart leaped, but then he realized it was the robbery case. Good for him, he thought, but these murders were more pressing. He wasn't getting the kind of cooperation out of Benson that he expected. Then again, that might have been the Captain's plan, pushing so hard for Benson to solve the theft. The murder had been shuffled onto Benson's back plate, leaving only Muldoon to investigate. And knowing Captain Hayle, he expected Muldoon to fail. Then, he would turn around and blame them both for allowing a dangerous killer to remain loose on the streets. And since the victim was an innocent debutante, the Captain would have the support of society's elite—the

'400'—and would finally be able to drum both Muldoon and Benson out of the Department. Boss Tweed be hanged.

He strode purposefully down the hall and pushed open Benson's door. The man sat at his desk, a young patrolman in the lone visitor's chair.

"Hello, Muldoon." Benson half-rose from his chair and motioned toward the occupied chair, as if offering him a seat. "Have you heard my news? I've solved the case. And now the Captain's given me a new one, another burglary. I rather enjoy them. Much better than looking at dead bodies. So, how's your case going?"

My case? Up until now, it had been Benson's, and he was just the assistant. He glanced at the young patrolman who looked at him as if he was the stranger here. Muldoon remained awkwardly standing, hat in hand.

"It seems to be going well," Muldoon said. "I may be getting close to solving it."

"Good, good." Benson sat back down, elbows on the desk, and hands spread over the open files. "We're just going over the details of the new case . . . oh! You don't know Stanley, do you? He's just been appointed. He's going to be working with me for a while."

And, what's going to happen to me? Muldoon pictured himself back out on the beat, replaced by 'young Stanley.' The kid might be all of nineteen. He couldn't even remember being nineteen. For Muldoon, life seemed to begin with the war . . . and then he was old. Or felt like it, anyway.

"Robert Stanley," said the boy, just barely rising out of the chair, and leaning forward to shake Muldoon's hand.

Muldoon forced a smile to his face, but his muscles felt frozen. It was clear he was being pushed out. Captain Hayle had decided on the lesser of two evils—him or Benson—and he'd definitely lost. In a wry sort of way, he felt rather proud that he was the greater threat to Hayle's equilibrium.

"If that's all, Muldoon?" Benson began. "We really need to get back to work."

Muldoon smiled, a slow crooked smile. "Aye, Benson. But I do have something to ask you."

Benson raised his eyebrows expectantly.

"Have you found the footman?"

"Oh," Benson said. "That's right. No . . . no, I haven't had time, what with these other cases the Captain's loaded me down with."

Muldoon couldn't believe it. Benson had so quickly forgotten the importance of this case. But then, Kelly McAllister was Muldoon's problem . . . not the detectives'. He nodded slowly. "Well, that's all right. I'll take care of it."

As he stepped out, he pulled the door nearly shut behind him, but left it open just a crack as Benson liked it. He could hear the young officer whispering excitedly to Benson, asking him if that was really the famous William Muldoon.

His spirits were low. Benson had taken on a new assistant, and was busily tackling fresh cases. At least he seemed to enjoy them. He was better off with burglaries anyway, Muldoon rationalized. The man hated visiting the morgue—he left it to Muldoon time after time. Perhaps he would be happier now, maybe drink a bit less. But, that didn't help him with this case. He didn't even have O'Malley, since the Captain wouldn't let him off the beat. No. Muldoon would have to go back to the Hamm's himself and question the staff. It would take longer, going it alone. And time was growing short.

He walked out to Bowery Street, caught a streetcar and rode the long distance to 32nd. A gray, ominous looking sky threatened more rain. He hoped it would hold off until the evening, but he doubted it would. As long as he got to the Hamm's before it broke, he thought. He traced his footsteps of days before, but instead of entering by the front, he stepped through the gate, and walked to the back servant's entrance.

Even back here the path was neatly cobbled. As he rapped at the door the first drops of rain splashed down.

CHAPTER 37

A large, buxom woman opened the door. She looked him up and down slowly, taking in his uniform. "You must be the policeman," she said with a strong German accent. "We are expecting you. If you will come in, I shall send the little girl to get the butler."

Muldoon nodded, took off his cap, and carefully wiped his feet on the mat before entering the kitchen. It wouldn't do to get on this woman's bad side. As he stepped into the house, he found that the cook was nearly as tall as he was, and easily as broad. She turned to point at the long table with the knife in her hand.

"Sit over there," she said gruffly. "I have my work to do, and it doesn't stop just because a policeman comes in."

Muldoon sat. The woman sent the little scullery maid to find the butler, then turned back to the pile of vegetables at one end of the table. Expertly, she swung the knife and chopped potatoes, carrots, and onions into small portions. Looking at her, Muldoon reflected on the woman's size and obvious strength, the muscles in her forearms rippled as she worked. She was large enough to take on Muldoon himself, if she had the skill. And a lesser man would be an easy target for a woman her size . . . let alone a girl like Margaret. But why? What would the motive be? He couldn't easily see one. How much did she owe her employer? Would she kill for him?

"Have you been here long? I mean in the Colonel's employ?" he asked

"Yah." She said. "I have been here for fifteen years."

Most of Margaret's life, he thought. "So, you must have known the first Mrs. Hamm?"

A smile lit up her rigid expression. "She was so wonderful. She hired me, you know. I was just new to this country. That was back in '51. My father and mother had died, from the yellow fever. I was all alone, and I had no job. But I was a skilled cook, so I answered the advertisement. And then I stood in the line for so long, waiting for my turn to come in. And I was afraid that when she sees me, and I am not from America, that she would say no. But she didn't. She asked that I come again, and that I prepare my best meal for her. I had to wait almost a week. She had other cooks who were to come before me, and I was the last one on her list.

"So, I waited, and my money was running out. Then when I came back here, I cooked a roast leg of lamb. I remember that, because she told me lamb was her favorite. And then I got the job."

Muldoon digested the information. So, her main sense of loyalty was to the first Mrs. Hamm, not to the Colonel. But, that didn't mean it hadn't changed over the years. She may easily have transferred her regard to the man. But, would she have killed the only daughter of her beloved mistress?

"Where did you come from? In Germany?" He tried a different angle.

"Oh, I was a farm girl first. I grew up on a dairy."

"Must have been hard work."

"Yah!" she smiled at the memory. "It was very hard. When I was younger, I milked the cows with my sisters. But when I got bigger, I had to deliver the milk. I had to load the milk cans on a wagon, and then the dog would pull it. My father liked the best dogs, strong dogs. He got the first one from Switzerland. They were big black dogs, with short fur. Grosser Shvietzer Sennenhunds, they were. That is one thing I miss in this house. The dogs.

"And then my mother sent me to school. To learn to cook. She wanted a better life for me. So, I went to Berlin and I learned to cook. But then they were talking about making one united Germany. My father, he didn't like that idea. See, we lived in a small region, called Oldenburg. My father, he didn't want to be part of one country. He said Berlin would be the capital. So, he said we leave before it was too late. But, my mother, she said it would never happen. And look, they are still talking about it, so she was right. And now my parents are dead. I think we could have stayed, and been better for it. But, I have my job, and I am happy."

She smiled as she spoke. The memories were good ones, it seemed, except the loss of her parents. She scooped up the pile of vegetables and poured them into a dish of water, where she swished them about, giving them a final cleaning. Then, she placed them in a pot of fresh water for boiling.

Just then, the butler entered the big kitchen. Muldoon swung around to look at him as he spoke.

"Ah, so you have met Mrs. Grossman, our cook. I am Thomas Burnes, the butler. I have been asked to aid you in questioning the staff." The man was tall and thin, exactly the type of butler Muldoon suspected worked in every house on 5th avenue. They seemed to like a particular sort of person as butler, one who had probably once been a footman. That meant good looking, thin, with long legs—a man who looked good in tails. And, that's just what Mr. Burnes wore—a clean, fastidiously well kept black suit, the coat's long tails draping behind. Muldoon was glad he was too big to look like a butler when he dressed in his finery several days previous. His suit, and this man's, looked an awful lot alike.

"If you would care to follow me," said the butler, and turning on his heel, he walked stiffly away.

Muldoon followed him as they entered the man's office, just up the hall. It wasn't a large room, but it was well furnished. The desk and single guest chair were old, but highly polished. He could imagine them moved out of the Colonel's office upstairs and placed here when the Master purchased something new.

"You may use the desk," said the butler, though he sat down behind it. He waved toward an empty chair and indicated that Muldoon should sit. "I have asked the staff to line up outside the door as their duties allow. I, of course, shall remain here while you question them."

Nodding, Muldoon pulled out his small notebook and stubby pencil. He dragged the chair over and sat. Resting his elbow on the desk, and facing the door, he said he was ready to begin. Really, he thought, there was little use in questioning them. Aside from the cook, he didn't think he would find anyone here large enough to take on Schneider, nor with a motive. But, he still must go through the motions. He may find something he didn't expect, especially where the footman was concerned. He thought he could get that information from the butler.

The first servant entered the room tentatively. She was the young scullery maid from the kitchen.

"Sit." Muldoon pointed at the chair just inside the door.

She smiled at him, shakily. He knew there would be little she could tell him. He couldn't ask questions about the family. The butler would never allow that, so he had to steer clear of anything that might shed light on the condition of Miss Margaret Hamm and her relationship to the missing footman. As he expected, the girl's answers to his questions did not help him.

The next several people he questioned were all kitchen staff. He needed to thank Mrs. Grossman for her help. But a tiny corner of his mind wondered if she feigned cooperation to throw him off her as a suspect. No, he thought. She had no way of knowing he was looking for a large man . . . or woman.

Next was Mrs. Hamm's maid. She was a pretty woman of about twenty-five. Muldoon surveyed her with appreciation. Even in her demure outfit, she glowed with a natural sort of beauty. Her blonde hair was neatly pulled back into a bun, a cap atop her head. She bobbed a little curtsy, then stood quietly, waiting.

"This is Mary Stephens," said the butler. "She is personal maid to the Mistress."

"How long have you been in the household?" Muldoon said.

"Not too long, sir."

"She came when the mistress's former maid retired." The butler leaned forward in his chair. "That's been almost two years."

Muldoon nodded, and noted it in his book.

"Did you notice any particular attitude toward the young lady, Miss Margaret, from any of the staff?" Muldoon asked carefully.

"Oh, no sir! Everyone was always very respectful like."

"Can you tell me about the other staff members?" He tried again. "Anybody you didn't particularly care for?"

The butler cleared his throat, and the maid looked up from her hands, which she clasped tightly before her. "Um, no sir. Everyone is quite wonderful."

"How about the footmen? You're a particularly lovely woman. Have you suffered from any unwanted advances?"

She blushed prettily, her gaze dropping again. "No, sir. I . . . I mean, not recently. Not since Martin left us."

Muldoon hid his interest, writing carefully in his book for a moment. "Tell me about Martin," he said quietly.

"He . . . he was very handsome, but . . . I believe he thought too much of himself. He always tried to get the girls to go for him. But he should have known we are proper girls, we don't do things that . . . that he wanted us to do."

"Like what?" Muldoon asked. He knew she responded so properly, not because she was virtuous, but because Mr. Burnes sat at his side. It would be hard to get the full measure of the footman with witnesses who couldn't speak freely.

"Well, he would come up behind me when I was working, and put his arms around me, and try . . . and try . . . to kiss me."

Muldoon nodded with what he hoped was an understanding expression on his face. "And other girls had the same trouble?" he asked.

The maid nodded. "Some more than others." He could sense the pride in her voice as she said it, and he knew the man's attentions weren't altogether unappreciated.

"Thank you," Muldoon said. "That will be all."

The story was the same with each of the younger servant girls. Several were less proper than Mary Stephens had been, but each was mindful of the butler sitting beside Muldoon.

He got much the same from the rest of the staff—the older women, the less comely girls, and the men—each thinking Martin Shelby a bit full of himself. After the last one left the room, Muldoon turned to the butler.

"It seems they are unanimous in one thing," he said. "Their opinion of Martin Shelby."

The butler nodded silently.

"He was fired?" Muldoon asked, though he already knew the answer.

"Yes."

"When, exactly?"

"On the first day of the month," the butler said.

"And who did the firing? Yourself . . . or the Master?"

"The Master," Burnes studied his fingers where they lay on the desk.

"Was that unusual?" Muldoon asked. "Who normally tends to the hiring and the firing in this house?"

"I do, except for the kitchen staff. That would be Mrs. Grossman. But the Colonel was angry that day. He called for Martin, and the fellow just strode into the Master's office like he owned the world. And then we could hear the yelling. The Colonel shouted at him, and he back at the Colonel. It was scandalous. To think of a servant speaking like that to his employer. So, he was fired."

Muldoon studied the man as he spoke. He knew it reflected badly on Burnes. He had hired the man, and as it turned out, the footman was far less than suitable.

"Thank you for your help today," Muldoon said. "If you think of anything further, you can contact me at Police Headquarters on Mulberry."

"I'm certain that won't be necessary," Burnes said as he showed Muldoon to the door.

CHAPTER 38

COLONEL Hamm had little to add when Muldoon returned to question him later in the evening. "Martin Shelby seemed quite acceptable, at least in the beginning," the Colonel said. "And then the man began pestering the maids. They became increasingly agitated, and had a hard time completing their work. The whole household was in disarray."

"And that's why you fired him?" Muldoon asked.

"Yes. He just wasn't working out," answered the Colonel, sitting behind his large desk.

The Colonel's office was one any man would envy. The desk was a large, dark walnut, with polished slate inlay. Its sides were ornately decorated, matching the carving on the fireplace. His chair was dark leather, the same as the chair opposite, and a long sofa sat at a slight angle before the hearth. A small table stood on its other side, an African mask lying on top. A lion skin rug graced the floor, and zebra hung over the sofa back. Several animal heads adorned the walls—gazelle, tiger, and various African fauna. This was a man who thought of himself as a conqueror, an adventurer, a controller, he thought. Or one who wanted to be. Muldoon watched the Colonel as he fiddled with a small sculpture.

"Did he make these same advances toward your daughter?" Muldoon asked.

Colonel Hamm jerked back as though hit. "No! How could you suggest such a thing?" But, something in his manner told Muldoon that was untrue, at least as the Colonel believed it.

"I am merely looking for a motive, if indeed your footman is the murderer."

The Colonel sat back again, the blood returning to his face. "Yes. Yes, I see. Well then, perhaps he did look at her in some manner. But, he never went so far as to touch her. Not like he did with the staff."

"When did you become aware of these unwanted attentions?"

"I can't say that I did. But, it's logical, isn't it? That what he wanted from the maids, he also may have wanted from my daughter."

Muldoon thought so, too. "And, you were angry?"

"Angry enough to fire the bastard!"

Muldoon nodded, writing again in his book. "Were you angry at the girls, as well?"

"Of course," the Colonel replied. He set a match to his pipe, and slowly puffed. Smoke curled upward, as if creating a blind behind which the Colonel hid. But Muldoon was a hunter, too. "He might not have gotten so carried away if the girls hadn't encouraged him," he said between puffs. Pulling up their dresses so he could see their ankles, and then bending over provocatively. A man might not be able to help himself."

Was he angry with his daughter, too? Angry enough to kill? But, why send the very footman who had caused the problem in the first place?

"One more thing," Muldoon said, thoughtfully. "Have you ever seen a man with the appearance of red eyes at night?"

For the second time the Colonel looked as if he'd been hit. He sat back hard in his seat, and Muldoon thought he could see a slight tremor in the hands resting on the desk. "No." The single word contradicted Colonel Hamm's demeanor.

"You're certain?"

"Like a . . . like an albino? No. I've never seen anyone with red eyes. Now, if you don't mind, I've matters I must attend to."

Muldoon thanked the Colonel and took his leave. He slowly walked back over to Fourth Avenue and the streetcar. The rain fell full force now, but he didn't notice it. He reflected on what he had learned from the master of the house. In the morning, he would have to go looking for Martin Shelby. He had put out some feelers, but hadn't yet heard any replies. The man had simply vanished. Perhaps he had left the City, but somehow Muldoon didn't think so. And why had Colonel Hamm refused to speak of the crimson eyed man? His behavior betrayed him. He'd most definitely seen the man. Probably knew his identity. Martin Shelby. Red eyes. Are they just one man?

CHAPTER 39

AIMING for an empty table against the wall, Muldoon threaded his way through McSorley's Saloon. He checked his pocket watch. Not too long until Barney MacDougal should arrive. He sat with his back to the wall, and kept his eye on the door.

Where the hell is Martin Shelby? He hoped MacDougal had more luck looking for the man than he had. He couldn't see a connection between the footman and Schneider. Shelby could easily kill the girl and her maid, but even without seeing him, Muldoon didn't figure he was big enough to take care of Schneider. Footmen generally weren't. Once he found the man, he'd find out what the link was. Maybe jealousy? Had he hired someone to do the killing for him?

The door opened and the two gas lamps flickering above the bar sputtered wildly. A small, greasy man slipped into the seat across from him. Muldoon raised his hand and signaled to the servant girl across the room. She nodded, left the room, and returned just moments later with two thick beef sandwiches and bowls of split pea soup. She set them in front of Muldoon, accepting a few coins in payment.

"We'll eat first, you think?" Muldoon pushed a plate and bowl toward MacDougal.

The man licked his thin lips, and bobbed his head several times. Snatching the spoon, MacDougal sucked down great scoops of soup, followed by huge mouthfuls of torn bread and beef. Muldoon carefully chewed his own meal, keeping an eye on the snitch. The girl returned with two tankards of ale. The man grabbed his, and thirstily poured its contents down his throat. At long last, he leaned back, and swiped the back of one dirty hand across his lips, a loud belch escaping his mouth. It was probably the first decent meal he'd had in days, Muldoon thought.

"You treat me right," the man squeaked in a thin little voice.

"So, MacDougal," Muldoon gazed at him, head cocked slightly to one side. "What've you found for me?"

MacDougal was one of the best informants he had. But, the man liked to bide his time, stretching the story. He suspected the snitch thought he earned more that way.

"Weeellllll . . . " MacDougal drew out that one syllable, long and thoughtfully. His accent was raw, the hard sound of America's native poor. "I done looked all over this town. It was hard work, it was. I had to walk all across it, because I ain't got any ochre for a cab, nor the street-car." He looked expectantly at Muldoon, as though listening for the clink of coins in his pocket.

"I checked all down here, because that's where a fella would expect to find someone trying to hide out from the law. But, it wasn't no good. So, I went down to the wharf. I thought maybe as he'd caught a boat, and he was gone-like. But, no one recalled as he'd seen a guy that matched his description. So, I crossed town again, and checked in the village."

Muldoon knew the man hadn't gone to all these places himself. Barney MacDougal had a gang of kids. They were thieves and beggars, the lot of them. Like something out of one of the Charles Dickens stories the paper ran. No doubt, MacDougal assigned each a district where the "kiddies" would ask for help finding a missing father, or sister, or puppy. They brought in odd lots of coins and trinkets expertly removed from men's pockets, or off women's wrists. "For the cause," as MacDougal said. And they brought information.

He shifted his eyes greedily toward Muldoon's unseen pocket, below the level of the table between them. "There wasn't a clue where the fella could've got to," he continued.

Muldoon's shoulders slumped, just a fraction. If he'd been in different company, he might have sighed. He had pinned hope on MacDougal's ring of urchins.

"Heh, heh, heh," the greasy man snickered. "Gotcha there, didn't I?"

Muldoon failed to see the humor, but he waited expectantly.

"Seems I hadn't checked the hospitals. So, I figured that's where I should go next. And you know what I found? A fella that looks an awful lot like the one you want. So, I tells myself, my friend Muldoon'll be interested in this fella."

Muldoon couldn't stop the slow spread of a smile as it moved across his face.

"But it mightn't be what you expect," MacDougal added, with a small smile of his own.

Sliding his hand out of his pocket Muldoon set several coins on the table and pushed them across to MacDougal. The little man snatched them quickly, thrusting them deep into his own pants pocket. With a smile, he touched his fingertip to his nose, rubbing it lightly, turned on his heel, and walked jauntily away. He did have his pride, Muldoon thought, MacDougal having indicated his position as a "nose," or spy, rather than a mere informant, or a snitch, with that momentary touch of his nose.

Muldoon left the pub, heading toward the East River and City Hospital. The hospital had been built on Blackwell's Island some years before. Though beautifully constructed, it was poorly administered, and had fallen into disfavor, treating illnesses like smallpox and paralysis. A patient in City Hospital almost never returned to society. Muldoon wondered in what condition he would find his suspect.

The island was inaccessible except by steamship. He had little trouble catching the first one available. He watched as the beautiful island grew large, reflecting on the irony of it. It was a pastoral scene set in the center of the city, but the island was far from idyllic. Instead, it was home to institutions—a prison, the hospital, and an asylum. There should have been a wagon waiting to take any paying visitors to one establishment or another. It was missing. He glanced up at the sky. The ever-present clouds hung low, but he didn't know how long it would be before the coach returned, so he chose to walk. He strode quickly toward the hospital, hoping to beat the rain. He wondered what he would find on this island of the forgotten, and the dying.

Muldoon entered the shadowed recess of City Hospital. "May I help you?" a young woman behind the front desk looked up from her paperwork. She wore a modest gray dress under a crisp white apron. Her mousy pale brown hair was pulled into a tight knot at the back of her head, just below a starched white cap. Despite the severity of her appearance, her features weren't altogether displeasing.

"I'm looking for a man, somebody I think might be a patient here," Muldoon said.

"A patient?" She glanced at his dark blue uniform.

"Aye," he answered. "A man name of Martin Shelby."

The nurse nodded briskly, and turned to her log, glancing rapidly through the list of patient's names. "There isn't anyone by that name," she said at last.

He leaned over the high desk and scanned the list, leaving little to chance. He refused to feel disappointment. MacDougal had found somebody here that matched his description, and Muldoon wouldn't leave until he had satisfied himself that the man was, indeed, not here.

"I'd like to see these," he said, pointing to several 'Unknown's.

"I . . . I'll have to ask the attending physician." The woman turned slightly pink. "You can't just go walking around the wards. It would disturb the patients." Again, she looked at his uniform. He knew she was right. Many of the patients would be afraid they were the object of his search. He waited impatiently as she went to find the doctor.

A few moments later, she reappeared, accompanied by a short round man.

"I am Doctor Dearing," he said with a pompous, but thin and wheezy, tone of voice. "What can I help you with?"

"I'm here for a Martin Shelby." Muldoon hoped his impatience wouldn't show through his thinly pasted veneer of calm. He needed to persuade this man to allow him access to the wards. "He may be a witness to a murder."

"As you know, we have nobody here by that name . . . " began the fat doctor, waving his hand vaguely toward the nurse's station. He removed his round spectacles, and wiped them furiously with his handkerchief.

"But there are several "unknowns" on your list."

Doctor Dearing replaced his glasses, setting them carefully on his protruding nose. He looked uncomfortably up at Muldoon, then pushed the glasses into a steadier position.

"Let me just take a look at the list," he said at last, realizing Muldoon wasn't going away.

His fat little finger traced each name as the doctor read through the list. Finally, he turned to Muldoon. "I think we can let you take a look at a few patients. But, you must have an escort. I can't have you traipsing through the place unaccompanied. There's no telling what damage you could do!"

Muldoon smiled, a slow smirk really, at the low opinion the man had of the City Police. He knew that opinion was probably shared by most of New York's inhabitants, rich and poor alike. An honest cop was a rare commodity.

"Nurse Duncan." The doctor turned to the nurse, who hovered nervously behind him. "Go find a girl to escort him."

"Yes, Doctor." She nearly ran from the room. She's afraid of him, Muldoon thought. The small, round man didn't seem threatening, but he appeared to run the place with an iron fist.

"You wait here, Sergeant," the doctor ordered. "I have patients to attend to. Nurse Duncan will bring someone to guide you to your little list of unknowns."

"Thank you."

The doctor harrumphed loudly, turned on his heel, and strode from the room. Alone in the entrance hall, Muldoon took the time to look over the list again. There were just four 'unknown' men on the sheet, compared to nearly five times as many women. Who were they all, he wondered? People who had just disappeared from the world— unwanted, unneeded, and unloved? And if they died, they would be buried in a pauper's grave, nothing but a number above their head.

He turned to the clicking of heels as Nurse Duncan returned, followed closely by a young black woman. The girl was tall and thin, her gray dress and white apron just an echo of the nurse's, the fabric faded, the white yellowed. They had obviously been cast-off, remade to fit the girl. The cloth hung limply from her skeletal figure. She looked at Muldoon with huge dark eyes.

"Mazey's the only one that can be spared at the moment," said the nurse, with new-found authority. "Now, please be quick about it."

"Aye, Ma'am," Muldoon said. He'd be quick. He didn't want to spend any more time in this hospital than necessary.

"If you please, sir," said Mazey, in a light, breathy voice. "Come this way." She turned, and beckoned Muldoon to follow her. They didn't speak as they walked through the halls. Though it was only ten years old, the building was rapidly deteriorating. Paint was already peeling from the walls. The floors were clean enough, but they were darkened in the corners, the buildup of years of grime that had gone unscrubbed, receiving only a cursory cleaning each day. As they passed through open wards, the gaze of glassy eyes followed him curiously. Some held terror, others just hollow, wracked with pain and illness.

"There's one there." Mazey pointed at a still figure near the end of a large open ward. The man lay on his side, blanket pulled up tight under his chin. Muldoon stepped around the cot, where he could see the face of the fitfully resting man. His spirits rose suddenly, could this be him? The man was fair, ash blonde hair spilling over his forehead. Light stubble covered his chin. Muldoon bent down close, but he couldn't make out the features under the beard.

"Can we wake him?"

"Yes," Mazey said. "He's got to be moved every now and again. Get his sheets changed." She waved at another girl busily scrubbing floors across the room, the strong scent of vinegar came from her pail of water.

"What you want?" asked the girl as she hurried over. She pushed a stray braid under the scarf tied over her curly black hair.

"Got to get this one up. May as well change his sheets now."

"Isn't it a bit early? The doctor might be angry."

"Maybe," Mazey faltered. "But Nurse Duncan says it's important to change them. She says that Miz Dorothea Dix says it makes them get better."

The other girl nodded, and then hurried from the room to get the sheets. Mazey leaned toward the patient. She placed a hand lightly on his shoulder. "Sir," she said quietly. "Sir, we got to make your bed."

The man slowly rolled over and looked at Mazey. Disappointment filled Muldoon. The man's eyes were blue. He was looking for an almost green hazel. He shook his head as Mazey gazed up at him. She patted the man's shoulder again, whispered quietly to him. Muldoon could just make out a few words, enough to know she was assuring him that the policeman wasn't there for him. He wasn't sure she'd needed to say anything. The man's expression remained blank as he looked, uncomprehendingly, into her eyes.

The other girl returned with a set of sheets in her arms, a second girl in tow. As they neared, Mazey turned back to Muldoon. "We'll go look at the next one."

Again, he was disappointed. They had entered the amputee ward. The 'unknown' lay quietly in a cot near the window, both legs removed below the knee.

"He was run over by a wagon," she explained, noticing Muldoon's eyes drop to the man's legs. "He's never waked, yet."

Muldoon nodded, but he wouldn't need to see this one's eyes. His hair was dark.

"Let's take a look at the third," he said. But he, too, was dark, as was the fourth.

Frustrated, Muldoon turned away from the last patient. His informant had been wrong. There was nobody here that matched Shelby's description. Perhaps that first man was the one he had referred to?

"I'm sorry you didn't find your man, sir," said Mazey, lightly touching Muldoon's elbow. Quickly she pulled her hand back, embarrassed by her audacity.

"Aye," he said. "I'm sorry, too."

They walked quietly through the halls, back toward the front entrance. "If you don't mind," she began, timidly. Muldoon turned to her, slowing his stride.

"Aye?"

"If you would tell me what he looks like, your man?"

"Tall and fair, dark blonde hair. His eyes are a greenish brown . . . and he has a slight cleft chin."

Mazey stopped, one hand held out in a little gesture, palm outward, fingers slightly bent. "We did have a patient like that!" she exclaimed. "But he's gone, now."

Muldoon's heart leapt, and then dropped to his feet with sudden disappointment.

The girl laughed lightly, a soft, tinkling sound. "Don't go looking like that," she said. "He is just over at the asylum."

Relief washed over him, and excitement again. He was close, so close.

"We never got his name, though. And he gets mad, like. So, the Doctor sent him over there."

Muldoon could kiss her! "Thank you, Mazey," he settled for instead, reaching out to take her hand. He squeezed it lightly. "You've really helped me."

As they reached the front door, he placed his flat policeman's hat back on his head, tipped it first to the nurse, and then to Mazey. The girl smiled shyly, a little giggle bursting from her lips. The nurse frowned at her, disapprovingly.

"You have work to do," she ordered. "I'm sure there's a floor to be scrubbed, or a bedpan to empty."

Spinning quickly, Mazey hurried from the room. The door clicked shut behind Muldoon, and he was back out in the cool spring air. Somewhere a bird called, a long mournful tone. Though it was in the middle of the city, the island almost lulled him into feeling as if he were in the country.

The asylum was beyond the prison. The prisoners, he knew, often helped at the asylum, cleaning, or helping to control aggressive patients. Mazey had said his man could be violent. He wondered what he could learn from him. Could his madness be the cause of the two murders? Somehow, Muldoon didn't think so. The girl had been carefully posed, her appearance well thought out. A man given to violent tirades was unlikely to have left her that way. Yet, the way both Karl Schneider and Margaret Hamm had been murdered, an arm about the neck, quick crushing pressure . . . certainly, a madman might do that.

As he approached the asylum he noticed the pleasingly arranged green trees and shrubs. They gave the appearance of a retreat, instead of a home for the hopelessly insane. The blue river flowed by, dotted with boats and an occasional steamship calmly plying the waters. The far bank was lined with stately mansions. He turned to the asylum. He knew it would be like walking into darkness from light.

He felt a sense of déjà vu as he entered, but the nurse behind the desk was heavy-set, a thick-jowled face sitting atop even wider neck and shoulders. She looked up as he entered, her watered-blue pig eyes glancing over his uniform.

"Man, or woman?" she asked flatly.

"Pardon?"

"Man, or woman? Nobody comes here unless they're looking for someone . . . or dropping them off." She looked him up and down a second time. "Since you're a copper . . . and you're obviously not dropping anyone off . . . then you're looking for someone. So. Now. Man, or woman?"

"Man," Muldoon said. She'd be only too happy to release a patient into his charge he thought. Usually it was the other way around. The police picked up the insane, and locked them into the Tombs. Then they were transported to the asylum, where they languished forever, or became well. Most, he knew, would die there. "I'm looking for a man named Martin Shelby."

The woman scanned her list of names, as had the nurse at City Hospital. "Ah yes," she said. This time, Muldoon wasn't disappointed. "The man brought over from the hospital. Came in with no name, but we got it yesterday. Some other man come by asking for him. The doctor, he calls in at him, and the 'unknown' turned to his name. It's him alright. So, we wrote in his name. Funniest thing, though. The other man, he didn't want to see him. Just wanted to know if he was here."

MacDougal, making sure I know the value of his information, thought Muldoon. The man had let him go to the hospital first, knowing Shelby was in the asylum. An extra coin more might have bought the right hospital.

The matron rang the bell, and Muldoon waited impatiently for the nurse to arrive. It was a large man, though, who entered the room. "This here is Daniel," the matron said by way of introduction. "He's from the prison, but he's one of our best. Takes care of the violents right well!"

Daniel tugged on his bangs, as though tipping a hat. "Sergeant," the man drawled, slight disrespect in his tone.

"Take the sergeant to see Mr. Shelby." The matron's eyes flashed with irritation at his behavior. The man nodded, quenching his rebellious look. The benefits he'd earned through good behavior could be erased at a moment's notice. Muldoon regarded her watery eyes with new respect. He knew the man would have to work hard to assure her it had only been a momentary slip.

Daniel beckoned for Muldoon to follow him. The matron glared pointedly at his hat as Muldoon passed her desk, but he only winked at her. He wasn't her inmate. He would keep it on his head.

There were no iron bars or metal doors in the asylum. The place had been sturdily built, but continued its pretense of health retreat on the inside as well as out. Doors were heavy and solid, and a big man, a guard, unlocked each as Muldoon and his escort approached, allowing them to move between wards. As he crossed through the place, he noticed the windows were barred, even though at first glance it did not appear so. They had been cleverly crafted, the bars disguised as metal frame between small, square glass panes.

"Martin Shelby," grunted Daniel, gesturing toward a closed door. Muldoon leaned forward and peered through a small viewing panel set in the center of the door. A man sat inside the shadowed room. He wore matching blue pants and shirt, nearly identical to the clothing worn by the other patients he had passed.

"He's violent?" Muldoon asked.

"At times," Daniel said. "Can't never tell what's going to set him off."

Muldoon nodded. Turning back to the window again, he asked, "can I talk to him?"

"Got to ask the doctor."

Daniel shuffled over to the desk where a couple of men played cards. They spoke quietly for a few moments, then one man hurried from the room. Daniel walked back slowly. "Got to wait. Doc's in his office. But Mac went to get him."

"Sure." He continued his silent perusal of the man in the room. Shelby sat quietly, making no sound or motion. He leaned back against the wall, legs drawn up under him, feet to one side. His arms were tight against his chest, protectively. His face devoid of expression, he showed no horror, no sadness, no anger . . . nothing.

Footsteps behind Muldoon signaled the arrival of the doctor. This one was completely opposite Dr. Dearing. He was tall and extraordinarily thin. He too, wore glasses, big things, on a pinched in face. A tired, harried expression occupied his features.

"I'm Doctor Moore. So, you're here for Shelby?" His voice was tired, too.

"Aye."

"Did he do something? Or are you here on behalf of his family?" The doctor looked pointedly at Muldoon's uniform.

"That's to be determined by this interview."

The doctor nodded, and then drew a thick set of keys from his pocket. Placing one in the lock, he pulled open the door, then motioned for Daniel to enter first. "We can't be too sure, with this one," he mouthed almost inaudibly.

Shelby turned his head just a fraction, the small movement an acknowledgement of their presence, but his eyes were occupied elsewhere. They remained riveted to some far-distant location only he could see.

"Martin," said the doctor, soothingly, taking a seat beside his patient on the lone bed. In the crowded institution, only the violents had their own room. A necessity, Muldoon surmised, protecting one patient from the hands of another.

Shelby tried to focus on the doctor.

"A man is here to see you," The doctor gestured slightly toward Muldoon.

Shelby didn't respond, just glanced downward towards the doctor's hand, where it hung in midair.

"He's very unresponsive," the doctor said. "I don't know if he'll ever get better."

"Tell me about him." Muldoon watched the ill man intently.

"He was just transferred a couple of days ago. He was at City Hospital. He'd been there about two weeks."

"Why was he there?" Muldoon noted the bruises on the man's face.

"He was beaten, very badly, but he recovered quickly. Not so, in his mind. He couldn't speak. He still only makes mumbling sounds, and then only when he's angry. He's most audible when angry. But he just repeats the same thing over and over again."

Muldoon raised his eyebrows inquiringly.

"Three. That's what it sounds like, anyway."

"Three?" asked Muldoon, baffled.

Suddenly Shelby's demeanor changed, his head shifted sharply as he turned to glare at Muldoon. "Three!" he shrieked, leaping from the ground and throwing himself across the small space. "Three!"

Daniel stepped in as Muldoon prepared to receive the blow, and caught Shelby tight around the waist. Something small dropped from the man's hands, skittered across the floor, and stopped to rest just short of the door. Muldoon stooped over to pick up the object while Daniel struggled to control the violent man. It looked vaguely familiar to him. He held it up and showed it to the doctor as the man ushered him out of the room, leaving Daniel inside. A second man pushed into the room, a straight-jacket in hand.

Martin Shelby struggled madly. "Three," he yelled again. "Three to one makes four. Three to one makes four. Three to one makes four. My little lamb. My poor little lamb. Three to one makes four." His words became garbled, until inaudible, just a long, anguished shriek emanated from his mouth.

"He's making some progress," the doctor said. "That's the most he's been able to say since he arrived."

Muldoon turned to the doctor. "What's this?" he asked.

"It's his lovie. As long as he has it, he's calm. He holds onto it tightly, like it signifies something important for him."

Muldoon looked at the short, chunky piece of whittled wood, one end broken. And suddenly he realized what it was. It was the stubby end of a longer piece of wood . . . and on the missing part would be the initials "A.R." But this piece lacked the distinctive swirls of the other two. As she inspected it closer he could see the beginnings of the design on the broken end. He looked in again at the struggling man, now howling as if in pain. The new attendant had wrestled Shelby's arms into the straight-jacket, and was pulling the cord tight. Shelby's face turned a violent shade of red as he screamed.

Could he have done it? Muldoon wondered. He was a tall man, but thin and elegantly built. He would look handsome opening a carriage door, or serving a tray at dinner. But he didn't have the build necessary to take on a man with the size and experience of Karl Schneider. No, he realized it couldn't have been Shelby. He had been hired, certainly. And somewhere, locked away in that horrified mind was the key to this case. Who had paid him to lure the young Margaret Hamm from the safety of her uncle's home? Had he known that she would be killed? He thought not. His 'poor little lamb' was probably Miss Margaret. And if her child was his, then perhaps he had loved her. That might account for his present condition. Then, the third marker, the murderer's calling card. Was a third victim yet to come? Or did the killer consider the black maid to be the third?

Shelby's scream had unsettled him, and he thought again of Meg McAllister's prophecy. She had said six. God, were there really six murders? Shelby said three plus one makes four. The maid could be the third victim he was counting. She had been killed during the kidnap. What had happened he wondered? Had the murderer met them at the train? But three plus one makes four? What the hell? His head began to ache, and the familiar yearning behind his heart began. He pushed away the scent of whiskey that existed only for him. He pushed away Meg's prophecy. He didn't believe in it. And then he pushed away the flicker of the oil lamp on the wall as it threatened to grow into flames in Pensacola and the cries of the insane ringing through the halls of the asylum tried to become cries of terror . . . women and children burning alive. And then he turned away from the soldier passing through the hall, his eyes fixed accusingly on Muldoon.

He slipped the wood piece into his pocket, shaking his head at the doctor. "It's evidence," he said. "If you can break into that mind, I'll find the answers I'm looking for."

"I don't think it'll happen," the doctor said.

"I didn't think so. But send for me if it does."

As Muldoon rode the steamship away from the island, he pondered his case. He had pinned so much hope on Shelby, thought he might be the murderer. Now, he knew, he'd followed the wrong lead. Not wrong, he amended. Shelby had been part of it. But his wasn't the mind behind the thing. He would have to think on it anew. He reached into his pocket, and pulled out his small pad. He flipped through his entries, wondering what he had missed. If he didn't find the murderer soon, another person would die . . . and he still didn't know the connection between Karl Schneider and Margaret Hamm. Somehow, he thought, it was something larger than either of them. And Saturday was hanging day.

CHAPTER 40

ALVA stepped out of her carriage, lightly taking hold of the footman's hand as he helped her down. She opened her parasol to protect her pale skin from the early spring sunlight. She knew it was vain, but she knew, too, that her looks were important in order to attract her future husband. Her maid followed close behind her. The footman always seemed to pay the girl special attention. Alva smiled as she realized he probably loved the girl. She ignored the little gestures that passed between the two, pretending she hadn't seen. The servants would be horrified if they knew she noticed these things. For some reason, they thought they were invisible. Perhaps they were, in other people's homes. Personally, she rather enjoyed the intricacies of their lives.

She sighed. The footman opened the door to yet another wigmakers' shop. The servants must wonder what it's all about, she thought. She could just imagine the whispering in the servants' quarters that evening. But, she wanted to do what she could to help find her friend's killer. When Muldoon had suggested she find out if Margaret Hamm's hair had gone to a wigmaker's, she had been appalled. Then she realized it made sense. Who would throw away valuable hair? But, would she recognize it? Certainly, she knew the color, but hundreds of women might have the same shade. Still, she had to try.

She entered the little shop with distaste. She had already made the rounds of the better establishments, and was working her way through the less significant shops. The proprietor was a thin, angular woman, with horsey teeth protruding from between her lips as she smiled. She came around the counter as Alva entered—all charm and helpfulness.

"Welcome, welcome!" The woman hurried to her side. "May I show you the best of my wares?"

She indicated a full wig on a stand. The hair was expertly coiffed, though a bit thin, ringlets falling below the shoulders. "This would simply look marvelous," she coaxed.

"No," Alva shook her head, her own ringlets bouncing prettily. "I'm not looking for me."

"Ah! You have a wonderful head of your own hair?" She moved slowly around Alva, surveying the girl's coiffure. "Perhaps you'd care to see some extensions?"

"Again, I must respond in the negative," said Alva smoothly. "I'm looking for something special. Something blonde. Not just any shade, but the palest of blondes, with just a touch of honey."

"You need it for a special occasion? A masquerade, perhaps?"

"It's a scavenger hunt," said Alva repeating the tired story she'd rehearsed. She smiled with feigned brightness, and twirled the now-closed parasol.

"Oh, I see!" the woman smiled gaily. "It's a game."

She strolled slowly about the room, pointing out hair piece after hair piece, but Alva was particular. It had to be just the right shade.

"Curled . . . or straight?" asked the proprietress suddenly, her wide mouth drooping just a bit as she thought.

"Naturally straight," answered Alva. "Though you may have curled it. And very, very long."

Suddenly the woman turned, one hand in the air. "I may have just the piece!" she exclaimed, eyes bright.

Alva smiled back, her heart pattering hopefully. The woman indicated the back door. Her skirts swished as she swayed over to open it.

"My girls are up here," she said.

Alva carefully ascended the steep staircase, and held her skirt high to avoid stepping on the fabric that was piled along the sides of each step. At the top of the stairs, a small front room held a tall cabinet and a desk. A Chinese man sat there, a long, empty pipe between his lips. He leaped up to open the door for her, bowing several times. The back room was poorly lit, long tables placed near the south-facing windows to gather as much light as they could. At each table sat a Chinese woman, some merely girls, others ancient old women. Carefully, each woman threaded a piece of hair into a needle and stitched it into a thin leather cap. Strand by strand, each hair was knotted securely. Then the process was repeated with yet another natural thread.

The first girl, Alva noticed, was creating tiny wigs with short bits of hair, pieces left over after styling.

"What are these?" She waved her hand toward the tiny wigs.

"Ah Miss," the woman fawned. "These will be sold to doll makers. Only the best, only the best."

As she gazed about the room, Alva was horrified to note how many boxes were filled with hair. They were separated by color and quality. Longer hair was much more valuable, she was certain. As she strode through the room, she imagined the dire situation that would force a woman to sell her hair. For a mere pittance, she would be shorn of her locks. Her hand strayed to the edge of a box. Several sections of dark, nearly black hair filled it, much the same color as her own. Each was banded at the top where the ends were neatly cut. A second band held the clump together at its center, and a third held it tight at the base. She pictured tears in some poor woman's eyes as she left the shop, a paltry sum in her hand, but maybe enough to feed her children that night.

She had never been so close to poverty. She shook her head, trying to clear the unwanted image from her mind.

"Beautiful, isn't it?" The proprietress clapped her hands. "Perhaps we could make this up for you? It matches your own hair perfectly."

A pretty Chinese girl smiled shyly, and bobbed a quick bow, then pulled the thick lock from the box. She draped it across her hands and held it up to the light where it streamed in through the greasy window. Alva shook her head and moved slowly toward the next table. An old woman sat there, her gnarled fingers pulling hair into place. Alva was appalled to think of the amount of work these women put into the hair pieces that she, and others like her, bought and cast aside on a whim. She would bring it up at her next lady's reform meeting.

The last table held pale blonde hair. She paused a moment, and glanced into the box. Each section was carefully banded, but none was right. They were either too curly, or too short. She shook her head.

As she turned to go, the proprietress opened a cabinet. "Oh, I have one more. I nearly forgot," she said. "A man brought it in a few days ago. But the color is so unusual, and it's wonderfully long. I just haven't decided what to do with it yet."

Long, honey-blonde hair. Horror-struck, Alva gazed upon the long hair in the woman's hands. She could see a pale pink ribbon woven into a thin braid. The little decoration hung absurdly from the band wrapped around the top of the lock. She stepped forward, drawn to the image, as if in a dream. She raised one trembling hand, but didn't touch it. She knew that braid—it was Margaret's. She'd worn her hair long, pulled back with a ribbon, with just that one thin braid. It was her everyday style. The one she wore when she was at home.

"Is that unusual?" Alva asked quietly. "To have a man bring in a hair piece?"

"Yes, it is rather," the woman answered. "But the quality is so good. It's worth top value."

Alva nodded. She could see the woman was right. She, herself, had bought such hair, though in a much darker shade.

"What did he look like?" asked Alva, her voice a near whisper. Clearing her throat, she continued, stronger now. "For the game, in case they ask."

Carefully she wrote down the description, and then paid the woman's price for the mass of hair. A girl wrapped it in a paper parcel, and Alva wrote Muldoon's name and address on it. She couldn't bear to carry it with her, except for the thin braid, which was deftly removed by the Chinese girl. That, she would take to Margaret's parents when they were ready for it. The rest of the hair would be delivered to Muldoon.

CHAPTER 41

No matter how many times Muldoon flipped through it, nothing he'd written in his notebook drew him any closer to learning the identity of the killer. He had a new sense of urgency, knowing that another person would die soon, perhaps already had. No, he thought. If another person had died, the body would have been dropped at the corner of Cross, where the thoroughfare entered Paradise Park. Or would it? He wondered. The first two bodies were for show, he knew that now. They had been placed on the street as a message for someone. Was it a warning to the next target? Or was there another reason the dead were brought to that spot . . . perhaps so the killer could watch from a safe distance as he, Muldoon, investigated the scene?

He wanted to talk with Benson, just to go over the elements of the case. But, the detective was busy with the burglaries that the Captain had thrown his way . . . accompanied by his new assistant. Muldoon wondered if he'd ever looked like that, so young and eager. He doubted it. He couldn't even remember feeling that way—certainly not since before the war. Maybe that's how he'd looked when he'd set out for Florida so many years before.

When he got back from Blackwell's Island, he'd gone down to the crime scene, and looked it over once again. Still, nothing sprang to his mind. He turned the clues over again and again, but they made no sense to him. The connection just wasn't there. They seemed like two distinct murders. That's how the Captain would see them. They just happened to be dumped at the same location. The chunky wooden sticks with the initials carved into them? Perhaps he'd simply missed the one under the window the night Schneider was killed. It may have laid there those couple of days, and maybe it wasn't even related to Margaret Hamm's murder. But, he couldn't believe he'd missed it! He backtracked in his mind. Somewhere, somehow, he'd missed something. Finally, he returned to Headquarters, tired and depressed. Detective Benson still wasn't about.

Muldoon leaned against Foley's desk, his weight heavy on his elbows. He knew the man couldn't help him, but he could commiserate a bit. He didn't go into any details, because too many things were twisted around in his brain.

"Having troubles?" sneered a voice behind him.

Muldoon spun about as Sergeant Collins crossed the room.

"You got one little case, and you can't figure it out?" Collins lips split apart in a replica of a smile.

"Nothing holding me back." Muldoon leaned nonchalantly, in what he hoped was a carefree pose, against the desk. "I've nearly got it figured out."

Collins chortled. "Sure, sure. I suppose you'll be marching upstairs to tell that to the Captain?"

"Aye." He wasn't ready, but he'd be damned if he told Collins that.

He caught a motion at the top of the steps, from the direction of Hayle's office. "I'll be out, Foley," Muldoon said quickly and ducked out the front door. Behind him, he could hear the trill of Collins' laughter.

He walked aimlessly, not knowing where to go next. He'd never felt so helpless in his life. At least he'd had a gun in his hand when he'd been in the war. He thought about Schneider. What had his search of the room told him? Not much. But he'd brought several things out with him. The stick . . . the killer's calling card. Some expensive wine. He thought about that for a moment. How had the man afforded such wine? Perhaps from his wrestling earnings? Certainly, that's how Muldoon purchased luxuries. But, could he afford such items? What about Schneider's clothing? He had well-tailored suits, and expensive gloves. Not all his clothes were so good. But, as he thought about it, he couldn't remember Schneider ever wearing the rough broadcloth that Muldoon usually wore. And, his own fights brought in top dollar. Perhaps it was time to look up that sister.

Benson had gone to let her know her brother had been killed. He'd said there was little chance that she'd had a hand in his murder, that she just wasn't the type. Now, Muldoon stood outside her modest home. It was a thin brownstone, ancient, built before the Revolution. The neighborhood was good, if a bit rundown, with spring flowers blooming in window boxes, and in urns set beside the door. He climbed the steps and knocked lightly, as if afraid to disturb the tranquility of the neighborhood. The curtains pulled to the side just a fraction, and a pretty, blonde-haired woman peeked out the window. Suddenly, the door flew open, and an old woman stepped aggressively out the door.

"You folks should leave her alone!" she exclaimed in a thick German accent. "She knows nothing about it!"

Muldoon stepped back. "Excuse me," he said, surprised. "I was just coming to show my respect."

The woman eyed him doubtfully. He glanced down, and realized her glare was directed at his uniform.

"I'm not here on official business. I'm William Muldoon, the wrestler." One little bend of the truth, he thought, just to get him in the door.

"Oh," she said. Then "OH! Come in, come in," and she held the door wide. She showed him into the small parlor at the front of the house.

"Gretchen," she called.

A few moments later, a young woman, perhaps seventeen, entered the room. "Yes, Mother," she said. Her diction was flawless, genteel. There was no hint of the German accent so evident in the older woman's voice.

"This is the wrestler your brother spoke about," she said. "William Muldoon. He has come to show his respects."

"Thank you," the girl said. "So few people have come. Just the policemen."

He allowed her to reminisce about her brother for a few moments. He hadn't actually liked the man. He didn't want to overstay his welcome, and it was getting close to dinner. If he stayed much longer, the women would feel obliged to ask him to stay, and politeness would require him to accept. Quickly, he posed the question he most wanted to ask.

"Are you set?" he asked. There was simply no other way to ask, no delicate way to put it. "Has your brother left you in good condition? Financially, I mean?"

"That is so good of you, to be concerned. But no, we don't need your help." The old lady had misunderstood him. "Karl left an inheritance. It's enough to maintain this house, and also to provide a nice dowry for Gretchen."

"I'm so glad. That takes a great weight off my mind," he lied, and tipped his head as if hurt they'd declined his offer.

He stood, and took his hat from the seat next to him. "I'm sorry," he said. "I only had a moment. Really, I have to get back."

The two women rose, and followed him to the door. Taking each by the fingers, he lightly kissed the back of their hands, first the girl, then her mother. They giggled like schoolgirls at his gesture. What a picture, he thought. The copper acting the part of a gentleman. Someday, he promised himself, he'd be wearing top hat and tails when he kissed a girl's hand.

As he walked down the street, he wondered where Schneider had come by his money. He certainly couldn't afford a brownstone, so how could Schneider? Not on his wrestling money, that was certain. The highest paid wrestler in this town was himself. He placed his hand in his jacket pocket, and lightly rubbed the bible he kept there. He pulled it out, and gazed down on its blue leather binding. Slowly, he began thumbing through the pages. He hadn't done so before, other than to flip quickly through for some loose bit of paper slipped between the pages. There hadn't been anything. He didn't know what he was looking for now, but he had nothing else.

His pace had slowed to a near halt when he found it. Pencil markings written in the margin. It wasn't particularly unusual for a man to write in his book, but this was a Bible, and he hadn't seen any other marks. He read the verse. Deuteronomy 20. "When you march up to attack a city, make its people an offer of peace." It made little sense to him, aside from its biblical context. He studied the marks written there. First was a long rectangle. Inside was a vague sketch of an eagle. It looked to him like the shoulder insignia of a Colonel. Next to it were several hash marks. The following pages showed the same hash marks, though the insignia wasn't repeated.

He puzzled over this for a moment . . . realization slowly dawned. Perhaps this was the connection. Quickly he signaled for a cab, leaped in, and directed the driver to the home of Colonel Hamm.

CHAPTER 42

THE Colonel didn't see him at first. The butler had shown him into the man's office, a disapproving frown on his face. The family was at dinner, so Muldoon waited. Nearly forty-five minutes later Colonel Hamm entered the room. He walked slowly to his desk, opened a humidor, and selected a cigar. He didn't offer one. Then, he motioned toward the sturdy leather chairs before the fireplace.

"What have you found?" asked the man as he lowered himself into a chair.

Muldoon sat, too. He admired the Colonel's poise during such distress. "Tell me about Schneider," he said.

Eyebrows raised, the Colonel gazed across the cigar held loosely between his teeth, struck a match, and touched it to the other end. He puffed slowly, drew in the aromatic smoke, and let it out in a cloud of gray.

"I know you paid him off," said Muldoon. He really wasn't certain, but he played the hunch.

Lowering the cigar, Colonel Hamm sighed heavily, resigned. "Yes, I knew the man."

"He was blackmailing you?"

"In a way. But he felt it was owed him."

Now it was Muldoon's turn to raise an eyebrow. He settled back in the chair.

"It was during the war," the Colonel said. "I was just a major, then. Karl Schneider was a sergeant."

He glanced up at a picture above the mantle, an oil portrait of himself in uniform.

"Twelfth New York Cavalry," he said proudly, yet tinged with something darker. "We went to North Carolina, and were stationed at New Bern. There wasn't much action down there, at least nothing we didn't create for ourselves. So, we raided. It was our main activity. We would leave our little enclave and scour the countryside for secessionists. Not all of us together, but in small units. Perhaps four or five at a time. We hit them fast, burned them out, and got back. You have to realize . . . I was just a young officer."

Muldoon reached into his pocket and tapped the dead man's bible. The Colonel hadn't been that young, he thought. He didn't speak, but let the story go where it would. The Colonel talked long into the night, reminiscing. But, Muldoon didn't see how anything could have led to blackmail . . . and to murder.

"Get back to Schneider," he said finally.

"Yes, well, it's not something I'm proud of."

"There's little to be proud of in war."

"It's what we did, my little unit and I." The Colonel shifted uncomfortably in his seat. He glanced up again at the portrait, but his time his pride gave way to resignation. He sighed deeply.

Muldoon listened quietly.

"We . . . we plundered."

Eyes narrowed, Muldoon leaned forward a fraction. The fire was dying now, but in the low flames he could see houses burning . . . women and children screaming. It was a picture he couldn't clear from his nightmares. He shifted his gaze back to Hamm. A gray soldier stepped up behind the man, placed an unfelt hand on his shoulder before fading away. Muldoon shared in whatever this man had done. Not directly, but . . .

The Colonel sighed, a rueful smile pasted to his face. He placed the cold, forgotten cigar between his lips, then pulled it out again, and turned it between his fingers.

"There were five of us," he continued. "I remember the first time. It seemed okay, as if everybody was doing it. We rode out with a huge force, eight hundred men led by Brigadier General Potter. It was a two-hundred-mile ride through Greenville, Tarboro, and Rocky Mount.

"On the third day out, Potter separated the force, and some of us went on to Rocky Mount. I stayed at Tarboro. We destroyed the town. It was a horrible sight to see. Steamboats, warehouses, the jail, everything was fair game. And the looting! We just went from building to building taking what we could.

"Major Clarkson took a force and followed some Confederates off into the woods on the other side of the river, but I stayed, my men and I. Maybe I should have gone. They were drawn into an ambush, and many of them died. Honorably. I stayed behind . . . and learned to loot. I wanted more than I could carry, and so did several of my men. So, we hauled what we could out into the forest, we buried it, and we mapped the location so we'd remember where it was. Of course, as the commanding officer, I kept the map."

He laid the cold cigar on the table and stood stiffly, then moved to the fire and stirred it with the poker. "Karl Schneider was my man, my trusted sergeant. He helped me bury the booty."

The Colonel reached atop the mantle and grasped a silver candlestick, one of a pair. He turned to Muldoon, proffering it. "One of my prizes," he said with a dismal tone to his voice.

Muldoon sat woodenly. He had no jurisdiction here. He might think it a crime, but so many had done it . . . and this man was a Colonel. Muldoon had no one to tell.

"Schneider was blackmailing you?" asked Muldoon again.

"Not really, no. It's more as though I was paying him his share. You see," the man turned again toward the fire, and placed one foot against the grate. "We continued raiding after that. My small group of five. We would ride on a house, take what we wanted, and set it ablaze. Then we would bury the goods, somewhere far out in the forest. After the war, I went back . . . and I brought it all here. There was only Schneider and myself left. He took his part, and I took mine. But he wanted more, he thought we should have split evenly, but I am, after all, the officer. So, we worked out payments. Otherwise, he said, my family would learn all about the war."

Muldoon nodded. He rose to stand beside the Colonel who had again grabbed the poker to stir the ash. Suddenly, Muldoon reached out and grabbed the man's arm. He flipped the hand over, bared the wrist, and revealed what he had just momentarily seen. The Colonel tried pulling his arm away, but Muldoon held it firm. There, on the inside of his wrist was a small tattoo, five dots, like those on a die.

"Our symbol," he said with a rueful grin. "Four of them, and me in the center."

"You all had it?"

The Colonel nodded. "Each different," he said. "To symbolize their position in our little group." Suddenly, Muldoon realized that this was why Schneider's wrist was flayed. The skin had been removed to hide the tattoo. Or was it to collect it? But, if Schneider's death had to do with the war, why kill the girl?

"Now, if you'll excuse me," said the Colonel. "It's getting rather late."

Muldoon glanced at the clock on the mantle. It was after midnight. He hadn't realized so much time had passed. Retrieving his hat in the hall, he exited the building, but not before he noticed the footman hurrying through the house. The man was dressed to go out, and carried his master's hat and coat. Outside, Muldoon darted around the house in time to see the Colonel climb into his carriage. He couldn't let the Colonel out of his sight. He ran to the street, and raised his hand to hail a passing cab. The driver slapped the horses and they moved quickly down the road, headed toward the poorer district.

CHAPTER 43

"Follow that carriage," Muldoon barked. He flopped back in- to his seat as the cab jolted forward. The horse wasn't as good as the Colonel's fine carriage horses. The distance between them grew, until he was afraid he'd lose them. Then, suddenly he saw the Colonel's carriage stop. The man got out and started walking. As his own cab neared, Muldoon leaped out and handed the cabbie his fare. He sprinted down the road, past the waiting carriage. Five Points, he knew, was ahead. In particular, the corner of Cross Street, where it opened into Paradise Park.

What was Colonel Hamm doing here, he wondered? Ahead of him, the man stopped in the center of the road. Muldoon could see him, the weak glow of the corner streetlamp silhouetting his figure. He moved to the right, into the shadows, hoping he'd be invisible in the darkness. He had no idea why the Colonel was here, and he wasn't going to be a target out in the open. Why had the man come here? Was it simply to see the location of his daughter's death? Could he be the killer? Or had the murderer sent for him, with some message he couldn't ignore?

Muldoon edged closer and scanned the shadows, but he couldn't see through the darkness. A nightwalker passed, then paused and brushed up against the Colonel, but he murmured something to her, and she stumbled on around the corner.

Minutes dragged by, and still the Colonel stood, waiting just outside Kavanagh's window . . . the spot where his daughter's and Schneider's corpses had been found. Suddenly, a slim figure broke from the darkness. Red orbs glowed where its eyes should have been.

"Hello?" Colonel Hamm greeted the shadow.

"Aaaargh!" the Colonel raised his hands, blocking a heavy arm as it descended. But the figure had hold of his coat. The Colonel spun about, quickly sliding out of the coat as it wrapped around the man's fist. He ran, not toward Muldoon, but into the Park.

"Damn," Muldoon breathed.

The figure shook free of the coat and chased after the Colonel. Muldoon ran, but there was too much space between him and the shadowed form. In the park, Muldoon could see the Colonel run to the fence. He grabbed hold as if he might climb, but then turned roughly to his left, glancing back behind him. The man ran hard, the killer just behind. Muldoon glanced wildly about the park, but he couldn't see the officers stationed there.

Colonel Hamm neared the police box, and then veered wildly away. He grasped a door handle, pulled hard, and flung himself in the door of a dilapidated building. A stocky, lumbering figure disappeared into the building behind the Colonel. Was that the same thin man he'd seen attack the Colonel moments earlier? Had the weak light and deep shadows of the night played tricks on his eyes?

As Muldoon neared the box, he could see two bodies sprawled there—the patrolmen Mickey O'Brien and Danny Denehey. Muldoon squatted beside Mickey. His neck had been broken. Danny's too. The force against the younger patrolman had been extremely powerful, and sudden. His neck bent oddly sideways, a scream frozen on his face. Neither man had put up much of a fight, as if they had known their attacker, or he'd come upon them very suddenly. Muldoon rushed across the street, and entered the dark chasm of the ramshackle building.

He paused, listening. The darkness was absolute. The sound of his own raspy breath filled his ears. A scraping sound broke the silence. A boot on a step? He moved toward the sound, where the stairway led upwards. He climbed the stairs slowly, his feet near the wall, where the steps squeaked less. The man's footsteps above echoed eerily in the hollow darkness. Somewhere above him, the man paused, a door screeched open. A rush of cool air filled the space, and Muldoon realized he had exited to the roof.

He hurried onward, still careful. Pulling out his nightstick he thought about the gun he'd left in his dresser drawer. He hadn't carried a firearm since the war. And now, when he could use one . . .

He reached the roof and stood silently beside the door. Somewhere out there, hidden by darkness, was a multiple killer. The man with crimson eyes. Somehow, he'd lured the Colonel here. How, Muldoon didn't know. The door was open. Carefully, he bent forward, just far enough to look out the door, and glanced about the rooftop. No one there. He stepped out. Crouched low, one hand on the rooftop below his feet. He peered into the gloom. To the left of the door several crates sat, abandoned. Behind them, he caught the glimmer of light off eyes! He stifled a shiver, then realized they weren't red. It was the Colonel. Muldoon raised a finger to his lips, hush.

He moved along the wall, away from the Colonel. The rooftop was flat and open, a square access building at its center. He reached the corner, and peeked around it. Suddenly, something sliced through the dark, smashing him hard over the head! Lights burst behind his eyes, blinding him for a second. He didn't know what he'd been hit with, but blood ran into his eyes. Sightless, he reached out and grabbed for the man.

His hand met flesh! He grabbed hard. A thick forearm. If this is Crimson Eyes, he thought, he's a man . . . not a shadow. And he knew how to fight a man. He slid his foot forward, and pulled the other man off balance. He'd lost his nightstick. Now, he relied on his skill. Blood streaming into his eyes, he fought blind.

The man had skills. He tried for various locks, but unsuccessfully. Muldoon countered each move. He maneuvered himself behind, and grabbed the man, one arm about his neck, the other pinning his arm to his side. The man thrust his body hard, trying to break free. Suddenly, Muldoon felt his body rising off the roof. Air rushed up toward him. Still blind, he fought to remain upright, but his opponent surged up and back. Muldoon prepared for the body slam, but felt an odd suspension. And then they plummeted off the roof. The man screamed, but Muldoon held tight, until a sickening crunch took his consciousness.

CHAPTER 44

April 29

WITH pain-filled steps, Muldoon limped from his bed over to a chair at the window. The short distance seemed so much further than it really was, when agony accompanied every movement. He gazed through the glass, watching as traffic sped by. He couldn't believe the case was over. Kelly McAllister had been exonerated.

He'd have died, had the other man not been beneath him when they crashed to earth. The other man. Sergeant Collins. He still didn't understand why, but he'd been in the war, too. A member of the 3rd New York Cavalry. And they'd been in North Carolina with the 12th. Somehow, he must have learned about the pact between Colonel Hamm and his men. But they'd never know now. Collins had died . . . Muldoon's arm around his neck . . . the way he'd killed the others. Karl Schneider, Margaret Hamm, and her maid, Lydia.

Three, now four deaths. Meg McAllister's prophecies had been wrong. Of course.

The Captain had come to see him in the hospital. He'd stood quietly, his hands deep in his pockets, and stared down at Muldoon, where he lay on his hospital bed. His right arm, and several ribs were broken. But, the massive body of Hugh Collins had absorbed the main force of the fall.

Finally, Captain Hayle cleared his throat, and congratulated him on a job well done. He set something on the table beside the bed, then left. Muldoon reached across with his good hand. His fingertips just reaching the cold metal, and he slid the thing close, until he could grasp it. A detective's badge lay on his open palm. With a deep sigh, he laid his head back into the softness of the pillow. The Captain hadn't been able to say the words. He imagined how they must have stuck in the man's throat. Muldoon, you've been promoted. No longer a sergeant over patrolmen, he was a junior officer in the Detective Force. He felt no pride in it.

Several days had passed, and now he was home, the case over. Kelly McAllister came home, too. But, the boy wasn't the same. He'd been terribly injured in his match with Schneider. Muldoon remembered the fight, recalled the sickening motion of the boy as he bent toward the ground. Nearly in two, he remembered thinking.

His spine had cracked, though not obviously at first . . . way down low. His legs were useless to him now. The kid was angry, and refused to look at anyone, even Muldoon. Perhaps, if he hadn't been locked away in the Tombs, without proper medical care . . . but he had been. And, now he lay in Muldoon's back bedroom. He ate little, and talked less. The only one he would see was his mother. Muldoon felt a deep sense of guilt, though he knew he couldn't have stopped him. The boy had wanted his break . . . and it broke him.

Muldoon would care for him, and for Meg.

As he gazed out the window, he thought about the case. One thing still bothered him. What did A.R. stand for? With Collins dead, he would never know. He sat in the window several hours, then limped back to bed.

CHAPTER 45

FIVE cards, all five of clubs. The cards were wrong, he knew that. How could he have a hand like this? He would be accused of cheating. But the man across from him smiled as he lay down his own cards. The gambler's mustache twitched, he had an identical hand, all fives. Reaching forward, the man pulled the pile of coins from the center of the table. Muldoon burned as if on fire. He stood, loosened his collar, and stumbled over to the next table. Roulette. He tossed down his money, and the ball was set in play, rolling, rolling. The wheel spun about. He grew dizzy watching, sweat dripped down his face. The wheel slowed, and with a skip and jump, the ball clattered to a stop. Five!

Turning away, Muldoon stared into the mirror above the bar. All about him, people laughed. He tried a third table, craps. Taking the dice in hand he shook them several times and sent them rolling. The far end of the table seemed out of balance, one leg taller than the others. The room spun about him as he watched the two cubes bounce across the table. Smacking into the end, they came to a halt. Fives. Laughter tinkled about the room as faces drew in and out of focus. The dice dropped into his hand, and again he flung them out. Fives.

"Why five?" he yelled. Sitting suddenly, he jolted awake. Had he really yelled aloud? He struggled from under twisted blankets, harshly reminded of his injuries. But, he knew the case wasn't over. Yes, Collins had performed the act, had probably been paid very well, but there was another, more sinister personality behind him. He pulled on his canvas pants and shirt, forcing the torn sleeve over his splinted arm, and left suspenders hanging loose. He drew on his shoes and a plain brown jacket. Pausing before the mirror, he splashed water over his flushed face, cupping his one good hand. The several days' growth of beard would have to wait.

As he turned to leave he thought about the pistol hidden in his top drawer. He pulled it open, took out the weapon, loaded it, and slid it into the waist of his pants.

He limped across his sitting room, flung open the door, and stepped into the hall.

"Sergeant Muldoon?" Mrs. Dunn called from her parlor.

Damn. He scowled as he paused at the door. He didn't have time for conversation. Somebody's life could be at stake! He stopped short as he recognized the form sitting closest to the door, her back turned to him. Alva Smith. Self-consciously, he rubbed the thick growth on his chin.

"Ah, there you are, Sergeant," Mrs. Dunn said. "Are you feeling better, then?" She eyed the cloth sling about his neck, the splinted arm hanging limply before his waist.

"I have to go out," he muttered. "Something I have to do."

He stepped further into the room. Alva turned to face him, shock registered across her features. She hadn't expected to see him so battered and bruised, even with stitches across his hairline where his scalp had been split by Collins' initial blow. He had yanked off the bandage—it wouldn't fit under his cap, and didn't provide protection for his concussion, anyhow.

"It's a pleasure to see you, Miss Smith," he said, surprised at how pleased he really did feel.

She rose to her feet. "Oh, Sergeant Muldoon," she said. "You're hurt, I mean . . . I knew, but . . . I didn't know how badly," she ended lamely.

He smiled ruefully, and then suddenly remembered he had somewhere to go. "I'm sorry, Miss," he said. "But I really must go. I don't have time . . . " He realized he was being exceedingly rude, and he didn't want to be rude to Alva Smith.

"Sergeant Muldoon," Mrs. Dunn said sharply. "Miss Smith came particularly to see how you are doing."

"I know. I'm sorry, but it's my duty . . . "

"And," the woman continued. "I realized that I'd forgotten a package she sent to you. It came the day of your . . . accident." She rose from her seat, went to a small lady's desk near the window, and returned with a paper bundle, carefully tied with string.

He glanced curiously across at Alva, where she remained, seated primly at the edge of her chair. An odd expression clouded her features, somewhere between pride . . . and dread? He couldn't tell. He accepted the package in his one good hand. Realizing his predicament, Alva rose.

She untied the string. "It's hers," she whispered.

As the paper fell open, he recognized the contents as a woman's honey-blonde hair. Quickly, he tried to hold it shut again, before Mrs. Dunn could see inside. She would be horrified, he was certain. Catching his glance at the older woman, Alva retied the package, being certain to double-knot it securely.

"This must be sent to Police Headquarters," he said to the matron. "It's evidence for one of my cases."

Mrs. Dunn took the package from him, a disappointed expression on her face. He came close to smiling. She'd probably thought the package contained some scandalous gift from Alva Smith. After all, she was a woman, and not above a bit of romance. He could see it in her eyes as they danced approvingly between him and Alva.

As she took the package from his cradled arm, a separate sheet fluttered lightly to the ground at his feet. Carefully, he bent his knees, and squatted so he could reach it without bending at the waist. His broken ribs hampered him, and he reached out to balance himself against the chair. As he knelt, he appreciated the view of Alva's shapely breasts, and her nipped-in waist. She blushed at the intimacy of his gaze.

Groaning, he stood back up. Alva took his arm with concern. "Do you need to sit?" she asked.

"No," he grunted painfully. "I have to go to Colonel Hamm's."

"Oh! I'm going there as well. Perhaps you would like to ride in my carriage?" She motioned toward the front of the house, where he was sure her carriage occupied a conspicuous position on the street.

He smiled, thankfully. He couldn't have walked far, and he'd be lucky to find a cab in this neighborhood. "Aye," he said. "I would like that."

They left the house in a hurry. Muldoon grabbed her hand and almost dragged her down the steps and into the carriage. He settled painfully into the seat across from her.

"Why are you going to the Hamm's?"

"Because," she cleared her throat, and started again. "Because I've had this made up." She held out a piece of jewelry, braided hair intricately woven into a lace circle, and attached carefully to a gold backing.

"What is it?"

"It's a broach!" she exclaimed, and offered it again, as though he could understand it better the second time he looked at it. But, it still made no sense to him. "Oh, for goodness sake, it's Margaret's hair. I've had it made into a broach for Mrs. Hamm. So she can remember her daughter."

He glanced at the object with distaste, and then glanced up at Alva, realizing the rudeness of his behavior. He might want a lock of hair from someone he loved who'd died, but he would hide it away somewhere, certainly not wear it. But, if this was something the upper classes did, then he ought to respect it. It was Alva's way of honoring the memory of her friend.

"It's . . . nice," he finally said.

She replaced the item in her reticule, and turned her face to the window. He'd insulted her, and she was showing him that she'd been offended. He pretended not to notice. He wasn't used to the conventions of her society. Instead, he unfolded the piece of paper that had fallen from the package of hair. It was Alva's note describing the man who'd sold the hair to the wigmaker's.

"You're sure of this?" Muldoon asked quietly, a dangerous tone to his voice.

Alva glanced back toward him, eyes flashing with irritation. But as she saw the note, she nodded, all anger forgotten. "Yes, it's the man's description. Is that who did this to you?" She laid her hand on his, where it hung limply from the end of the sling. Instantly she pulled her fingers away, as though burnt by the contact.

"No."

"No!" she exclaimed. "Then he's . . . " her words trailed away, helplessly, as the awful realization entered her mind.

"Then who did you kill?"

He grimaced at her characterization of his fight. "Hugh Collins. He was a police officer, a sergeant, like me. I think he was paid to kill your friend, and to kill Mr. Schneider."

"How . . . how awful! Somehow, that seems worse than if he'd killed them for his own reasons."

Muldoon nodded. He felt the same way.

"And he was a policeman, too. What a disgrace for the City."

He agreed. It certainly wouldn't look good at the next review. Captain Hayle would be particularly mortified, after all Collins was his man. Muldoon allowed himself a grimace of a smile.

"So, you're going to the Hamm's for . . . " Alva asked.

"To warn them."

CHAPTER 46

A pretty maid opened the door, one he hadn't seen when he'd last been here interviewing the servants. She glanced at Muldoon doubtfully, as if he didn't belong at the front door. He half expected her to tell him to go around to the kitchen, except for Alva at his side. A flicker of recognition lit her eyes as she glanced at Alva, and then looked again at Muldoon. Her face again blankly schooled, she turned back to him, as if it weren't unusual to see working-class men and aristocratic ladies arriving together on the doorstep.

"If you please," she said with a little curtsy. "The mistress is in the morning room."

They followed her across the wide entrance, and entered a room to the left. Elizabeth Hamm stood at a marble-topped table before the window, carefully arranging flowers in a crystal vase. She turned as they entered, her eyes fleetingly glanced over Muldoon, an echo of her maid's earlier action. Dismissing him, she turned to Alva.

"Miss Smith," she said. "It is so good of you to come." Muldoon didn't believe her—he could see the distaste in her expression. He glanced at Alva, wondering if she sensed it, too. He hoped she didn't.

"You know Sergeant Muldoon, of course," said Alva. "Um, Detective Muldoon. We ran into each other on the way here. It seems he has business with your husband."

"He will have to wait," she said, and gestured vaguely back toward the hall. "Perhaps in the Colonel's office. He's busy just now."

He watched as she continued to trim excess leaves and thorns from a long stem and placed the rose in the vase. Then she reached for another. His gaze was drawn to the bundle of greenery lying carelessly on the table, a ribbon loosed from around it, and its pretty bow on the table by their side. As her hand dipped, she pulled another stem free, a little "oh" escaping her lips as a thorn pierced her. A tiny drop of blood fell from her fingertip to where the bow lay and landed on a piece of wood around which the bow had been formed.

Muldoon leaped forward, snatched the bow off the table, and pulled out the piece of wood. It was roughly whittled, chunky, only part of a whole. As he turned it over, the initials A.R. blazed into view. If he fitted the pieces together he knew they would make a walking stick, this, the balled top, just right for a hand to hold.

"Where did you get these?" he demanded, waving at the flowers.

"Why . . . from my husband's . . . from the Colonel's friend," Mrs. Hamm answered, confused. She pulled back from him, eyes large in her pretty, oval face.

"Ring for the butler," Muldoon growled, low and urgent.

"I . . . I can't!"

"Why not?"

"The servants have been given the day off. It is a Sunday. They won't be back for several hours. All except Bess. I needed somebody to answer the door, and to get lunch."

"Then ring for her," he said. "Where are your children?"

"They went for a walk," her voice rose wildly. "With the nanny. Why, what's wrong?"

Muldoon turned to Alva. She backed away, as if afraid of him. He reached out to her, and grabbed her arm with his one good hand. "Get her out. And the maid. Get out now!"

Alva nodded dumbly, and ran to yank on the bell pull and summon the girl.

"They're upstairs?" Muldoon turned again to Elizabeth Hamm. Blood drained from her face, and she wavered on her feet as Alva took hold of her.

"Yes," she said. "In his treasure room . . . at the top of the stairs."

"Go," said Alva, and she pushed him toward the door. "We'll be fine."

He ran to the stairs. It was a grand staircase, two open flights up. On that top floor, he would find the killer . . . and Colonel Hamm, perhaps already dead. He gripped the banister tightly with his good left hand and pulled his aching body up the stairs.

As he neared the top, he heard voices, one the raised, frightened one of the Colonel—the other, the calm, measured voice of Sean Kavanagh. Muldoon pulled the gun from his waistband, cocked it, and inched toward the door. Inside, he could see a collection of silver and jewels, weapons, and works of art.

Kavanagh moved about the room, a can of lamp oil in his hand. The far end of the room already blazed, flame licked up the edge of a painting, some priceless European piece. Muldoon stood, transfixed by the flame. An image floated in the red-yellow flicker, women and children screaming in the fire. All of this contraband, he knew, had been gotten this way. He'd seen other men do the same thing, but he hadn't ever condoned it. The guilt of not stopping it weighed heavily on him. And then, unbidden, soldiers appeared amidst the contraband. He tried to tear his gaze away from them, but their accusing, empty eyes held him.

" . . . And then you left me," Kavanagh said. Muldoon tried to listen, tried to tear himself away from his visions. "I couldn't believe it! Whatever happened to Corporal Matthews? Did you leave him, too?"

"He died," the Colonel said. "At Plymouth."

"You saw him?" Kavanagh snorted derisively. He poured the final drops from the can. "Can I believe you? I suppose you thought I was dead, too?"

"Yes, I did," the Colonel said.

"Well, I wasn't, and neither was Johnson."

"We looked for you both. You must believe me! Sergeant Schneider and I looked among the wounded, but you weren't there. Mathews was injured, but we got him out . . . only to die of yellow fever at New Bern that summer. I saw him buried."

"I know you didn't look for me," Kavanagh snarled. "I lay there, among the wounded and the dead. And you walked right past me, you and Schneider. I called to you, but you didn't turn. You didn't look at me. But Schneider . . . he did. He saw. And you didn't turn around."

"How could I know? He never told me he'd seen you."

"You could have looked harder. You could have turned around, seen faces the other direction. Like he did."

"But we were retreating," Hamm moaned. "The Albemarle had sailed in. She sank one union ship, and chased the rest off. Then she turned her guns on us. If we'd stayed we would've been killed, or surrendered with General Wessells."

"Like I was." The statement came hard, brittle. Hatred dripping from those three words. "That's why I had Schneider killed. I knew I couldn't do it, so I hired the biggest guy I could find. And a copper, too!" he laughed.

"But why kill my Margaret?"

Their words penetrated Muldoon's trance. He glanced about, trying to find the Colonel. Finally, he saw him—the Colonel knelt behind a Romanesque pillar. His right wrist was handcuffed to a heavy chain wrapped about the column. He rattled the manacles, trying desperately to pull away. His other arm was drawn backward and hogtied to his ankles.

"I killed her to make you suffer. Like I did when I was in Andersonville Prison." Kavanagh laughed, an evil, rasping sound.

"But you didn't lose a daughter." Terror snaked through the words, intermingled with what seemed genuine loss.

"You don't know what I suffered!" Kavanagh's face twisted with anger. "The place was awash with hatred . . . and ugly things. And then we had the Raiders. It was a little gang of us . . . of course, I was the brains. And Johnson was my man, along with six others. Until Johnson got too almighty big for himself. For months, we ran that camp. And then I let him hang. All of them. Because they'd tried to cut me out!

"It was so funny. The guards didn't even know they were helping me, they had a trial and everything. They even built the scaffold. And then the Raiders hung for their crimes . . . for my crimes. Ha ha!" He laughed a twisted choking sound.

Kavanagh dug into his pocket and pulled out a match. He struck it and held it a moment before flicking it into the pooled oil. The light reflected off rose-tinted spectacles. Blue flame ran quickly across the floor, spread toward the growing fire at the back of the room. The air filled with smoke. It gathered near the ceiling, and poured toward Muldoon where he stood near the door.

"I took some of the gallows and fashioned it into a cane. I carried that cane for years. It was like a beacon for my anger. Then, when my plan came to me, I broke it into pieces, and carved A.R. into the wood. A.R. for Andersonville Raiders. One piece for each of you. But then, I learned that my vengeance was cheated. Matthews was dead. So, I took your daughter in his place. You deserved to hurt more than anyone, for stealing all of this from me." He waved at the contraband.

Suddenly he stepped toward Hamm and drew out a knife. Muldoon ripped his gaze from the visions that consumed him as surely as the fire would if he didn't find the strength to let them go.

"Stop!" Muldoon yelled.

Kavanagh scooped up the oil can and flung it at Muldoon. Pain screamed through his arm as it hit. He doubled over, then quickly drew the gun upward again. But not before the crazed man grabbed the Colonel's shackled wrist. Twisting it painfully, he bared the tattoo, and set the blade an inch above the black dots. Expertly avoiding tendons and veins, he peeled back the flesh, and cleanly removed a little square. The Colonel screamed, and collapsed heavily against the column.

"For my dice . . . " Kavanagh said, a heavy rasping sound as smoke filled their lungs. He coughed a laugh as he slid behind the kneeling man and held the knife to his throat. "Throw down the gun," he yelled.

Muldoon wavered.

"Now," Kavanagh roared. "Kick it over here."

Muldoon dropped it, and kicked it lightly away. The moment the gun slid off, Kavanagh sprinted toward Muldoon and slammed hard into him.

"Oooof," Muldoon grabbed hold of him with his good hand, even as pain exploded from his broken ribs. He raised his right arm high, deflected the other man's knife off his wooden splint. Behind him, flames spread out onto the landing, eagerly seeking new fuel. Alva stood silhouetted by the fire, eyes widened in horror. No, he thought. Get out! Quickly she ripped the fragile fabric of her dress, stepped free from its encumbrance, and dropped the heavy hoops to the floor. Wearing only her chemise and pantaloons, she ran toward him and leaped on Kavanagh's back. She wrapped her legs about his waist, fingers digging into the flesh of his face, screaming wildly in his ear.

Kavanagh spun about, and smashed the girl into Muldoon's side. Tearing pain ripped through his body, and he fell to his knees gasping for breath. She loosened her grip, and dropped into a heap on the floor. Kavanagh screamed, then stumbled from the room, his fists balled into empty sockets, trying to stop the bleeding. He disappeared onto the flame enveloped staircase.

"I . . . I," said Alva, staring at her bloody hands. "His eyes."

They didn't have time for her to think about it. Muldoon grabbed her wrist, made her loosen her fingers from their gory treasure, and dragged her to the Colonel's side. The man pulled frantically at the shackle, and tried urgently to slide his hand from its tight prison. He gazed wildly at Muldoon. The raging fire burned around them. The air burnt their lungs, sweat streamed from the heat, and their clothing clung damply to their skin. Muldoon yanked at the manacle, but he couldn't find the key. He pushed against the pillar trying to break it, but it withstood his might . . . his injured body didn't have the strength.

"Cut it," the Colonel said, flatly.

Muldoon grabbed a sword from a rack a few steps away, but let go quickly. It had already heated up from the flames. Swiftly, he pulled the sling over his head and wrapped it around the hilt, then pulled the weapon from the rack.

"No!" Alva backed away as the sword swung down, and the Colonel's trapped hand fell with a thud.

The older man screamed, and nearly lost consciousness. Alva grabbed hold of him, and pulled him to his feet. She ripped a piece off her pantaloon and quickly tied it tightly around the arm to slow his bleeding. Muldoon thrust the blade into the fire, heating it. He placed its heat against the raw flesh, cauterizing it to stem the bleeding.

They rushed onto the landing, but flames fully engulfed the stairs.

"This way," Colonel Hamm grated through clenched teeth, and led them to the left. Muldoon pushed the heavy door open, they burst through, and he shut the door on the heat and flames behind them. They were in the servant's quarters. Smoke curled under the door, the only sign of the inferno on the other side. A thin staircase rose behind what seemed to be a closet door. Tucked in behind it, a second flight of steps dropped in a tight, incredibly steep spiral. This was the servants' staircase, meant for speed, not comfort.

The Colonel ran swiftly down the steps, followed more carefully by Alva. Muldoon brought up the rear, afraid he wouldn't fit around the tighter corners. As they passed the next landing, he could see flames where the servants' quarters blazed. Above him came the report of a gun as the forgotten revolver was engulfed in flame.

"Aaaargh!" Muldoon roared, as pain ripped through his leg. The heavy weight of a body crashed into him from the second-floor landing! He reached down to grab the knife where Kavanagh had shoved it deep into his thigh. He was quick, and caught the man's hand while it still held the knife's hilt. He squeezed tight, until he could feel the crunch of thin wrist bones. Kavanagh screamed and let go of the knife. He shifted his hand to the man's collar and grabbed a fistful of fabric. Leaning back, he supported himself against the near-perpendicular steps. He pulled the man from the landing, and held him, writhing, above the empty recess below. Then he snapped his head back, then forth, and slammed his forehead hard against Kavanagh's. Blood splattered across the space, streaming from Muldoon's scalp as his stitches ripped free. The man went limp.

He thrust Kavanagh away from him, flung him like a rag doll back into the hallway. The limp body skidded across the floor and banged to a stop as he hit the wall. Grabbing the hilt, Muldoon yanked the knife from his thigh, and staunched the flow of blood with his one good hand. Above him timbers crashed. Without a thought, he sat and slid down the steps as he'd done as a child. But, before he reached the bottom, he heard the wail of a man, caught in the conflagration above.

MULDOON stood outside, supported by Alva Smith. Smoke poured from the once-stately mansion, billowing into the afternoon sky.

Colonel Hamm sat on the grass staring dismally at his burning home. He cradled his handless arm as though it were a child. His wife stood behind him, eyes hollow with shock.

"I never did sell any of it, you know . . . the treasure," he said. "I couldn't."

CHAPTER 47

THE strains of an Irish lullaby helped clear Muldoon's mind as Meg McAllister sang quietly in her sitting room. He rested in a big chair Mrs. Dunn had brought down from the attic and had positioned in front of his fireplace.

"William?" Meg stopped singing and peeked through the open door between apartments.

"Hmmm?"

"May I speak with you?" She came around to the front of the chair. "I . . . you're . . . "

She dropped to the floor and knelt before him, both hands on his knee as if in supplication. Clearing her throat, she began again. "You've done so much for me. I'll never forget it. You . . . you've saved my boy."

"Not soon enough, Ma." He shook his head slightly. "If only I'd figured things out sooner."

"No, you did everything you could."

If only, he thought. This world is full of 'if only's.' If only he'd saved those women and children from the burning house in Pensacola. If only he hadn't gone to war in the first place, then he'd have been home when his own house had burned. Then, maybe his parents would still be alive. And maybe Patrick Ryan wouldn't have disappeared on Santa Rosa Island. If only he'd known Kavanagh was bent on murder, then Kelly McAllister could have got out of the Tombs sooner. Poor Kelly, he thought. If only he'd had a doctor look at him after the bout, then maybe the kid would still be able to walk. But he hadn't. Now Kelly lay in his bed and might never walk again.

"I'll take care of him, Ma. You have my word," he said.

"I know you will. You're a good boy."

She reached up and traced the tips of her fingers along the side of his cheek. "So serious, William. You're always so serious. I wish you would smile."

He gave a half-hearted attempt, and she smiled in return.

"I hope someday your smile returns to you." She stood and began to turn away, but her hand reached back toward him, and she paused. "And not that crooked one . . . "

She turned away, and then back again. He could see a change in her bearing.

"You must tell me, Billy," she said in the husky voice that wasn't quite her own. "Tell me what happened."

His Irish blood ran cold.

"Who were the three? Who were the first to die?" she asked.

"Karl Schneider, Margaret Hamm, and her maid."

She nodded, but still faced away. "And the two by your hand?"

He hadn't thought of it that way.

"Collins and Kavanagh. But that's only five. Your prophecy is wrong."

Her head tipped to the side, almost as if trying to hear some far away sound. "Wasn't there one before?" she asked.

"No." He thought back over the case. "Yes. Kavanagh's partner. The one who swung in Andersonville Prison."

"Six." She spun around and fixed him with her stare. "Did you find the man with the cane?"

"Kavanagh."

"No, an older cane," she said.

He shrugged, avoiding her eyes.

"Then he'll return for more. He's a bloodthirsty one, and his thirst is unquenchable."

Her hand dropped, and the dark veil lifted from her eyes. She smiled weakly, and went back to her own room, pulling the door nearly closed behind her.

No, he thought, I don't believe in it. The prophecy was wrong, it had to be. He believed in an ordered, scientific world. One in which men had motivations, and studying the clues would reveal their mistakes, and ultimately lead him to the criminals.

Pain stabbed through his body as he stood up and moved over to the fireplace. He rested his forearm on the mantle, and stared into the embers that glowed on the grate. He tried to think of nothing, to still his mind, but he couldn't. His curled fingers rubbed the polished wood, and then tapped against something that skittered unevenly across the mantle and dropped to the floor.

It was a single die, the number six on top. He bent painfully and picked it up. Somebody had carefully carved a wooden block, and then covered it with rawhide. Six tiny leather squares were stitched neatly together, and stretched tightly over the cube. He turned it over. Each square of flesh had been tattooed with a single dot, two dots, then three, four, five, and six. Some had been marked long ago, the ink faded to gray. Others were newly marked. But they were tattooed, not printed. The ink had been injected into the skin. As he turned it over, the number six stood out . . . it was dark brown.

He'd seen a similar, unfinished die on the windowsill in Kavanagh's apartment. Was this the same one? How had it got on his mantle?

His mind turned to Biggs and his evil gang. They weren't in-volved with Kavanagh and his crimes, but they were still up to something. Perhaps something even bigger. He would have to keep an eye on them.

He set the die back on the mantle and returned to his seat. The sputtering fire had caught again, and a small flame leapt and danced, hungrily devouring what fuel it found. Muldoon's hand strayed to a glass on the table next to him. The doctor had left it there. Half-full. It would make the pain tolerable, he'd said. Muldoon picked it up, and swirled the amber liquid.

Author's Note

I stumbled upon William Muldoon while at the University of Maine. I was researching the history of wrestling, and became intrigued with the idea of a champion wrestler and police officer as the central character in an historic novel. Muldoon was, in truth, both of these in the later 1800s. I moved to New Jersey, and spent long hours in New York City, walking through the neighborhoods Muldoon once lived in. The Five Points no longer exists. It was demolished as a way to get rid of NYC's most notorious criminal center of its time. Paradise Park was at the juncture of Cross Street, Orange Street, and Anthony Street. Today, Orange Street is now Baxter Street, Anthony Street became Worth Street, and Cross Street is gone. The Park's location (and the Five Points, from which the district took its name) can be found today at the intersection of Baxter and Worth. The approximate district borders are Broadway, White, Bowery, and slightly south of where Pearl crosses Park Row.

Most of the details of the city are accurate. Some street names, in addition to those mentioned above, have changed. For instance, Chatham became Park Row. Police Headquarters was located at 300 Mulberry Street, Harry Hill's was on Houston Street, The Black and Tan was on Bleecker St. Other actual locations include The Tombs, Billy McGlory's Armory Hall, McSorley's Saloon, the hospital, prison, and asylum on Blackwell Island, and Sister's Row. The various neighborhoods all existed, and most can still be found, though in slightly different incarnations.

Of the cast of characters, like William Muldoon, many of them actually lived in 1867 New York City. I have taken some liberties, including making some of them older than they actually were. Alva Smith was rather younger, and probably never met Muldoon. She would later become Alva Belmont, an important leader of the Woman Movement. Bob Gamble was the coroner. Frank Stephenson was proprietor of the Black and Tan. William Tweed, was indeed, "Boss" of New York City's Democratic machine. Billy McGlory owned McGlory's. Harry Hill discovered Muldoon as a wrestler, and was owner of Harry Hill's. Dick Fox was editor of the Police Gazette, and Ada Everleigh was the mistress of The Seven Sister's. In addition, the Andersonville Raiders were a prisoner-of-war gang at Andersonville Prison and were hanged for their criminal activities during their captivity. Also, the election of April 23, 1867 was to select delegates to the New York Constitutional Convention for discussion and ratification of the 14th Amendment.

William Muldoon was in the Civil War as part of the 6th New York Infantry. They fought at Fort Pickens, on the island of Santa Rosa, just off of Pensacola. While the account of the battle on October 9, 1861 is fictionalized, it is loosely based on real events. Like the characters listed above, real soldiers include Colonel William Wilson, Major Vogdes, Captain Hildt, and Jimmy Dolan. The military strategies in this novel were used in the actual battle. Today, Fort Pickens can be approached by foot, by bicycle, or by boat. The island, and fort, took a lot of damage from recent hurricanes, including Ivan and Katrina. Like my forays into New York City, I spent time in Pensacola, Florida and at Fort Pickens.

Among the many works I utilized in researching the characters and locations of this novel perhaps my favorite is *The Historic Shops & Restaurants of New York* by Ellen Williams and Steve Radlauer. This little book is pocket-sized, though rather too fat to fit in a pocket. It was my traveling companion as I toured the city, helping me locate historic buildings, especially those where I could get a drink or a bite to eat! My primary inspiration was the Police Gazette with its wonderful tales of 'blood sport,' and 'horrid murder.'

L. Mad Hildebrandt is a writer of historic thriller-mysteries, fantasy, and science fiction. She received her Ph.D. in history from the University of Maine and teaches online for Rowan College in Pemberton, NJ. She is a veteran of the United States Coast Guard. Born in Denver, CO, Mad currently lives in New Mexico with her husband, cat, and three dogs.

www.lmadhildebrandt.com

www.facebook.com/lmadhildebrandt

www.twitter.com/madhildebrandt